Searching For Answers

By
Truly Grace

Contents

Chapter 1
Saying goodbye is hard

Mary Davis sat up in her bed, propped on pillows. She knew she had only a few hours to live, possibly a day. Her nine-year-old daughter, Jessie, slowly turned the doorknob and walked over to her mother's bed. Jessie understood her mother was very sick, and she had to see her at least one more time.

Mary turned her head toward Jessie and reached her arm out for Jessie. Mary said in her weakened voice, "Come here, Jessie. I'm glad to see you." Jessie was straining to hold back the tears, but she couldn't stop a tear from dropping down her cheek. She walked over closer to her mother, and she put her arm around her mother's neck. She just wanted to stay like that for as long as she could. She just lay there and held her for a moment. Tears began to flow from Jessie's eyes, and her voice cracked as she looked into her mother's eyes and said, "I love you, momma."

Mary lifted her arm and placed it across Jessie's back to hug her with all the strength she had. Mary remained calm and said, "I love you, Jessie." Then she asked, "Jessie, do you remember me telling you about how wonderful it will be in Heaven?"

"Yes, Momma," Jessie whispered, her heart full.

Mary continued, "It's okay, Jessie. I will go there soon, and I will be well. It might be sad for you and the other children for a little while, but I need you to always remember that I will be happy there. I won't have any sadness or sickness. Someday we will meet together in Heaven."

"Oh, momma!" Jessie cried. Her heart broke as she said it, but she knew this was part of what was happening.

Mary pulled Jessie back from her and said, "It's okay, child. I want you to be brave. You are the oldest, and I need you to do something for me."

"Okay, momma," Jessie said, feeling a deep sense of responsibility already heavy on her young shoulders.

Mary took some deep breaths from her oxygen cannula that was in her nose, then she said, "Bring me the big wooden box from the third drawer of the dresser." Jessie gently lifted the box from the drawer and laid it on the bed beside her mother.

The soft flow of the gospel music was playing on the radio. Mary's frail hand, trembling slightly, clutched the edge of the wooden chest, its surface worn, but beautiful, like something from another life.

"I know you are scared, Jessie," She whispered, her voice barely above a breath, but this chest, everything inside it... It's for you. For all of you." Jessie's wide eyes stared up at her mother, her small fingers tracing the intricate carvings on the chest as if searching for something she didn't understand.

"Mom, is there a way for you to get better? It's possible, right?" Jessie asked, her voice thick with hope.

But Mary didn't answer right away. Her mother's gaze drifted over her, distant, as if seeing something far beyond the walls of the room. Then she forced a faint smile. "I wish I could promise you that. But sometimes... the things we leave behind matter more than the time we have left."

Jessie didn't fully understand, but the sadness in her mother's eyes made her heart twist in a way she couldn't explain. There was a heaviness to the air, like they were both living in a moment they couldn't change, but had to face anyway.

"Everything in here is for you and your siblings," Mary continued, "but most of it, most of it is for after I'm gone. There are things in this chest you need to know, I couldn't say out loud. You will understand when the time comes."

Jessie didn't speak, but her fingers tightened on the chest as if she were holding on to something much larger than the special box in front of her. It felt like holding on to everything her mother was leaving behind.

Mary coughed weakly, a thin veil of pain clouding her face before she closed her eyes for a moment. "You are going to have to be strong for them, Jess. There is a reason for all of this."

A chill ran through Jessie's bones. She didn't know what her mother meant by the "reason." She didn't know if she ever would. Nothing in their life would ever be the same again.

Mary managed to smile and put her hand on Jessie's cheek. She said, "I need to rest now, Jessie. It's getting late. You go to bed and get some sleep." Jessie leaned over and kissed her mom and walked toward her bedroom while clutching the box with both hands. The box was a little heavy for her, but she managed to hold on to it. She couldn't let go of it.

Jessie sat on her bed and placed the box in front of her. She stared at it for a moment, and like most people, her curiosity got the best of her. She slowly opened the box. There was an envelope with Jessie's name on it.

The envelope was not sealed, so Jessie took the letter out and began to read it.

"My darling Jessie, I have always been proud of you. You were always a good daughter. I believe the Lord has great things in store for you. You will understand more about that as you get older. Always put your trust in the Lord, read your Bible, and keep learning about Jesus. It is very important. I know you miss your dad when he is gone. He is a brave soldier who loves his family and serves his country. In this box are copies of birth certificates for all the children. There are things that you will understand more when you are older. Keep your family close in your heart and remember that your dad and I always love all of our children.

With all my love, Momma."

Jessie picked out some of the items in the box and realized what her mom had said, that she would know what to do when the time comes. She sat still for a moment, holding the papers, but nothing made sense yet. She put the items and papers back and closed the box. Jessie whispered out loud to herself, "I wonder when I will be old enough to figure all this out?" She began to yawn and said to herself, "I'll ask Momma in the morning."

At 11 pm, Mary was still awake. The moonlight was shining in her bedroom window. She was hoping to see the love of her life one more time. A few tears dropped from her cheek as she thought about her Joe. Her eyes were heavy with tears, but she still waited. Then a manly hand reached for her hand. A man stood before her in a dark dress, green pants, an olive green shirt with a black tie, and a dark green jacket with two rows of ribbons.

Mary looked up and asked, "Joe, is that you?"

"Yes, honey, it's me," he answered.

Mary's voice was weak as she said, "I didn't think you would be able to come home."

Joe sat down on the bed beside her and said, "Baby, of course I would be here for you."

Mary said, "Joe, I will be going on soon. I know you have to go back to the service. Find nice places for the children to stay. Find someone who will love them."

He said, "Mary, just rest and save your breath. I'm here now. Don't worry about anything."

"Joe, I love you and always have."

Joe squeezed her hand and said, "I know. I have always loved you, Mary."

With all the breath she had, Mary said, "Joe…" Her voice was barely there, but it was full of everything she had left. Tears filled Joe's eyes as he bent over to give his Mary one more kiss as she took her last breath and closed her eyes. It was a quiet goodbye, but it was everything they needed to say.

Joe knew that there was nothing more he could do. He just sat on the bed and held her hand. He stayed there, wishing there was something, anything, he could do.

Joe gently called the Hospice nurse, who was waiting in the living room. Her name was Julie. She was five feet ten, slim, but strong. She had a gentle voice as she said, "Mr. Davis, I will take care of everything with your wife while you go talk to your children."

"I don't think I should wake them," he said.

Julie asked him, "Do you think your oldest daughter will want to see her one last time? They were very close."

He said, "You may be right."

Joe went into Jessie's room, and for a few seconds, he wasn't sure what to say or do. Jessie must have felt his presence. She opened her eyes and said, "Hey, Daddy."

Joe walked over to Jessie's bed and knelt on the floor. Jessie wiped her dad's damp face and asked, "Is Momma gone?"

"Yes, honey," he replied.

Jessie put her arms around her daddy's neck and held him tight. Joe squeezed her, not wanting to let go, but knowing he had to.

Julie gently knocked on Jessie's bedroom door.

Joe said, "Come in."

Julie said, "I'm sorry to bother you, Mr. Davis, but the mortuary men are here to pick up Mrs. Mary. Do you and Jessie want to see her before she leaves?"

Joe looked at Jessie. Jessie said, "I want to see her and tell her goodbye."

Joe held her hand as they walked together to see Mary. Jessie's steps were slow, but she didn't let go of her dad's hand.

Joe leaned over and kissed Mary on her forehead. Jessie held her mother's hand and, with tears flowing down her face, she said, "Goodbye, momma. I remember what you said, so I'll see you again someday." Her voice was shaky, but she held onto the promise her mother gave her.

Jessie reached over and held her dad as the men took Mary's body to the hearse.

Joe walked Jessie back to her room, and he sat down beside her on her bed and held her until she fell asleep. He didn't sleep himself, just sat there with her, lost in his thoughts, trying to process everything that had just happened.

Joe was tired from the long jet ride home, but his thoughts were racing. By 9 am the next morning, he called his mom and told her what had happened. She lived two counties away, but she and Joe's dad, Richard, immediately drove over to help. She asked, "Joe, did you call Mary's family?"

"Funny thing," Joe said. "They all went together on a tour to see Europe before Mary got really bad, but I don't know how to reach them."

Jessie heard what her dad said. She said, "I will pray that they will come home."

Joe's mom, Naomi, said, "It couldn't hurt. It's a good idea."

Joe said, "I have thirty days to make arrangements for the children, then I have to go back to my unit."

Naomi said, "I'll help you get started. Let's start with the children. I'm sure you want to keep them together, but we live in a small two-bedroom apartment. I'm sure we can take good care of Jessie. She will have to go to a new school, but Jessie has a great personality, so I'm sure she will make friends quickly. Your aunt June lives on a small farm, and she and Keith never had children. I feel sure she would love to take the boys. I'll ask her when she gets here."

"What about Patty?" Jessie asked. She stood in the doorway, listening quietly.

Naomi didn't have time to answer because the phone rang.

Joe said, "Hello."

"Hey Joe. This is Rick and JoAnn. I felt a strong urge to call and see how you all are doing. We have been touring for a month, but it is time to come home and rest."

Joe said, "I have some bad news."

"What is it?" JoAnn asked.

"Mary was sick when you left, and last night she passed away."

There was silence on the phone. Joe asked, "JoAnn, did you hear me?"

Rick's voice came on the phone. "Joe, please hold the funeral for a few days. We are on our way."

Joe said, "Sure, Rick. We'll see you both in a few days. Mary's brother was with them on the tour."

Joe looked at Jessie and said, "You did well asking for God's help."

Jessie smiled and said, "Momma told me that I could count on him."

Friends and family were called, and two days later, Mary had a beautiful celebration of life. The family was surprised that about a hundred people attended. Joe didn't expect so many people, but it was clear how loved Mary had been. The family heard a lot of stories from the people who came to the funeral. Mary had attended church every Sunday until she became unable to go. She visited the sick and elderly, and she did some volunteer work at the hospital sometimes. A few people talked about Mary's sense of humor. When patients expressed fear or anxiety about going into surgery, Mary held their hand and told them jokes. The patients would laugh and start to relax. Joe told them that Mary had great humor. Sometimes she would tell Joe a joke and forget the punchline. She would hesitate. Joe said, "I asked her what happened. She'd tell me, I'm not sure, but this is what I think happened, and I'm sure she made something up."

She was good at that. After everything was over and the friends went home, Joe decided to talk to JoAnn about raising Patty for a few years. JoAnn looked at Rick with hope in her eyes. He nodded, and JoAnn said, "We'd love to have her with us as long as you need."

The next afternoon, Joe called Jessie and Patty into the kitchen to talk with them privately. They all sat at the kitchen table together. Jessie asked, "Is this about where we are going to live?"

Joe knew that Jessie was fairly mature for her age. He said, "Yes, honey."

Patty, who was seven, was surprised. "Where will we live?" she asked.

Joe said, "Patty, you may not understand right now, but I have to go back to the Army. That is where my job is, and it is far away from here. I cannot take your children with me because it is dangerous. You will go to live with your grandparents, Rick and JoAnn, until I come back."

Patty began to cry. She said, "I don't want to live with them."

"They love you, Patty, and they will be good to you," Joe said patiently. "They're family."

"I want to live with you and Jessie, and the brothers," Patty said, crying harder.

Joe said patiently, "I know, honey, but I need your help. I need you to stay with them until I finish my work." Then he concluded, "We will all be together someday when I finish my work."

Then he asked, "Will you love me and help me with this?"

Patty wiped her tears and said, "I will."

Two days later, the children packed what they could take and said goodbye to each other and their dad. Joe was trying to hold back the tears, but his eyes were watering. His parents and Mary's parents tried to comfort him and promised him that the children would be taken care of.

Joe's mother said to Joe, "Don't worry, son, just concentrate on your job and be safe. We will be waiting for your safe return."

Joe hugged his parents, Mary's parents, and his Aunt. He held onto them tightly for a moment, knowing how much it meant. Jessie and Patty grabbed their dad for one last hug. Joe told the children, "I will keep a check on you, so be the good kids I know you are."

The girls were crying as they got in the cars to go with their grandparents. They waved at Joe from the back seat until the car was out of sight, and he stood there, watching them go.

Jeremiah was four, and he didn't understand why he was going away. Joe picked him up and held him in his arms. Jeremiah's small hands gripped Joe's shirt, not knowing what was happening but trusting his dad. He said to Jeremiah, "I want you to go live with your Aunt June and Uncle Keith on their farm. You will like living there. I have to go back to work, but I will see you boys, as soon as I can."

Jeremiah shed a few tears, and he squeezed his dad's neck. Joe said to Jeremiah, "You help take care of your brother when you can." Then he concluded, "I love you, son. I'll see you, okay?" Jeremiah didn't say anything, but his little arms wrapped tighter around Joe's neck. Jeremiah kissed his dad on the cheek as he lowered him into the car seat. Joe held his baby son, Dusty, and kissed him as he put him in the other back car seat. Dusty was too young to fully understand what was going on. He was a year old.

June said to Joe, "We don't have children, so I'm glad we have this opportunity to have some to love. I promise you that we will take good care of them."

Joe said, "I appreciate this." His voice was soft but filled with gratitude.

He waved at the children as they drove down the road. Joe turned and went inside the house and sat down at the kitchen table. He just sat there for a moment, staring at the empty space around him, feeling the quiet settle in like a heavy blanket. Joe's best friend, Jerry, knocked on the back door. Joe got up and let him in.

Jerry said, "Do you want to talk, Joe?"

Joe answered, "I don't know. I just sent my children off in four different directions, and I wonder if I did the right thing."

Jerry said, "Joe, you did what you had to do. You didn't give them up for adoption; you left them temporarily with family. Mary would be happy with what you did."

"Thanks, Jerry."

Jerry said, "I know you have a lot to do, but you need to eat, so I will take you out to eat. I won't take no for an answer."

Joe said, "I hate to ask, but do you think you could keep an eye on the house until I return?"

Jerry said, "Of course."

Joe stayed in the house a few more days. He had to be by himself and mourn for his Mary. It was the silence that bothered him the most; the silence felt louder than anything else. He straightened the house, left a note for the children in case they came home before he did. He packed his duffel bag and then made a final trip to Mary's grave before he left to go back to his Army unit.

Joe arrived at his unit hours later. He got on the phone and called his friend Jerry.

"Hello," Jerry said.

Joe said, "It's me, Joe."

Jerry asked, "Are you all right, Joe?"

Joe answered, "Yeah, I guess. I just…"

Jerry asked, "What is it, Joe?"

"I just feel weird, Jerry, like something bad is going to happen."

Jerry tried to comfort Joe. "Joe, you just lost your wife and had to leave your children. Your world has been turned upside down. No matter what happens, you should know that your children are in good homes and they are safe. You will see them again, and the pain of losing Mary will get easier in time."

"Thanks, Jerry. I just needed to talk to a friend."

"I'll probably feel strange for a while, but I think Mary would want me to carry on."

"Sure she would," Jerry replied.

Joe said, "I gotta go, Jerry. Thanks for listening."

Jerry said, "Sure, keep in touch."

After they hung up, Joe could not shake the feeling that something was going to change for him, and he knew what he had to do. It was a feeling he couldn't explain, but it was there, like a whisper he couldn't ignore. He began to pray, his thoughts turning to the things he couldn't control, asking for guidance in the unknown.

"Lord, I am thankful that you have taken care of my children, and you have always taken care of me. I know my Mary is with you, and I know she is well and happy. I don't know what the future holds for me, but I am trusting in you to guide me the way you want me to go. Thank you, Father. AMEN"

Chapter 2
Life is a mystery

Thirty days later, Joe sent a letter to his parents, Naomi and Richard.

It read:

"I am doing fine. I have a new assignment, and I will be going overseas soon. I'm not sure if I'll be able to write or receive letters, but I will try my best to stay in touch. Please reach out to Patty and the rest of the family, and send them my love. I miss you all, and I'm keeping you in my thoughts."

He also enclosed a heartfelt note to his daughter, Jessie.

"Hey, honey, I hope you're doing well. I miss you and the other children so much. I'll be going out of the country for a little while, but know that I will be thinking about you every single day. Don't forget to read your Bible and be the good girl that I know you are. Keep up with your prayers. I'm so proud of you. Stay strong, and remember, I love you always. Dad."

Jessie was beyond excited to get her dad's letter. She ran to her grandparents and exclaimed, "This is the first letter I've ever gotten!" Naomi, her grandmother, smiled warmly and replied, "You'll get many more letters in your lifetime, honey, whether by mail or e-mail." Jessie, who was already familiar with computers, knew exactly what her grandmother meant.

Three weeks later, Naomi received a phone call from Joe.

"Hello."

"Hey, Mom, it's Joe," came the voice on the other end.

Naomi's face lit up. "Joe, this is such a nice surprise."

Joe responded, "I can't talk long, and I can't tell you where I am or what I'm doing, but I just wanted to let you know that I'm fine. I also wanted to thank you again for taking care of Jessie and helping me find good places for Patty, Jeremiah, and Dusty. I hope the boys remember me when I get home."

Naomi, her voice full of warmth, reassured him, "It will all work out in God's time."

"I have to go, Mom. Send my love to everybody."

"I will, Joe," she replied.

Then, in a quieter voice, she added, "Joe..."

"What is it, Mom?"

Naomi tried her best to keep the tremor from her voice as she fought back the tears, "Joe, please be safe, and take care of yourself."

Joe responded softly, "Don't worry, Mom. Remember, whatever happens, God has my life in His care."

"Bye, Mom. I love you."

The line went dead, and Naomi whispered, "Joe... Joe…" She wiped away the tears, trying to maintain composure as her husband, Richard, walked into the kitchen where Naomi stood by the phone. Richard immediately sensed the sadness on Naomi's face.

"Is something wrong, honey?" he asked gently.

Naomi looked up at him, her voice trembling as she replied, "That was Joe. He couldn't talk for long. While we were talking, the phone went dead."

Richard, having served in the Army, understood that these things happened. He wrapped his arms around Naomi and said, "I'm sure Joe was limited on time. That's all. He'll call back when he can."

A week went by. Then two weeks. Three months slipped away without any word from Joe.

Then, one fateful day, Naomi saw a man in a military uniform walking up the drive to the door. Her heart dropped. She called out for Richard in a voice that trembled with fear.

Richard immediately rose from his recliner and hurried to the front door. He opened it just as the man knocked. Naomi's voice quivered as she whispered, "Richard."

"Try to stay calm, honey," Richard urged her.

He opened the door, and the man handed him an envelope marked with a military address. Naomi's hands began to tremble as she watched Richard take the envelope. Her knees weakened, and Richard gently took her by the arm to steady her. He led her to the living room chair, where they both sat. Naomi asked in a shaky voice, "What does the letter say?"

Richard slowly opened the envelope, his face growing somber. His voice dropped as he explained, "It says that Joe Davis is missing in action. The military doesn't believe he's in enemy hands, but they don't know for sure where he is."

Naomi gasped, her heart heavy with dread. Richard continued, "They've started an investigation. We still have hope, Naomi. We must hold onto that."

Tears welled in Naomi's eyes. She wiped them away and whispered, "What will we tell Jessie?"

Richard replied gently, "We will tell her the truth, but we have to be very careful, very gentle with her."

That evening, after supper, Richard sat down with Jessie. "Honey, we need to talk to you for a minute."

Jessie, who had been playing, looked up nervously. "Did I do something wrong?" she asked innocently.

"No, Jessie, you haven't done anything wrong," Naomi reassured her. "We just need to talk about something important."

Richard, his voice calm and loving, said, "Let's go sit in the living room." He sat down next to Jessie on the couch.

"What's going on, Grandpa?" Jessie asked, her eyes searching his face for answers.

Richard took a deep breath and spoke slowly, "Jessie, we got a letter today from the military…"

Jessie's eyes widened with worry. "Did something happen to my dad?"

Her voice trembled as her eyes filled with tears.

Richard reached out and gently placed a hand on her shoulder. "Jessie, your dad is somewhere, and the military doesn't know exactly where he is right now."

"What do you mean, Grandpa?" Jessie's voice cracked with confusion.

Richard paused for a moment, choosing his words carefully. "He's missing right now, but they are looking for him. There are a lot of people in the military, and sometimes some of them get lost or go missing in action. We'll just have to wait until we hear from them or from your dad."

Jessie, ever the brave girl, nodded, her face set with determination. "Well, I guess we don't have a choice, do we?"

Richard smiled softly. "You're a very brave girl, Jessie. I can see why your mom and dad are so proud of you."

Jessie gave a small, brave grin, then excused herself and walked slowly to her room.

Naomi, determined to help Jessie process her feelings, bought her a journal. When she handed it to her, Naomi said, "You can write down your thoughts and feelings every day. When your dad comes home, you can share them with him."

Jessie held the journal in her hands, but a tear slid down her cheek as she spoke quietly, "We haven't heard from Dad in so long. I don't think he's coming home."

Naomi's heart ached, but she placed a gentle hand on Jessie's shoulder. "Have you been praying for him, sweetheart?"

Jessie wiped her tears away and nodded. "I prayed for him every day, but then I thought… maybe he's not coming back."

Naomi took a deep breath, her voice full of faith. "I know your parents taught you to pray and to trust in God. You need to keep praying. Pray for your dad, for your strength, and for courage. Never forget that God hears every prayer and knows every need."

Jessie, wiping away another tear, nodded. "Okay, Grandma. I'll keep praying."

Naomi smiled softly, "That's my girl."

Months continued to go by without a word. Richard drove down to the nearest military base at the end of every month, but there was no word. The same empty silence greeted him each time. Each visit, Richard would return home with his hopes just a little more faded, the weight of waiting growing heavier with each passing day. The years went by quickly. Jessie turned seventeen and fell in love with a boy in her History class. His name was Eric. Eric was tall, around 5 feet 11, in the twelfth grade. He was built strong from playing football for three years in school. He was very handsome with dark brown hair and blue eyes that seemed to shine with every smile. He had this way of making Jessie feel special, like she was the only one in the room.

He and Jessie dated for a few months, but one evening, Eric took Jessie to a park with a waterfall. It was a quiet, secluded spot, just the kind of place Jessie loved to go to clear her head. There was a concrete bench close to the waterfall. They sat down, side by side, the sound of water cascading over rocks filling the air.

"Let's sit down," Eric said, a soft smile on his lips.

"Okay, this is a beautiful place, Eric," Jessie said, looking around, appreciating the peaceful atmosphere.

"I'm glad you like it," Eric said, his voice a little more serious now. "I hope you will remember this place."

Jessie didn't have a clue as she said, "I probably will. Is it some special place for you?"

He smiled and tried to keep from laughing. He put on a serious facial expression, then pulled out a small box from his pocket. He opened it and held it in front of Jessie. She sat speechless for a moment.

Eric asked, "Jessie, I know we haven't been together for a long time, but it didn't take long for me to fall in love with you. I know I want to spend the rest of my life with you. Would you marry me?" His hand trembled slightly as he waited for her answer.

She was still, as if in shock. She looked into his blue eyes and said, "I remember the first time I saw you in the lunchroom, when you spilled your milk on my plate. You laughed, and your smile was so warm, I knew I'd never forget you." Jessie paused, feeling overwhelmed by the moment. "I've been in love with you ever since that day. Yes, Eric, I'd love to be your wife!"

They shared a passionate kiss as lovers do. Eric kissed her again, his smile wide and bright, almost as if he couldn't believe what was happening. He was filled with joy, not just from the moment, but from the thought of spending the rest of his life with her.

Eric pulled back and said, "We have so much to talk about."

Then Jessie's smile faded. Eric asked, "Is something wrong? Did I say something wrong?"

Jessie couldn't hold back a few tears as she said, "It just hit me that I haven't told you about my life. You don't know a lot about me."

Eric said, "I know that your mom passed away when you were very young. I know you were raised by your grandparents. I know you have two brothers and a sister. I'm pretty sure you never murdered anyone."

Jessie couldn't help but laugh out loud when Eric said that she didn't murder anyone. She said, "Eric, I've carried so much for so long. My dad has been missing for over seven years. I don't know where my sister, Patty, lives, and I haven't seen her or my brothers in almost eight years. It feels like the weight of it all just sits on me, like I'm stuck in this limbo, not knowing how to fix it. I promised my mother before she died that I would keep us together, and she said I would know what to do when I was older, and the time is right. It feels like I'm waiting for that right moment to act, but it hasn't come yet. After we graduate and I save enough money, I have to find my family."

Eric smiled, put his arm around her, and said, "I know what to do."

Jessie's eyes lit up. He had her full attention now.

He said, "My dad is a financial consultant. I will talk to him about how to save the money we need to live on, and I will also explain to him that we need enough money to travel and find your family, I mean our family."

Jessie asked, "Do you think your dad can help?"

Eric smiled, "Of course. That's what he does."

"Oh, Eric, you're so amazing!" Jessie exclaimed.

"I know," he said with a grin, clearly pleased by her excitement.

They made eye contact, both quiet for a moment, their hearts in sync. Then, they burst out laughing, the joy of their shared plans filling the air. Eric and Jessie hugged for a few seconds, holding onto each other as if nothing in the world could separate them.

Then Eric said, "We have to make a few plans before we even make wedding plans."

Jessie said, "Like what?"

Eric said, "Who should we tell about our plans first? I think we should do it together when we tell my parents and your grandparents."

"I agree," Jessie said with a smile. "Let's go tell my grandparents. I think they will be very happy."

"Okay," Eric said. "It's close to graduation, so we must tell them, but we plan to graduate first."

Jessie asked, "What will we do for jobs, Eric?"

"Good question," he replied. "I plan to work at the hospital and go to school to be a doctor."

Then he asked, "Do you have any goals or dreams?"

Jessie said, "Funny you should say that. I would like to go to nursing school. Maybe I could be a nurse practitioner."

"That's perfect!" Eric said with excitement.

Jessie said, "Eric, it won't be easy. It will be long hours and possibly TV dinners or sandwiches for years."

Eric laughed. "It will take some hard work and a lot of love and patience."

Then he asked, "Can you love me enough to go through this?"

Jessie said, "I love you enough to go through fire."

"Really?" Eric asked, raising an eyebrow.

Jessie laughed. "Well, maybe a small fire," she teased.

Eric laughed so hard, he almost fell off the bench. He grabbed Jessie's hand and said, "Let's go talk to your grandparents."

Jessie held onto Eric's hand as they walked in the door. Both grandparents were standing in the living room. Jessie said, "We'd like to talk to you both if you have time." Richard said, "Of course, we have time for you. Let's sit down." Jessie got a quick glimpse of her grandpa winking at her grandma. She couldn't help but wonder if they already knew what was coming. She leaned over to Eric and whispered, "I think they know."

"They probably had an idea about us since we are together so much," said Eric. Jessie smiled a little at that. It felt good knowing that their love wasn't a secret anymore.

Jessie sat with Eric on the couch. Her grandparents sat in the chairs across from them. The air was calm, but there was a quiet tension as everyone got ready for what was about to be said. Eric took a deep breath and finally said, "I love Jessie, and I want to marry her."

Richard said, "Okay."

Eric's voice squeaked slightly from nervousness, and he didn't even hear what Richard said. He was focused, his heart racing. "We will wait until after graduation, and I have a job to support us. We can live at my parent's guest house temporarily. We have plans to continue our education, and I love her very much and promise to take care of him."

Richard said, "Eric, we've known you since you were a little boy. You have a good family, and you've always been a good kid. We know you love Jessie. Even though you're still very young, we believe that you can have a wonderful life together, and I feel sure you'll be good to her."

Eric could feel his heart pounding through his shirt. "Yes, sir."

Richard nodded. "We do want you to wait until Jessie is eighteen in a few months."

"Yes, sir. We talked about it, and we agree," Eric said.

Naomi asked, "How do your parents feel about the marriage, Eric?"

Eric said, "We decided to share this with you two first, but we are going to tell them right away."

Jessie said, "I think we should tell them tonight."

Eric asked, "If it's okay with you, I'd like to take Jessie with me to talk to my parents."

Richard thought for a moment and said, "It's a lot of driving for you going back and forth. You might want to wait until tomorrow and get some rest."

Eric said, "I don't mind."

Richard laughed. "Okay, bring Jessie back before ten. She still has school tomorrow."

"Yes, sir."

Eric and Jessie talked with Eric's parents later that evening. Eric explained his plans, feeling nervous but determined. As they waited for a response, the minutes stretched on, feeling like hours for both of them. After what seemed like a long pause, Eric's parents looked at each other and nodded. Eric's dad, Jim, said, "Eric, I'm proud that you've thought this through and have plans to further your education. You're both very young, and this is a lifetime commitment. But I believe that you both have love and faith in the Lord, and that will get you through the tough times and bless you with good times. You have our blessing."

Eric's mother walked over to him and Jessie, hugging them both. "We're happy for you," she said, her voice full of warmth.

Eric drove Jessie home and kissed her at the door. She walked in and saw her grandparents standing in the kitchen doorway.

She asked, "What was that wink about earlier, Grandpa?"

Richard grinned, "What wink?"

"Come on, Grandpa."

"Well, Jessie, your grandma and I could see the sparkles in your eyes every time you mentioned your young man's name. We knew it was bound to happen."

"Oh, Grandpa!" Jessie said, laughing. She hugged them both and went to bed, feeling like everything was falling into place.

Five months later, Eric and Jessie had the wedding they both dreamed of. They stood by the willow oak trees and red maple by the lake. It was September, and the leaves were beginning to change colors, giving the whole scene a golden, glowing feel. Jessie knew the timing was perfect. She felt like her life was beginning a new chapter, just as the leaves were beginning to change. A small boat went by in the distance, and as the soft ripples of the water met the shoreline, Jessie knew she and Eric were meant to meet and be together.

Jessie had often thought about her mother, missing her every day. But today, she felt an overwhelming sense of peace and happiness. For the first time in a long time, Jessie felt like her mother was smiling down on her, proud of the woman she had become. Even her mother's death had led her to this moment, to this love, and for that, Jessie was grateful.

Eric and Jessie didn't start out with a lot of money, but Eric's parents wanted them to have a honeymoon to remember. It was a gesture they knew would make a big difference for the young couple, who had worked so hard to get to this point. Eric walked over to his dad at the reception and handed him an envelope. Eric opened it and found a reservation for a cabin in the woods in Tennessee. There were also five $100 bills enclosed in the envelope, a generous gift that made Eric's heart swell with gratitude.

Eric had a close relationship with his dad, and it didn't bother him at all to hug his dad in front of everybody. It wasn't just about the money or the honeymoon; it was about the love and support his family had always shown him. Eric immediately strolled over to Jessie, who was waiting for him. When he showed Jessie what his dad had given them, Jessie didn't hesitate to jump up from her chair. She nearly ran to Eric's dad, wrapping her arms around him tightly, thanking him through tears that were now streaming down her face.

Then she turned to hug his mother, thanking them again with heartfelt words. The love and gratitude in the air were undeniable, and it was clear that both families cared deeply for each other.

Eric and Jessie returned from their honeymoon, and Eric carried Jessie over the threshold of his parent's guest house. As he kissed her and said, "We are home," there was a sense of new beginnings in the air.

Jessie smiled, but there was a touch of disbelief in her voice as she said, "I hope this is not a dream because I don't want to wake up."

Eric chuckled softly and said, "It's not a dream, but we do have to work on our dreams in the morning." He paused, becoming a little more serious. "It may be tough for a while, honey."

Jessie, determined and unwavering, looked up at him. "I will work hard. As long as we are together, we can do anything. My mother always said, 'When you trust in the Lord and serve Him, He will always get you through.'" Her words were comforting and filled with a sense of faith that had carried her through much of her life.

Morning came, and Eric went back to the hospital where he worked as an orderly. It wasn't glamorous, but it was work that gave him a sense of purpose. Sometimes, after work, Eric would help his dad by cleaning his office and straightening files, or whatever else was needed, earning a little extra pay that helped cover their expenses.

One evening after working at the hospital, Eric began to feel like there was something more he was supposed to do. There was this desire bubbling inside him, a calling to serve his country. The thought didn't come lightly, but he couldn't ignore it. He stopped by his dad's office, and since there were no clients in the building, Eric asked if he could talk to him.

"Sure, son. What's on your mind?" his dad asked.

"Dad, I feel like I need to be a part of something bigger, and I want to join the Navy."

Jim, his dad, looked thoughtful for a moment before responding. "Son, there comes a time in some men's lives when they feel the need to serve their country. You can serve your country in the military, but you also serve your country when you work a job that helps people. You can also serve by volunteering your time to community services. The military is a great place to serve, but make sure it's what you truly want to do, because it's a different life. You should talk to Jessie, and you should pray about it."

Eric nodded, "I have plans to talk to Jessie about it tonight, and I have prayed. It feels like God is leading me to go into the Navy."

Jim smiled and put a hand on his shoulder. "I support the decision you make, son."

Eric drove up to the door of the guest house, his hands gripping the steering wheel. He just sat there for a moment, feeling nervous about telling Jessie. His mind raced with questions. "Will she be mad? Will she threaten to leave me? Will she cry?" The thought of her being upset worried him, but he knew he had to share his feelings with her.

Jessie opened the front door and called out, "Eric, is everything okay?"

"Yes, honey. I'll be right there," he replied, trying to sound calm, though his voice had a slight tremble.

Eric walked slowly to the door, each step feeling heavier than the last. He walked in and gave Jessie a quick peck on the cheek, trying to mask his anxiety.

Jessie immediately picked up on his nervousness. "Okay, Eric, what's wrong?" Her voice was gentle but filled with concern, and Eric knew he couldn't hide it from her any longer.

"Let's sit down," Eric said. Jessie became very quiet and stared straight at Eric, waiting in anticipation. Her heart raced a little, and she wondered what he was about to say. She could tell this was something important to him. Eric began explaining, "Honey, I've been thinking lately that I should join the service and serve my country. I've been thinking that maybe I would join the Navy. I love boats. I love the ocean, and I love this country. I feel like it's something I am led to do."

Jessie was quiet for a minute, and then she asked, "How long do you think you would be gone?"

He said, "Around eight weeks for boot camp, then I'm not sure how long for school."

"What would you do?" asked Jessie.

"I want to be a medic or a doctor," Eric answered.

"Wow! I think that would be a long time apart!" Jessie said, her voice trembling slightly. It suddenly felt like everything was changing, and she didn't know if she was ready for it.

Eric said, "Sometime after boot camp and school, you can come stay in an apartment, and we will be together."

Jessie said, "I don't know, Eric. I know you need to go where you are led to go, but I don't think the Lord would separate us for a long time."

Eric said, "I will do a lot of research, and no decisions will be made in haste."

Eric said, "I thought you would be mad."

Jessie replied, "I'm not mad. I'm a little scared."

"Why?" Eric asked.

A few tears trickled from her eyes. "You know my dad went in the service, and I never saw him again."

"Oh, Jessie, I'm sorry, I guess I forgot how you felt about that."

Jessie looked straight into Eric's blue eyes and said, "You know what, Eric? I believe you would make a great medic, but I think you would make a great doctor."

Eric asked, "Thanks, honey, but what's your point?"

Jessie continued, "If you went to college, we could be together and save money as we go. I can work and go to school part-time, or I can work two jobs and go to school later. After you finish school, maybe you can go to the Reserves and be a doctor." She paused for a moment, hoping her suggestion made sense. "That way, we won't be apart for so long, and we can still have our future together."

Eric stood up and walked around the room, not saying a word. Jessie said, "Eric, I'm sorry if that was a bad idea."

Eric rubbed his hand alongside his chin, then he looked down at Jessie and said, "Jessie, my dad said something like that, and it makes sense when you say it."

Jessie smiled. It was a relief to know that they were thinking about the same things. It felt like a weight had been lifted, knowing they could figure this out together.

Eric said, "We have goals and dreams, but it won't be easy. It will be a lot of work, but we can accomplish our goals by the time we're about twenty-six or possibly twenty-seven."

Jessie said, "It sounds almost too good to be true. I hope nothing happens to stop us."

"Like what?" Eric asked.

"Oh, you know, like sickness, death, and stuff."

Eric took her hands in his. "I understand, but I truly believe that if we trust in each other and trust in God, we'll make it through anything that comes our way."

Jessie nodded. "I guess you're right. We just have to stay strong and keep our faith."

Eric smiled, feeling better after talking through it all. He knew it wouldn't be easy, but he also knew they could make it work if they were both committed to each other. "We'll do this together, Jessie. Whatever happens, we'll handle it. I know we can."

Eric called his dad and told him his new plans that Jessie helped him with. He said, "Dad, it feels right now."

Richard said, "Eric, I think that is a great plan."

"Thanks, Dad," Eric said, feeling relieved to have his father's approval.

Eric continued, "I realize it will be tough, but Jessie and I are strong, and we both count on the Lord to see us through."

Richard was quiet for a moment, trying to make sure Eric could not hear the crack in his voice. He cleared his throat and took a deep breath before continuing, his voice soft but full of emotion. "Son, I have never been more proud of you."

"Wow! Thanks, Dad. I'm not sure what I did," Eric replied, his heart swelling with gratitude.

Richard said, "I believe you are sincere when you say you trust in the Lord, and you are so mature for your age."

Eric wasn't sure what to say, so he was quiet for a moment, letting his father's words sink in. Then his dad continued. "Eric, I know you can accomplish your goals, but I would like to help. If you and Jessie would consider staying in the guest house for a few more years, or until you finish school and get the career you need, your mother and I would love to have you both, and that would save you some money."

Jessie was standing nearby, listening to the conversation, and Eric held his hand over the phone to tell Jessie what his dad had offered. He gave her a look, silently asking for her opinion.

He asked Jessie, "What do you think?"

Jessie removed Eric's hand from the phone and said loudly with excitement, "Thank you so much!" Her face lit up with a smile that made Eric's heart feel full.

Eric laughed and said, "Dad, it looks like we will be staying a while. I hope you don't get tired of us."

Richard chuckled on the other end. "I don't think we'll see much of you with the schedule you have."

Time went by quickly. After one year of medical school, learning about drugs and patient care, Eric didn't feel the same about his educational goals. He found himself thinking more and more about what he really wanted to do with his life, and the medical field wasn't sitting right with him. He talked to the college counselor and explained that he knew the world needed doctors, surgeons, and specialists, but he did not want to have a career of ordering drugs for patients. He was searching for something that felt more fulfilling.

The counselor offered other options. When the counselor explained physical therapy, Eric became excited. "That sounds right up my alley, but I must talk to my wife." Eric couldn't wait to share this with Jessie. It felt like a real possibility, and he knew she would be supportive, but he wanted her opinion. He thanked the counselor and drove home quickly.

Eric explained how he felt to Jessie. "I've been thinking a lot about it, and this physical therapy thing really excites me. It's a way to help people and be hands-on without having to deal with all the drugs and prescriptions. I feel like this could be the right path for me."

Jessie had a lot of questions. "How long would it take to finish? And where would we go?"

Eric said, "The school is in Alabama. As a matter of fact, it's in Birmingham. It won't take as many years to graduate, and we can apply for a grant or loan. Plus, we can get you started in nursing school. You've been a nursing assistant long enough, and your training will help you with your schoolwork."

"Eric, are you sure this is what you really want to do?" Jessie asked, her voice full of concern. She could tell that this decision was big for him, and she wanted to make sure he was sure about it.

Chapter 3
What won't kill you will make you stronger

Eric hugged Jessie and said, "Jessie, God is teaching me so many lessons. At first, I was worried, but I read in the King James Bible, 1st Corinthians 14:33: 'For God is not the author of confusion, but of peace, as in all churches of the saints.' Jessie, I'm not confused, I'm just figuring things out." Then he asked her, "Does this make sense?"

Jessie said, "I think so. It's just scary at times when things change." Eric asked, "Jessie, did you know and understand about the Lord when you were a baby?" "No," Jessie replied.

Eric said, "You grew up and changed when the Lord made Himself known to you." "Okay, I trust you, Eric. Let's do this." Jessie applied for a grant and received a partial grant that would help her get started in school as a physical therapist assistant.

When she explained to Eric what she had decided to do, he hugged her, lifted her in the air with a big hug, and then kissed her on her lips. With a smile from ear to ear, she asked, "So are you happy about my decision?" Eric said, "I think it's wonderful, and we might have some classes together." Jessie said, "I think I can do a class or two online, but I'm not sure of all the details yet."

Eric said, "Honey, it's still going to be tough at times. It will kill us or make us stronger." Jessie looked at him with her lips tightened and said, "Don't talk like that. We'll make it, by the Grace of God." The Lord works in mysterious ways. She believed with all her heart that no matter what challenges came, they could face them together.

Jessie knew it would be best for her if she started working on the night shift so she could go to classes during the day. She had no idea that she would be working with a bully on that shift. The first night at work, one of the nurse's aides came over to Jessie and whispered to her to be aware of Judy.

The nurse's aide, Alice, told Jessie, "She's mean, bossy, and makes people quit."

"Oh no!" Jessie said out loud. "What have I done?" Alice said, "Do your best to stay away from her. I'll help you when I can. Judy likes to work by herself anyway. She thinks she knows it all."

Jessie asked, "Why hasn't she been fired if she is so mean?" Alice answered, "I guess it's because we are always shorthanded and they keep the ones they have."

Jessie said, "Well, I have to work here for now, so she will just have to get used to me."

"Good luck," Alice said. Just then, Judy walked around the corner of the nurse's desk. She said smugly, "Well! It's Alice in Wonderland. Are you lost?" Alice turned her head and walked away.

Then that mean-mouthed Judy looked at Jessie. She said, "You are new on this shift. Just so you know, I don't like it when people get in my way, so don't ask me for help."

Jessie said, "Oh, I won't. I don't think you'd be much help anyway!" And Jessie walked over to the nurse's desk. The nurse was sitting at the desk and heard the conversation. She said, "Hi, Jessie."

Jessie turned and recognized her friend Julie. Jessie said, "I'm glad to see a friendly face."

Julie said, "Don't worry, Jessie. I heard the conversation. Good for you." Jessie said, "I may have started off on the wrong foot."

The nurse said, "No, she will torment you if you let her. Alice and I will help you." "You've got this, Jessie. Just stay strong. Don't let her break you."

Jessie didn't want to bother Eric with this challenge, but she knew she would be praying a lot. Jessie had to change pads, keep residents dry, and check several vital signs during the night. She stayed busy.

Judy remained hateful when she spoke to Jessie and Alice. The nurse informed Jessie that she could make a complaint and write her up if she wanted to. Jessie said, "We reap what we sow. It will come back to her someday, if she doesn't get right with the Lord." Jessie knew that her patience and kindness would eventually outshine Judy's bitterness.

One evening, an elderly resident sat up in her bed and then started walking to the bathroom. She began to lose her balance and screamed out. Jessie was close by and ran in, catching the lady before she hit the floor. Jessie eased her down to the floor. Judy walked by and looked in the room. She said, "I'm going to report you for letting her fall."

Jessie said, "Okay, but can you help me get her off the floor?" She said, "You dropped her, you get her up." The lady said, "I know you did not drop me to the floor. Thank you."

Jessie said, "You're welcome." The lady said, "That girl is mean." Jessie said, "Yep, it looks that way. I'll stay with you until the nurse gets here and helps us." Jessie turned on the call light, and the nurse arrived within two minutes. Jessie explained what happened. The lady who fell also explained Judy's behavior. The nurse said, "I have to write this up and turn her in."

The next morning, Judy was called into the office and, as expected, she was fired. Jessie told the nurse, "I'm sorry she lost her job, but she went too far this time." "It's hard, but sometimes people need to face the consequences of their actions."

Things were tough for a while because Jessie had to do her classes and work extra nights until another worker was hired. Two weeks later, a young man was hired. He was twenty years old, tall (about five feet eleven), and muscular. It was obvious that the man worked out.

Jessie told Eric that a man had been hired to work with her, so she should be getting a little more time off. Eric was not happy. He asked Jessie if he was good-looking. Jessie said, "Eric, I love you, and I just want to get through the classes so we can have a career. I am not interested in this man, and I don't want any stress at home!"

Eric said, "Okay."

Low and behold, about three weeks later, the young new hire started flirting with Jessie. He got brave one evening and tapped her on her bottom. She turned and looked at him and said, "I am happily married and just trying to get through each night. My husband would not appreciate you touching me. He would come here and kick your butt, and send you into outer space, but I may do it myself if you try anything like that again!"

The young man said, "Okay, okay!" Jessie decided not to mention it to Eric because she knew he would meet this guy, and there might be trouble. She had come too far to quit now. "I'll handle this myself," she thought.

Time went by quickly. Jessie had studied hard and was ready for her final exams. Eric said, "You have worked so hard, honey. I'm so proud of you." Jessie said, "I haven't passed yet."

"You will do fine," Eric reassured her. Jessie said, "It's a lot of pressure, Eric."

Eric faced her and put his hands on her shoulders, and said, "If you don't pass it, you will study a little and take it again." Jessie took a deep breath and walked into the room to take her test. She felt a mix of nerves and determination, but she knew she had given it her best shot.

Jessie passed her tests and began looking for a new job. She looked in the newspaper, listened on the radio for jobs, and then got on the internet. There were several PTA (physical therapist assistant) jobs, but they were a long distance from her house. She went to work that night as usual, serving as a nurse's aide. She tried to keep a smile on her face, but the nurse noticed the sad look on her face.

She walked over to Jessie and asked, "What's wrong, my friend?" Jessie answered, "I've got my license as a PTA, and I'm having trouble finding a job locally. I like it here, and I got a lot of experience and friendships, but I need to practice in a new field of work."

The nurse said, "Hmmm, I think I heard of a job opening in the hospital that serves home health residents." Jessie's eyes lit up. "Thank you so much. I will check that out tomorrow."

The nurse said, "Jessie, if you don't find what you are looking for, try the colleges around. You might have an opportunity as a teacher. I'm not sure about that, but it's worth a try. If not, you could teach after you get some experience."

Jessie stood up and hugged her friend. Her friend concluded, "I would miss you, but I understand that you need to pursue your dreams. Just don't forget us once you're out there doing what you love."

When Jessie got off work in the morning, she was still very excited. She drove directly to the hospital. She went in and asked for an application. After she filled it out and turned it back in, she asked the lady behind the desk if they were hiring. The lady said, "We are hiring, but we have a few applications and resumes to go over, so you will be notified if they want you to come in."

Jessie opened her mouth with the intention of telling the lady how much she needed this job, but a voice inside her told her to wait. Jessie thought to herself, "I am not going to beg for a job. I have to be patient."

Jessie began to notice that her eyes felt heavy. She had worked all night and had to work again tonight, so she decided to go home and get some sleep. That evening before she went to work, she talked to Eric. She said, "I miss seeing you every evening and lying beside you."

Eric said, "I miss you too, but things will get better eventually."

Jessie told Eric that she looked for a job today at the hospital, but she had to wait for an answer. Eric reminded Jessie, "Don't forget to ask God what He wants you to do. He blessed you through school, and He can lead you to the right job."

Jessie smiled and said, "Thanks for the reminder." She closed her eyes for a moment, whispering a prayer for guidance.

The next morning, Jessie went to two home health agencies to apply for a job. When she started to go out the door of the second agency, a lady walked out of her office and called Jessie back. Jessie turned and looked at the lady.

She asked, "Ma'am?"

The lady said, "I am Mrs. Marks. I was looking over your application. I see that you are recently out of school."

Jessie said, "Yes, ma'am."

Mrs. Marks continued, "Jessie, normally we hire people with experience, but I have a feeling about you. We could use some young, fresh ideas, and I think you would be an asset to this agency. We have a Physical Therapist you would work under. If you think you'd be interested in working here, I will introduce you to him right now, and we will discuss your salary."

Jessie tensed up and tried to contain her excitement as she said calmly, "I would be interested as long as I could work during the day and give notice to my other job."

Mrs. Marks said, "We don't have a third shift."

Jessie was thrilled to be making more money and learning more about her career. She could hardly wait to get home to tell Eric. Jessie knew it was going to be difficult to work out her notice because she was so anxious to start her new job. She couldn't help but smile as she imagined what it would be like to focus entirely on her new career.

Little did she know that she had a lot to learn about her life as well as her job. On Jessie's last night of working out her notice, Mrs. Quinn, a resident, started crying. Jessie went into her room and asked her why she was crying.

Jessie was surprised when Mrs. Quinn said, "I don't want you to go away. I will miss you!"

Jessie held her and began to cry. She explained that she had worked hard to get this opportunity, and she told Mrs. Quinn that she would come back to visit her. Mrs. Quinn said, "Okay, I will look forward to that." She continued to cry.

Jessie was feeling uneasy when she walked out of Mrs. Quinn's room. Jessie heard an alarm go off. She ran to the end of the hall and saw a resident going out the door. It was five a.m. Jessie would be going home soon, but she screamed out for the nurse as she went out the door after the male resident. He was angry and yelled at Jessie, "I want to go home!"

Jessie reached out for his arm and said, "Come with me, I'll take you where you need to be." The resident was still angry and swung at Jessie, hitting her on the side of her face with his fist.

Immediately, Jessie's face turned red and blue from a severe bruise. She fell to the ground, and now she was mad. Jessie knew this resident couldn't help himself, but she was not going to be defeated. Jessie grabbed both his arms and said, "I will take you home." The resident became calmer as he looked at her. She didn't lie. She took him to his room, which was his home.

The nurse was standing at the door as she witnessed Jessie holding on to the man. She shrieked slightly and covered her mouth with her hand. She said, "Oh my goodness!"

Jessie said, "It's okay, I got him."

The nurse said, "Jessie, your face is swollen like a big blue balloon!" Jessie remembered that the man had slugged her, but she didn't know how badly. Jessie felt the side of her face and said, "Ouch, that's smart."

The nurse told Jessie, "Let's fill out a report, and you will have to go to the ER." Jessie said, "I start my new job tomorrow. I can't go in like this."

Jessie went to the ER as instructed. She notified Eric, but told him to go to school because she was okay. As she went to the ER desk to sign in, she saw Eric sitting in the waiting room. He jumped up from his seat and ran over to her.

She explained what happened, and for some reason, she began to cry. Eric held her for a few seconds, then he snickered and tried to keep from laughing out loud.

"What are you laughing at?" Jessie asked.

He tried to answer her but started laughing.

Jessie stared at him with anger, then she began to laugh. She said, "Don't make me laugh, it hurts my face." Eric could not contain himself. He burst out laughing.

"It's not funny!" Jessie said as she held her face and tried to keep from laughing. Eric said, "I'm sorry, honey, I know it hurts, but I can't believe that man got away with slugging you in the face."

Jessie tightened her lips as she often did when frustrated and tried not to laugh. Eric and Jessie went back to the exam room together.

The nurse said, "Your X-rays show that nothing is broken, but of course, blood vessels have burst and will have to heal. I hope you got a good punch into the one that did this."

Eric and Jessie held their posture until they went out the door, then Eric doubled over from laughing so hard.

Jessie said, "Okay, it may be a little funny, but not that funny." Eric snorted as he tried to quit laughing. Jessie said, "It isn't that funny."

Eric didn't say anything. Jessie said, "It isn't!"

The next day, Jessie was afraid she would lose her new job if she called in, so she went in with her swollen face. Mrs. Marks met her at the door and asked her what had happened. Jessie told her story.

Mrs. Marks said, "Well, I admire you for coming on to work. I think you can learn some paperwork and train with the PT if you feel like it."

Jessie agreed.

Seven days later, Jessie's face was beginning to get some of her olive skin color back. She went out to a lady's house with the PT to meet her and start her therapy. The lady was young, thirty years old.

She was recovering from a recent fall. She held her one-year-old baby in her arms while Jessie explained what she was going to do.

Jessie asked if she could hold the baby. The lady handed her the little girl. Jessie had a strange feeling come over her as her heart melted. She leaned over and kissed the little girl's forehead and handed her to the grandmother. Jessie thought about the lady and her baby all day.

Jessie came home and prepared dinner for herself and Eric. As they sat down to eat, Jessie was unusually quiet. Eric watched her push her potatoes around on her plate, and he asked, "What are you thinking about, Jess?" She was deep in thought and didn't answer.

"Jess!" Jessie looked over at Eric and asked, "What did you say?"

Eric repeated, "What are you thinking about?" Jessie blurted, "I want a baby!"

They looked at each other without saying a word, then Eric asked, "Um, what did you say?" Jessie let out a big sigh and explained, "I know it's a lot to think about, and maybe it's the wrong time, but I feel like I want a baby." Then Jessie started to cry.

Eric got up from his chair and said, "It's okay, we can talk about it." Jessie said, "I have so much on my mind and heart. I think about having children, but I know it would be hard on you, going to school for close to six more years. I think about my dad, and I wonder where he is and why I haven't heard anything from the military, and I think about my family and wonder where they are. I'm not sure why this all hits me at once."

Eric said, "I knew this was coming someday. You will need answers, and we will search for them together." Eric continued, "I'd love to have a baby too, but maybe we can wait just a little longer to have time to get insurance at your job. We can keep making inquiries about your dad, and we should start looking for your family, starting with library records, hospital records, churches, and maybe schools. We could put ads in the newspaper."

Jessie asked Eric, "What do I do if I find them?"

Eric said, "When you locate any of them, you go see them when you can, or call them, or send a letter. Right now, you might want to concentrate on your new job. Soon we will start searching for answers."

Jessie gave a sigh of relief and said, "That sounds like a good plan." She wiped her tears away, feeling a little more at peace knowing that Eric was there to help her figure things out.

Months passed. Jessie's face healed. Eric had a little over five years of school left to complete. Things were going well until that cold winter day in January. A thin layer of ice was building on the roads, and snow was beginning to cover the ice in their driveway. Eric and his classmates were sent home early.

When Jessie arrived home, she found Eric sitting on the couch by the phone. He had a concerned look on his face. She walked over to Eric and asked, "Is something wrong?"

Eric said, "Sit by me. I want to talk to you."

Jessie said, "Eric, you are scaring me."

Eric said, "It's not bad news exactly."

Jessie asked, "Well, what is it?"

Eric said, "I received a call from Jim today. He's a friend I knew who joined the Army. I told him about your dad a few months ago. He told me about a man he met in the hospital on post around a year ago. His description sounds like your dad."

Jessie said, "I want to go see him!"

Eric said, "Jessie, we need to stay put with the ice on the roads, but we will check into this. I want you to be prepared, if it is your dad, he has remarried."

Jessie said, "It couldn't be!"

Eric held her hand and said, "Jessie, if you want to know, you will have to be prepared and calm because we don't know the whole story yet."

Jessie stood up from the couch. She was very quiet as she looked around the room. She spoke quietly, "I've waited so long. Could this actually be my dad?" Her heart raced with hope and fear mixed together.

That night, Eric tried to sleep, but it felt like waves in the ocean with Jessie tossing and turning. He knew she was anxious to find answers about her dad. He was turned away from Jessie, just glaring at the wall. He said a silent, "God help her."

The sun came up, and Jessie jumped out of bed. She said, "Eric, I need to find out about that man and see if he is my dad."

Eric said, "Okay, give me some time to see if I can reach my friend."

"Hey, Jim."

"Hey Eric, how's it going?"

"Good. You know, we talked about a man who fits Mr. Davis' description?"

Jim answered, "Oh yeah. I don't think his name is Davis, but I'm not sure."

Eric asked, "Can I get the phone number or address?"

Jim said, "I really can't give out information, but let me make a call, and I'll call you back before the end of the day."

Eric said, "Okay, Thanks."

Jim said, "Sure, talk to you soon."

Eric called out to Jessie. She was in the kitchen preparing breakfast. "I'm in the kitchen," she said.

Eric walked to the kitchen and began to tell Jessie about the phone call. He said, "Jessie, Jim said he doesn't think it is your dad, but he will make a call and get back to us before the end of the day."

Jessie said, "I'm kinda glad I don't have to work today, especially since the roads are still bad."

Eric asked, "Jessie, did you hear me?"

Jessie responded, "Yep, I heard you."

Eric knew Jessie was disappointed. He said, "Maybe he'll have some good news when he calls."

Jessie said, "Maybe."

Three hours later, the phone rang. Jessie walked toward the phone and then stopped beside it. She just stared at it and listened to it ring. On the fourth ring, Eric answered it.

"Hello." He heard silence for a second, then a voice came on.

"This is Jim. I managed to get in touch with that man's wife. She said she will call you in about an hour. Her name is Kathy."

Eric said, "Thanks, Jim."

Jim said, "Good luck."

Eric told Jessie what he said. He noticed that Jessie began to tremble.

"Now, Jessie, try not to worry."

Jessie said, "I'm trying." Her hands clenched, and she tried to breathe deeply, telling herself that she couldn't let herself get too hopeful too soon.

An hour passed, and the phone didn't ring. Jessie sat on the couch close to the phone and just stared at it. Fifteen minutes later, the phone rang. This time, Jessie snatched it up.

"Hello?" Jessie said quickly.

Someone at the other end said, "Hello, am I speaking to Jessie?"

"Yes, ma'am," Jessie answered.

"Jessie, my name is Kathy. I understand that you have been searching for your dad."

Jessie answered, "Yes, ma'am, I have."

"I met the man I married in the hospital. He was in the Army, and he was hit by a hit-and-run driver. I was one of his nurses. He did not remember what happened in the accident, and he wasn't sure how he got to the hospital. We talked every day, and we fell in love quickly. There was no identification on him, so we called him Mr. Smith. I'm going to send a picture of him to you in a text. He may not look the same due to some reconstructive surgery, but if you think it is your dad, I will ask you to give me time to explain this to him. Also, keep in mind that he doesn't remember his past, although sometimes his head hurts when he says he has brief flashbacks."

Jessie's voice was quivering slightly as she said, "I understand."

A moment later, a text message came through on Jessie's phone with a picture of the man. The phone was silent on both ends. Eric asked, "Jessie, what do you think?"

Jessie stood silent, looking at the picture on her cell phone. Eric said, "Jessie."

Jessie turned slowly toward Eric and said, "This is my dad." She repeated it, "Oh my gosh, this is my dad!" Jessie put her face close to her phone and asked, "Mrs. Smith, can I come see my dad?"

"Of course you can, but we will have to be careful not to upset him or rush him. Do you understand how important it is, Jessie?"

Jessie replied, "Yes, ma'am. I will be patient. We have ice on the roads now, and I just started a new job. I'm off on the weekend, so if the weather is good, I will make the trip, and that will give you some time to talk to my dad."

Mrs. Smith said, "That sounds fine, Jessie, and by the way, you can call me Kathy."

"Thank you, Kathy," Jessie replied. She felt a mix of excitement and nervousness building inside her. It felt so real now, but she wasn't sure what to expect.

The weekend was near, and the roads had cleared. Jessie had called her boss and explained that she had found her dad, who had been missing for several years. She explained that she loved her job and did not want to lose it. She asked if she could have two more days added to her weekend to meet and talk with her dad.

Her boss was touched by Jessie's story and told her to take a week and enjoy the reunion. He said, "I'll be anxious to hear about it when you get back."

She thanked him and told Eric that she should pack.

Eric said, "Jessie, I just happened to have a break at school this week. I would like to go with you, if that's okay."

Jessie said, "Oh, Eric, that would be wonderful!" They packed their bags, grabbed a GPS, and loaded the car.

Jessie sat quietly in the passenger side of their jeep, her fingers twisting the hem of her sweatshirt as the car neared the Tennessee line. Jessie's anxiety grew heavy. She began to wonder if he would even want to see her. Would his wife feel threatened or sympathetic? Jessie rehearsed different things to say. "Hi, I'm your daughter." Felt too blunt. "We used to be close." Too pushy. What haunted Jessie the most wasn't that he couldn't remember her, but that he had remarried a woman that she had never met. Now she was traveling to Tennessee to face a stranger who used to be her hero.

Jessie thought about writing a letter because that might be easier, and something he could read and process in his own time, but she longed to look him in the eyes, just in case a flicker of recognition remained. The fear of rejection tangled with her fragile hope that love, however buried, could still find a way through. She knew the moment she arrived, everything would change, but she wasn't sure how.

When Eric and Jessie arrived, Jessie stood in front of the small house, clutching a photo of her and her dad on a fishing trip when she was very young. The door opened, and her dad's new wife answered.

"You must be Jessie and Eric," Kathy said with a smile. She invited them in. Her father stood in the living room, puzzled, but kind. Jessie took a deep breath, offered the photo with trembling hands, and said softly, "I don't know if you remember me, but I remember everything about you."

In that moment, she wasn't asking to reclaim the past, only to begin something new.

Jessie's father took the photo from her hand and studied it carefully. His brows furrowed, eyes narrowed as if trying to pull something from deep within a fog. He didn't speak at first, just stared, tilting his head slightly. Then, with a sudden inhale, he flinched and brought a hand to his temple. "I've seen this before." He murmured, voice strained.

Jessie froze, unsure if it was real recognition or just a polite response. His wife, Kathy, stepped forward instinctively, placing a supportive hand on his arm. "Sometimes he gets these flashes," she explained softly to Jessie. "But they come with migraines. It's like his brain fights to remember."

A tense silence filled the room as Jessie's father sat down, the photo still in his lap. The stream in the woods. Big rocks. A cane fishing pole. His words were halting. "Yes," Jessie said as she kneeled beside him. "You taught me how to fish with a cane pole. I was five years old."

He winced again, squeezing his eyes shut as if the memory was too sharp, too sudden. "Your name is Jessie." His voice was barely audible.

She nodded, unable to stop the tears. Eric moved over and put his arms around Jessie to comfort her. It wasn't full recognition, but it was something. A flicker of the past is trying to resurface.

Jessie's dad opened his eyes again, looking at her with a mixture of confusion and awe.

"You were my little girl?"

Jessie nodded again, this time with a small, trembling smile. His wife sat across the room watching with emotion, not jealousy, but something closer to heartbreak and understanding.

"I don't remember everything," he said slowly, "but I feel something… when I look at you, like I am supposed to know you, like I want to."

Jessie reached out and held his hand, knowing that healing wouldn't come all at once, but for the first time in a long while, she felt like maybe there was still a place for her in his life, even if they had to start from the beginning.

Kathy asked Eric and Jessie to stay the night in their spare bedroom. They agreed.

The next day, after Jessie's emotional reunion with her father, she sat on the porch with him and gently asked, "Do you remember Patty? Or Jeremiah... Dusty?"

Her father's expression tightened as he searched his memory, but came up empty. Jessie pulled out her phone and showed him a picture she took of the kids from a photo album. She had kept the album since her mother passed away.

Patty was seven, Jeremiah was four, and Dusty was two, I think, just learning to talk pretty well.

His words trembled as he held the phone, and then he pressed it close to his chest as if it might trigger something buried deep inside. "I wish I did," he said, his voice cracking. "But even if I don't remember them... they are mine too, aren't they?"

Jessie nodded. "They didn't come with me because when Momma passed away, the kids went with different family members, and I haven't seen any of them in a long time, but I do plan to look for them in hopes that we will all be together again someday."

Jessie said, "I can hardly wait for them to meet you, Kathy."

Chapter 4
Plans change unexpectedly

While at work, Jessie shifted her weight from one foot to the other. The worn rubber soles of her sneakers squeaked slightly on the tile floor. The clinic was quiet for a moment, a rare lull between appointments. She used the pause to roll her shoulders and stretch her neck, the ache from hours of lifting and guiding patients never quite went away. Her job as a physical therapist assistant at the agency paid steadily, but it wasn't the kind of work that left much room for dreaming, at least not for now. Still, she clung to the dream anyway and prayed for patience. She believed that things could improve, even if it took time.

Eric continued to juggle classes during the day and work for his father in the evenings. Most evenings, he came home with textbooks under his arm, too exhausted to talk, but always smiling when he saw her. Jessie admired his determination. They both knew it wasn't a glamorous life, living free in the guest house. Eric wanted more for Jessie, but Jessie never complained. They were saving money and watching prices like hawks. They both had a plan: save every cent and pay off debts. One day, a few years down the line, they'd have enough to buy a small ranch, land, freedom, and sky. She dreamed about waking up to open space every day, without the weight of bills and endless hours. They both worked so hard, but Jessie knew they couldn't keep at it forever.

More than that, they would have the resources to finally start looking for Jessie's siblings and hopefully visit her dad more often, if he was up to it. Jessie made inquiries and tried here and there to find her family, but without time and money, it always ended the same way: another dead end. She didn't talk about it often, not even with Eric, but that quiet hope sat heavy in her chest every time she stared out the window during her breaks. She thought quietly to herself, "This shouldn't be that hard. They were raised with family. Where are they?" The thought troubled her, a constant ache she couldn't ignore.

Jessie and Eric were building a life, brick by brick, with hands that were tired but steady. Jessie reminded herself of that on the hard days, the days when a patient snapped at her or Eric came home too tired to eat. The ranch, the search, they were far-off glimmers, but they were real enough to keep her going. This wasn't the end of their story; it was just the part where they learned how much they could carry. Jessie was used to carrying weight, whether it was physical or emotional. She'd learned early on that she had to be strong, strong for herself, for Eric, for the dream.

And Jessie had always been good at carrying things. A few weeks ago, Jessie recognized a name on her patient intake list, and her stomach twisted. Judy Hanes. It had taken her a second to believe it could be the same girl, the one who used to call her names, refused to assist her with patient care, and whispered cruel things behind her back when they worked at the nursing home. Judy had been sharp-tongued and smug, always finding ways to make Jessie feel smaller during those long, grueling shifts. Jessie never fought back. She remembered what her mom had taught her about the importance of kindness to others. "You never know what someone's going through," her mom had said. Jessie had just taken it and kept working, determined to outlast everything that tried to break her down. But now, seeing Judy's name again, Jessie wasn't sure if she could ignore the past this time.

Now, years later, Judy was one of her patients, recovering from a bad fall, needing help to walk again. Jessie didn't say anything when they locked eyes for the first time, but she could tell Judy remembered her, too. There was a flash of discomfort, maybe even shame, in the woman's eyes. Still, Jessie just nodded, smiling politely, and got to work. She guided Judy through her exercises with the same calm tone she used with all her patients. No bitterness. No grudge. If Judy noticed the grace in that, she didn't say so. But Jessie could see her soften a little more with each visit. This was Jessie's way now, let the past go, focus on the present, and move forward.

On Judy's fifth visit, it seemed obvious that she had concerns. She looked down at the floor and then back at Jessie. She said, "Jessie, I remember working with you at the nursing home a while back." Jessie sat quietly in the chair in front of Judy and did not interrupt her. Judy continued, "I was going through a tough time. My parents were getting a divorce, and I was angry at the world. I want you to know that I am very sorry for the way I treated you." Jessie said, "It's in the past, but I wish you had talked to me. I would have listened." Judy hung her head and shed a few tears. She said, "I was angry, and I did not trust anyone." Jessie surprised Judy when she reached forward and gave her a tight hug. Then Jessie said, "You can talk to me, and I will still listen, but we must concentrate on getting you stronger and back on your feet." Judy cracked a smile and felt better than she had in years. She had a friend and someone to work with her to get better. For the first time in a long while, she felt like she wasn't carrying the weight of her past alone. Jessie said a quick prayer in her head, she knew God could hear her. "Thank you, Lord, for this moment."

Jessie had a jar of coins on top of the fridge, something she had started years ago when every penny counted more than people knew. It had once held gas money, emergency rent, and occasional fast food indulgences on the days she was too tired to cook. Over time, it became a symbol of something more. When she finally paid off her little hatchback last summer, counting out change and crumpled bills at the credit union, it felt like a turning point. A small one, maybe, but it was hers. Since then, she started saving again. Every dollar went into a separate envelope now, "ranch fund" scrawled in

Sharpie on the front. She didn't count the money too often; she just kept adding to it. "One day," she told herself, "One day all of this waiting will lead to something worth every tired night and quiet compromise. It was planting seeds for something bigger. She knew things like this took time. Healing, forgiveness, and even finding her way back to the people she'd lost."

And if she could treat Judy Hanes with kindness, after all that history, then maybe she was strong enough to face whatever came next. She knew that she needed to give thanks to the Lord, but she might not ask for patience again. She thought out loud, "I will just trust God and ask for guidance."

Jessie sat at the edge of her bed, her fingers tracing the end of her long, thick brown hair, eyes fixed on the floor. Her thoughts raced about the bills piling up, the maps and letters she collected, and the family she was trying to find, possibly scattered across the states. Every morning, she woke up with a plan. In the afternoons, she felt nauseous, and every night she went to bed feeling like she was failing. It felt like there was never enough time, enough energy, or enough of anything to make progress. She had kept most of it from Eric, not because she didn't trust him, but because she didn't want to burden him with the weight she could barely carry herself.

Then came the second line on the test. Faint, but unmistakable. Pregnant. The word echoed in her chest like a warning bell. A new life when she was barely holding her own together. The fear came fast. What if they couldn't afford this? What if chasing down the pieces of her past meant sacrificing the future of their child? She sat in silence for what seemed like hours before finally deciding to tell him. She had wanted a baby but wasn't sure this was the right time.

That night, as Eric came through the door, Jessie stood in the kitchen; her back turned, trying to steady her breath. "I need to talk to you," she said quietly. When he looked up, his face instantly alert with concern, she broke. The tears came without warning, spilling down her cheeks, as she choked out the words, "I'm pregnant, Eric, and I… don't know what we are going to do. I've been trying to figure out the money, how to keep looking for them, how to keep us okay, and now this… I'm scared. I didn't want to tell you like this." Eric crossed the room without a word, pulling her gently into his arms. "We are going to have a baby!" he said with excitement. She expected tension, maybe frustration, but all she felt was warmth. He held her until her sobs softened, then leaned back just enough to look at her. "Jess," he said softly, brushing the hair from her face, "You don't have to do everything alone. I know you have been trying to protect me, but I am here. We are in this together." He paused, giving her a quiet smile. "I have the inheritance from my grandfather, remember?" And there is still money in savings. We are not broke. We can figure this out, both the baby and your family." He continued, "You know you have hospital insurance from your job at the agency." Jessie said, "Oh yeah. I forgot for a moment."

Jessie blinked up at him, the weight in her chest easing slightly for the first time in days. She had forgotten, or just ignored, that she didn't have to carry the financial burden by herself. Eric kissed her forehead and held her again, and this time she let herself lean fully into him. It wasn't the end of the fears or questions, but for the first time, she didn't feel alone in facing them.

Back in Tennessee, Jessie's dad had gone to bed early. He had been restless for hours, pacing the floor for almost an hour. Kathy was concerned and asked Joe, "Is something bothering you?" Joe said, "My mind is racing, and I am tired." While Joe was sleeping, he began to wrestle with his thoughts. He tossed and turned. Then he yelled out, "Mary!" Kathy woke him with a gentle tap on his arm. Startled, he asked, "What happened?" Kathy said, "You were having a dream. You called out the name Mary." "I'm sorry, Kathy. I thought…" Kathy said with a gentle voice, "It's okay, Joe. Jessie said you were married to Mary, and she passed away years ago."

Joe said, "I thought I could see her."

Kathy said, "That's great, Joe. Maybe you're starting to remember."

Joe said, "I want to go to sleep, Kathy."

Kathy patted Joe on his arm and said, "Get some sleep, Joe. You'll feel better in the morning, and we can talk then."

Later that night, Eric and Jessie sat at the kitchen table with a notepad between them, steam rising from mugs of hot cocoa they had forgotten to sip. Jessie still felt raw from earlier, but lighter somehow, as she had finally put down the heavy backpack she didn't realize she was wearing. Eric held her hand as they talked, about the baby, about what she needed to continue her search for her family, and about how they could make it all work without losing themselves in the process.

"I know it's not going to be easy," she said, her voice low. "There's no road map for any of this. I'm thankful that we found my dad, even if he doesn't remember his family, but we still don't know where my sister and brothers ended up. I want to find them, but now..." Her hand instinctively moved to her stomach. "Now everything is changing."

Eric nodded, his thumb gently brushing the back of her hand. "Then we'll change with it. It doesn't have to be either/or. We'll make a plan, step by step. We can slow things down if we need to. We can use the inheritance to get you a few plane tickets or hire someone to track them down if it gets too hard. And for the baby, we'll prepare together. We can set up a bedroom as we go. You don't have to put one part of your life on hold to protect the other."

Jessie looked at him, searching for any doubt or resentment, but found only steady love in his eyes and a smile. It wasn't blind optimism, it was faith, in God, in her, in them, in the uncertain road ahead. Her heart softened again, not with grief this time, but with gratitude. For once, she didn't feel like she was standing in the middle of a storm alone.

They stayed at the table long into the night, sketching out rough plans and lists, dreaming a little, worrying a little, but doing it together. Eric's hand in hers reminded her that they would walk every road side by side, even the ones that hadn't been built yet. For the first time, Jessie allowed herself to feel a small bit of hope. She knew it wouldn't be easy, but with Eric by her side, it felt like they could handle whatever came next.

Jessie was in deep concentration, working with a client, Kenneth. She moved slowly, her fingers firm but gentle as she guided Kenneth's arm through its range of motion. The hum of fluorescent lights overhead mixed with the soft rhythmic creak of the treatment table. Her brow furrowed in concentration, her mind focused fully on the physical task before her.

Kenneth, reclining on the mat, winced slightly. "You always get that serious when you're working," he asked, his voice light, attempting to break the silence. She didn't respond right away. She hadn't even heard him at first, too deep in her thoughts. He called her name again, this time a little louder.

"Jessie!"

Her eyes blinked into focus. "Sorry," she said, her voice clipped but kind. "Just concentrating."

Kenneth gave her a sideways look. "You okay?"

"I'm fine," she replied, almost too quickly. The rule echoed in her head: Don't get personal with clients. Maintain boundaries. Keep things professional. But something in Kenneth's tone was disarming, genuine in a way she hadn't expected. Something about him didn't feel like a stranger. She hesitated, her hands pausing mid-movement. "Can I ask you something weird?" she asked quietly, not looking directly at him.

Kenneth raised an eyebrow. "Sure."

"I haven't heard from my family in years," the words trembling out before she could stop them. "The last time I spoke to them…it was when they took my sister and brothers from our house, where I lived as a child. My sister was going to live with our grandmother, but I guess they might have moved. I haven't been able to find a phone number or address. My brothers went to live with my aunt and uncle, but I was very young, and I don't remember exactly where they lived."

Kenneth listened, not interrupting.

"I just don't know how to find them. I don't even know where to start. No numbers. No addresses. Nothing."

Kenneth didn't rush to offer solutions, he just stayed quiet, allowing Jessie the space to speak her heart. It wasn't often she let herself get this vulnerable.

"Your parent's house," Kenneth said, after a pause. "It still belongs to your dad, right?"

Jessie nodded slowly. She didn't give any explanation about what happened to her dad.

"Then go there."

She looked at him, uncertainty and surprise in her eyes.

"I'm serious," he continued. "If no one lived there, maybe there's still mail, old papers, or something with a lead. You'd be surprised at what people leave behind."

Jessie looked down, her hands reflexively resuming the movement on Kenneth's arm. "I never thought of that. I didn't think I had the right to…I don't know."

Kenneth said, "You do. It's part of your story too."

Jessie's mind raced at the suggestion, something simple yet powerful, a possible first step in the journey to finding her family.

Jessie was thrilled when her client suggested she visit the house she grew up in; it might have clues about the whereabouts of her long-lost family, especially addresses that could help her in the search. Excited about the possibility, she couldn't wait to tell Eric when she got home.

The house was a four-hour drive away, and without hesitation, Jessie and Eric decided to make the trip together over the weekend. When Jessie stepped out of the car, it hit her like a wave. She was surprised by how little the house had changed over the years. The wind chime still hung lopsided over the window, the smell of cut grass, and the faint scent of diesel from the neighbor's old truck. It was all still here.

To Jessie's surprise, the neighbor who had promised her father years ago to look after the place was still tending to it. He warmly welcomed them and asked Jessie how her father was doing. Jessie turned away and ran to the bathroom. The neighbor, Tom, asked, "Did I say something wrong?"

Eric answered, "No, sir. Jessie is having morning sickness, but she has it in the afternoon."

Tom said, "I'm sorry she doesn't feel well, but congratulations."

Eric said, "Thanks."

In a few moments, Jessie returned to the kitchen. She looked at Jerry and said, "I'm sorry about that. It came on suddenly." Then she explained gently that her father had lost his memory some time ago in an automobile accident. Jerry said, "I wondered why I haven't heard from him."

Jessie asked, "What do we owe you for taking care of our house?"

Jerry said, "I made a promise to Joe to look after the house until I heard from him. I was glad to do it. I guess I need to know what you need me to do now."

Jessie said, "We owe you a lot. I'm so thankful that the house is in such good condition. Someday, I hope to pay you back for your kindness." Jessie glanced over at Eric and asked, "Do you think we can take responsibility for this house?"

Jerry interrupted, "I'm glad you want this house. It has a lot of memories for me. You need to know that your dad and mom left a will. It's in a safe at my house. I will bring it to you." He turned and walked out the door.

Jessie turned toward Eric. "I didn't think about a will. It may not even be our house anymore," she said, her voice beginning to tremble.

"Now, Jessie, don't get stressed. I'm sure we can still look for the papers you need."

Jerry returned to find Jessie crying. "Why are you crying, Jessie?"

Jessie answered, "I guess I'm emotional due to my pregnancy and a little concerned about the will."

Jerry said, "I'm sorry if I worried you, but your dad asked me to keep it safe. It is still your house, but it is to be a home for your family unless all of them agree to sell."

Jessie sighed in relief. Jerry said, "There's more."

Jessie's eyes widened. "What is it, Jerry?"

Eric asked.

Jerry said, "Joe and Mary set up a trust fund for all the children."

Jessie said, "I didn't know my parents had that much money."

Jerry said, "Your parents were married almost eleven years, but the year you were born, they made a decision to put back money for your college, then as the others came along, they did the same."

Jessie said, "Any little bit helps. I'm thankful for my parents' love."

Jerry let out a hearty but kind laugh. "I wouldn't call ten thousand dollars for you 'a little bit.'"

Jessie looked at Eric, then at Jerry, and a few tears dropped from her blue eyes. It was hard for her to even grasp the idea that her parents had managed to save this much money, money she had never known about, money that now felt like a lifeline.

"They didn't have time, I guess, to get that amount of money to the others, but they have accounts with about four thousand each. Come to think of it, with interest over the years, it could be more."

Jessie said to Jerry, "I didn't know my parents had any money. I wonder why Daddy had to be in the military service."

Jerry quickly answered. "He wanted to serve his country, Jessie. Some people have that calling. It's a strong feeling you get. Some people serve by working in civilian life, and some serve in the military."

Eric said, "I understand that."

Jerry said, "I'll leave this house in your hands now, but know you can call me if you need me."

Jessie said, "We will see you again, Jerry. I can never thank you enough for what you've done for my family." Then she reached up and hugged Jerry with a tight squeeze, which made Jerry smile, and at the same time, rub a small tear from his eye.

Inside the house, Jessie began searching through old belongings, drawers, and papers, hoping for anything that could lead her to her family. Her efforts paid off when she stumbled upon a few promising clues, including hints about the whereabouts of her sister Patty.

Hope flickered in Jessie's heart. This could be the breakthrough she had been waiting for. Jessie knew that Patty had gone to live with her mother's parents, Rick and JoAnn, but she hadn't been able to reach them by phone. Now she had their address and hoped they still lived there. There was an emergency number if Joe needed to reach his parents. Jessie immediately pulled her cell phone out of her pocket and dialed the number. It rang three times, then went to voicemail. Jessie put her finger on her phone and, discouraged, was about to press the red button to hang up, but then she decided to leave a message. The weight of the moment sank in; this was the first real lead she'd had in years. She had to take the chance. She left her message on the voicemail: "Hi, I'm Jessie, and I'm trying to locate my grandparents, Rick and JoAnn. I haven't heard from them in a very long time. If I have the right number, please contact me," and she left her phone number just in case it didn't show up on their phone.

Jessie continued to rummage through papers and her mother's dresser, hoping that something would help her. With every drawer she opened, the sense of urgency grew. The clock seemed to tick louder in her mind. Within minutes, Jessie's phone rang. It was the emergency number she had dialed earlier. Jessie stared at the number for a second, took a deep breath, and answered. "Hello."

The voice at the other end said, "Jessie, this is Grandpa." In that instant, Jessie was so excited that she let out a shrill squeak.

She said, "Grandpa, is that really you?"

"Yes, honey," he said. "You called our friend, Harry, and when you called, we happened to be visiting him and his wife, Estelle. I am so glad to hear from you. Are you and the kids all right?"

Jessie, trying to hold back the tears, managed to answer in her trembling voice, "Grandpa, there is so much to tell you. I have been looking for Patty, Jeremiah, and Dusty for years. Eric and I are going to have a baby, and we are working, and we are trying to find the rest of the family." Then Jessie could not hold back her emotions as she began to cry.

Grandpa Rick said with a gentleness in his voice, "Jessie, everything will be okay. We know where Patty is living with her husband, Mark. I think we can locate the boys, but I will need some time to check into that. Give me your address, honey, and we will visit you and Eric next weekend, and we will talk about everything. Is that okay?"

Jessie said, "It is wonderful!"

Eric had stepped outside and walked around the house. Jessie shouted, "Eric, where are you!?"

Eric could sense the excitement in his wife's voice. He stepped up onto the steps that led to the kitchen. He asked, "What is it, Jessie?"

Jessie was wiping the wetness from her cheeks as fast as she could. Still excited, she said, "Eric, I talked to my grandpa, and he and grandma are coming to our home next weekend, and they will tell me where Patty lives!"

Eric hugged Jessie and said, "That's great, honey!"

Jessie collected a few pictures, and she and Eric spent the night sleeping in her old bed. Jessie couldn't sleep for a while. She kept Eric awake, asking questions that he couldn't answer.

"Eric, where do you think Patty lives?"

Before Eric could tell her he didn't know, she asked, "Do you think Patty will remember me?"

Eric was quiet and waited patiently. He knew Jessie was just nervous and excited. Jessie didn't even realize that Eric didn't answer her questions. Then she asked, "Do you realize that my parents left me enough money to put a good down payment on our ranch?"

Now she had Eric's full attention. "Wait a minute, Jessie. We have that money and the inheritance that I have, but we have to be careful and make good decisions. We have some time to work all that out."

Jessie said, "You're right, Eric. We'd better get some rest before we travel back home tomorrow."

Jessie closed her eyes but found it hard to doze off. For the first time, she felt the possibility of everything falling into place: the ranch, the family, and the future she had always dreamed of.

While Jessie prepared for the long-awaited visit, she had no idea that her father was starting to remember. He had lived in a quiet fog, but now moments of clarity were returning, like shafts of light breaking through the mist. He began to speak of his late wife and sometimes even the children they had together. Faces. Names. Laughter. He couldn't hold on to the memories for long, but they were coming back.

His current wife, Kathy, was trying her best to help him through it all. She watched his flashes of recognition with a mix of hope and heartbreak, unsure of what would come next. Kathy had never mentioned this to Jessie. She wasn't sure if it was something Jessie wanted to hear or if the memories would just bring more pain.

As the weekend approached, Jessie stood on the edge of Discovery, unaware that the family she sought might be closer than she realized, and the past she thought might be lost was quietly trying to find its way back to her.

The late afternoon sun spilled through the lace curtains in their cozy little living room, where Jessie waited, her heart pounding like a drum in her chest. She listened for cars and watched the door, as she clutched a lukewarm cup of coffee she hadn't touched in twenty minutes.

Then finally, there they were. An older man with tired, kind eyes and a slow, steady gait. His white hair framed a weathered face. When their eyes met, something clicked, something deep in Jessie's chest that she hadn't felt in years.

"Jessie?" he asked, his voice gravelly, but warm.

She stood quickly. "Grandpa!"

They hugged, awkwardly at first, then tighter, longer. She hoped she wouldn't cry, but she did. He held her like he'd been waiting for years for this. He explained that Grandma was lying down at the local motel, resting. She had a bad migraine, and she wanted to be her best when seeing Jessie.

They sat down at the kitchen table, and after a few quiet minutes filled with small talk and sips of fresh coffee, he took a deep breath. "I know you've been searching for a long time," he began. "And I should have reached out sooner. I just didn't know exactly where you were and if you even wanted anything to do with us."

Jessie shook her head. "I always wanted to find you. All of you."

He nodded, his hands trembling slightly as he reached into his coat pocket. "Well… I can't fix the past, sweetheart, but I can help now."

He slid a paper across the table. A phone number, written in neat handwriting.

"That's your sister, Patty. She lives in Georgia with her husband, Mark. She's got a little girl now. She's been hoping you'd find her someday."

Jessie stared at the number, her throat tightening. "You… you talked to her?"

"I've kept in touch with her over the years. She has asked me to let her know if I ever hear anything about you." He smiled gently. "She's going to be so happy, Jessie. Call her when you are ready."

Tears welled up in Jessie's eyes again, but she blinked them back. "Thank you."

"There's more." He added. "Your brother, Jeremiah. He's still in Alabama. He's a preacher now; he has a small church just outside Montgomery. Last I heard, he is doing well, staying out of trouble."

Jessie smiled. "That sounds like Jeremiah. He was a good little boy."

"I don't have a number for him, but I can give you the name of the church he was at last. It's a start."

Jessie nodded, overwhelmed with emotion. Her heart raced with the weight of it all. For so long, she had felt disconnected, like a piece of her life was missing. But now, for the first time in ages, she felt like she was getting closer to the missing pieces.

For the first time in years, the world didn't seem so fractured. Threads were forming; connections she thought were lost forever were suddenly within reach. She had the chance to find them, Patty, her brothers, maybe even more pieces of her family she never thought she would see again.

Her grandfather placed his hand over hers. "You've got a long road ahead, Jessie, but you are not alone." Her chest tightened as she held his hand. She could hear the weight of his words, but a part of her felt ready. She wasn't alone anymore.

Flickers of Light

The morning was quiet. Too quiet, Kathy thought, as she stood at the kitchen sink, rinsing dishes that didn't need rinsing. She glanced into the living room, where her husband Joe sat in his usual recliner. The TV was on, low and tuned to some old Western, but his eyes weren't watching it. He had been like this for a while now, drifting, alive but unmoored. Most days, he couldn't remember what he had eaten for breakfast, or that he had four children, or that his first wife, Jessie's mother, was gone. But some days were different.

Kathy dried her hands slowly, watching him. There was something off today, a change she couldn't put her finger on. His posture seemed different, more alert, less weighed down. He sat forward slightly, hands resting on his knees, his brow furrowed like he was trying to solve a puzzle just out of reach.

She walked over quietly. "Joe, are you all right?" He didn't answer at first. His eyes were fixed on a framed photo on the mantle. It was old, Jessie, as a little girl, standing beside her mother in front of a tree that had long since been cut down.

"I know that dress," he said suddenly, his voice low and uncertain. "The yellow one. Mary… she made that dress."

Kathy stopped in her tracks. He almost never said her name. It was as if a veil had lifted from his mind, and the memory of his first wife had found its way back into the daylight.

"Yes," she said carefully. "She did. That was one of Jessie's favorite dresses, wasn't it?"

A long silence fell. He nodded slowly, still staring at the photo. "Used to cry if it was in the wash. Mary said she wore it out twice over."

A long silence fell. The air felt thick with the weight of the memory. The old memory hung in the air like sunlight through dust.

"She used to sing," he murmured. "Mary. Every morning, in the kitchen. Eggs frying, radio playing something old. She had this soft voice, kinda off-key, but it made you feel like… everything was okay."

Kathy sat beside him. She didn't know how to respond. Part of her longed to hold him in this fleeting moment of clarity, but the other part of her felt this aching void where they used to be.

"You haven't mentioned her in a long while," she said gently. Kathy's heart tightened as she realized how much Joe had lost, how much they had both lost.

He turned toward Kathy now, eyes a little clearer, more present. "I remember things in pieces. It's like they're in a fog, but sometimes", he tapped his temple, "the wind shifts."

"That's good," Kathy said softly. "Maybe it means more will come back."

"I hope so," he whispered. "I want to remember the kids. Jessie… her sister and the boys. I know their names sometimes, but I can't always see their faces."

Kathy reached over and took his hand. She felt the fragility of it all, the uncertain path they were both on.

"You don't have to rush it," she said. "Just hold on to what comes. We'll figure out the rest together."

He looked down at her hand in his and nodded. "I want to see Jessie. I feel like I haven't seen her in years."

Kathy hesitated. She hadn't told Jessie about the moments of clarity Joe had been experiencing. Maybe she hadn't been ready to face it herself, but now it seemed like time was catching up with them.

"I'll try to reach her," she said, her voice steady. "When you're ready."

"I think I'm ready," he said, almost to himself. "Or at least I want to be."

Kathy sat on the edge of the bed, phone in hand, hovering over the contact labeled Jessie (cell). It had been so long since she'd reached out to her, but now, with the hint of her father remembering, Kathy knew she couldn't keep avoiding it.

The last time she called it, it had gone straight to voicemail, and she hadn't tried again. She told herself it was out of respect. In truth, it was fear.

But Joe had changed that. Yesterday morning, when he looked at Jessie's picture and said her name like it still meant something, Kathy knew it was time. He was reaching out, and so should she.

With a deep breath, she tapped the call button. It rang once, twice, then, click.

"Hello?" Jessie's voice was cautious, distant.

Kathy cleared her throat. "Jessie, it's Kathy."

A pause.

"Kathy, is something wrong?"

"No, no, not wrong. I just…" She hesitated. "I wanted to talk to you about your dad." The line was quiet for a second too long.

"I thought he didn't remember anything," Jessie said finally.

"He didn't," Kathy admitted. "But things are changing. Slowly. He's… starting to remember pieces. Your mother. You. The boys and your sister. Yesterday he asked about you for the first time in a while."

Jessie didn't speak, but Kathy heard the quiet catch in her breath. "I didn't want to reach out until I was sure," Kathy said gently. "But I think you should come. If you want to."

Another pause. Then Jessie's voice, shaky, soft. "Yeah, I think I do."

When Jessie hung up, she sat frozen on the steps at her front door, phone still in her hand. The sun was setting, but her thoughts were far from the warm glow of the evening.

Her dad remembered her. Or at least, something about her. Jessie had mourned her father while he was still alive. It was the only way she knew how to cope, but in the back of her mind, she never wanted to give up on him. And now Kathy was telling her he was coming back.

Jessie wasn't sure how to feel about that. Part of her was very excited and wanted to run to him. Another part, one that had learned to keep wounds buried, wasn't sure she could handle another disappointment. She felt torn between hope and fear, but she knew this moment could be the one she had prayed for.

She spoke to Eric about her concerns. He looked at her with love in his eyes and asked, "This is what you prayed for. Can you go on faith?"

Jessie stood up tall and straight. "You are right. It's what I asked for, and I can handle whatever happens with God's grace!"

"That's my girl!"

She looked up at the sky. "I'm coming to see ya, Dad," she whispered. Then she went inside and called her grandfather. She said, "I am going to see Dad first. I will call Patty very soon."

Kathy met her at the door, arms crossed tight over her chest, eyes red-rimmed but warm. She smiled.

"Jessie. You made it."

"I'm so glad you came. He's in the living room. He's been having more... moments. Clearer ones."

Jessie stepped inside, her footsteps soft on the hardwood floor. When she entered the living room, he was sitting in the recliner, hands folded in his lap, eyes distant. He looked up.

"Jessie!" His throat closed.

"Yeah, it's me."

"You had that yellow dress. Your mama made it. You wouldn't take it off," He paused. "Even when it was muddy."

Jessie nodded, her eyes filling. "That was my favorite."

He reached for her hand. He was dry, warm, and shaky. "I remember you... and Patty. And Jeremiah. Dusty too. He was just about to turn two when I left to go back to my unit."

Jessie swallowed the lump in her throat. "You remember all of us?"

"Not everything. Just flashes." He admitted. "Mary, your mama, she's been in my dreams. Singing in the kitchen. I can see her face again, clear as day. Her hair always smelled like lemons."

Jessie laughed through a tear. "It did."

"I forgot so much, baby girl," he whispered, tears slipping from the corners of his eyes. "But I'm trying to come back. I want to."

She knelt beside the recliner and wrapped her arms around him gently. He held her like a man who thought he never would again. There was something in the way he held on, like he was scared to let go, but at the same time, relieved he didn't have to anymore.

Kathy stood in the doorway, wiping the tears from her face. She didn't want to interrupt, didn't want to crowd the moment, but her heart was racing. This was hope. Real hope. But it was delicate, like a bird's fragile wing. When Jessie pulled back, her dad looked at Kathy.

"She'd been taking good care of me. I don't know what I'd be without her."

Jessie glanced at Kathy and nodded. "Thank you for not giving up on him."

Kathy's smile was small but sincere. "He's worth fighting for. And so are you."

Jessie kissed her dad on the cheek. She said, "I believe in you, and I believe in God. That is where you get your strength and faith from. Don't give up." Her voice cracked slightly at the end, but she held it together. She meant every word.

Later that afternoon, the house was quiet again. Kathy had gone to make tea, and Jessie sat with her dad in the living room, the lamp casting a soft amber glow between them. The stillness of the moment was comforting. Jessie could almost hear the years that had passed, but now it felt like there was hope for more time to come.

He was more alert than he had been earlier, his eyes clearer, his posture stronger. It was one of his "good windows," as Kathy called them. Jessie knew this was the moment. She shifted a little in her seat, hands folded nervously in her lap.

"Dad," she said gently. "There's something I want to tell you."

He looked at her, his expression calm but curious. "Yeah?"

"You… You're a grandpa."

His brow lifted. "I am?"

Jessie smiled. "You already have a granddaughter. Patty has a little girl. Her name is Julie. She's two. Julie, Patty, and her husband, Mark, live in Georgia. I plan to visit them soon. I finally found Grandpa Rick, and he told me about Patty."

His jaw tightened slightly, not in discomfort, but in the kind of emotional tension men like him carried when their heart cracked a little. He looked down at his hands, then gave a small, almost disbelieving shake of his head.

"I'm a grandpa," he repeated, his voice gruff.

"Yeah," Jessie said, watching him closely. "And… there's more."

He looked up.

"I am pregnant. Just a few months along."

Silence.

His eyes widened, not with fear, not even with shock, but with something softer, something rooted. A kind of pride that sat heavy in his chest.

Jessie expected a lot of things: questions, confusion, maybe even a lecture. But instead, he leaned back, let out a loud breath through his nose, and nodded slowly.

"Well, I'll be damned." He muttered.

Jessie laughed, the sound shaky. "Is that a good 'Well, I'll be damned' or a bad one?"

He looked at her then, his eyes glistening enough to show that it meant something. "It's a good one," he said, voice rough with emotion. "It's a real good one."

He rubbed his hands together, then stood up, pacing slowly across the room like he needed to work the weight of it through his limbs. He paused at the window, looked out at the sunny yard, then turned back.

"I missed a lot, didn't I?"

Jessie nodded, swallowing a lump. "Yeah, but you are here now. You couldn't help what happened to you."

"I won't miss this." And that was all that he said. But it was enough. It felt like a promise, a quiet vow to be part of the family again.

It was getting on in the afternoon. Jessie gave her dad another kiss on the cheek and said, "I will be back to see you soon, and we can keep in touch over the phone when you feel like talking."

Kathy walked in and asked, "What are all the smiles about?"

Jessie said, "I just informed Dad that he has a granddaughter and another grandchild on the way. That means you're a grandmother. I'm not sure how you feel about that."

Kathy said, "I could not have children of my own as much as I wanted some. I am thrilled to be a part of your family. I will be a good grandmother."

Jessie said, "I know you will. You will both be great. I have to get home and make plans to start my search and find the family. I will keep in touch."

Kathy hugged Jessie and said, "This was a great visit." Her voice trembled with the kind of quiet joy that came from seeing the family whole again.

Chapter 5
The Search is On

Jessie was almost home as she turned off on the back road to get out of heavy traffic. She spotted a brown paper bag on the side of the road. As she came closer to the bag, it seemed to move. Her first thought was to speed up and get on down the road. "Maybe there is a snake that crawled in there," she thought out loud. The last thing she needed was to deal with a snake on a random back road. Her curiosity got the best of her, so she slowly pulled over to the edge of the grass behind the bag. She opened the car door and walked very cautiously toward the bag. Then she heard a familiar sound. She wasn't afraid now. A small meow broke through the silence. She leaned over and opened the bag. She looked in and spoke out loud as if speaking to the bag. "Eric is going to kill me." She picked up the bag gently. It must have weighed two pounds.

Fifteen minutes later, she arrived home. Eric had just pulled up in the drive. He walked over to see Jessie, and he noticed that she was bending over, reaching for something in the back seat. Eric said, "Hi." Then he asked, "What 'cha got there?" She turned and opened the bag wide so Eric could see. "Kittens!" he said. "What are we going to do with one, two, three kittens?" Jessie said, "I don't know, but I couldn't leave them in this bag on the side of the road. Someone threw them out!"

Eric looked at the kittens, then he looked at her, then he looked back at the kittens. "I see that I have a wife who will bring home strays." They looked at each other and laughed. He said, "You go find a box to put them in, and I will drive to the store and get some cat food."

"Thanks, Eric."

"Try not to get attached. We may need to find a home for them." Jessie whispered to the kittens. "Don't worry, he's a good guy. I'm just glad you weren't snakes."

Eric arrived back home within thirty minutes with three cans of cat food, some powdered milk, and a box of cat litter, with a plastic pan to put it in. As he walked in the door, Jessie said, "I need to talk to you."

Eric asked, "You don't have any more surprises, do you?"

"Not really, but I do have good news." She explained what had happened while she was visiting her dad. "I believe he is getting his memory back."

"Wow!" Eric remarked. "What's next?" Jessie answered, "That's what I wanted to talk to you about. I think we should talk about getting a place of our own, and I need to visit Patty and try to find my brothers while the trail is hot."

"What?" Eric asked. "Where did you hear that?"

"Some western movie." Eric chuckled.

At the supper table, as it is often called in the south, Eric and Jessie had a lot to talk about. Mostly Jessie. Jessie said, "Things are finally happening. I was blessed to be reunited with my dad; he is starting to remember his family, and we are having a baby to start our family. I assured Dad that I would be back to visit soon, but I need to see Patty and find the boys. I don't want to seem like I am complaining, but it almost seems overwhelming. I'm not sure what to do." She paused, stirring her drink thoughtfully. "So much is happening at once, it's hard to keep track of it all."

"I would think that praying about it would be the first thing to do," Eric answered. "Then one thing at a time. We have money to put down on a small farm or ranch, but we can wait on that a little longer. We have a roof over our head, so we can continue to save a little more money. We can check our finances every month and look around for a place we really like, and then when we find it, we can start making plans for that."

"What do you think the best thing to do now is?" Jessie asked. Eric said, "I'm not crazy about you being on the road with pregnancy sickness, but I think you should start your visit with Patty. Maybe you can go see your dad once a month until the baby comes or once every two months, and in the meantime, keep in touch by phone."

"That makes sense, Eric. I feel better," Jessie said as she gave out a sigh of relief. "I was thinking that I might take a leave of absence and go visit Patty."

Eric said, "I know you have a lot to talk about, but she is just a state away. Labor Day is coming up, and you will have three days off. That would be a good time to visit." Then he asked, "Why don't you call her in the morning and ask if that is a good time to visit? Then get her address, and we will figure out how long it takes to get there. You will have at least one full day to visit and get reacquainted. You could even take her a kitten."

"That's funny," Jessie said with a sarcastic smile.

"I'm not kidding," Eric said.

Jessie wasn't listening. It was like the clouds opening up, and the heaviness of her heart's worries went up to the sky. The weight that had been sitting on her chest for weeks seemed to lift just a little. She felt relieved knowing what she needed to do. She went to her bedroom and knelt on her knees in prayer, asking God for guidance and thanking Him again for Eric in her life. It wasn't just about the decisions she had to make; it was the peace she had finally found in her heart.

The sun shone through the opening of the bedroom curtains, and Jessie knew it was morning. It was only 6 am. She had calmness about her this morning. It was time to get up, eat breakfast, and get ready for work. Her idea was to call Patty on her morning break and give her the news.

She felt a quiet, peaceful start to the day, like everything was falling into place.

At ten am, Jessie walked outside to the wooden chair on the porch where she worked. She dialed Patty's number for the first time. After four rings, she heard Patty's voicemail, "You have reached Patty. Please leave your name and number, and I will call you back." Jessie left a message. "Hi Patty. This is your sister, Jessie. I'm at work, but I will be home around five this evening. Please call me if you can. I'm so anxious to talk to you." Jessie released a deep breath as she hung up and released the tension on her shoulders. She hoped Patty would call back soon, but she knew it could take time. Jessie went on to work, a little disappointed that she still had not heard Patty's voice.

That evening, when Jessie arrived home, she immediately began to prepare a meal for her and Eric. Eric's dad knocked on the door. Jessie opened the door and said, "Hi, come in." Eric's dad, Jim, looked straight into Jessie's eyes and said, "No, I just wanted you to know that I am taking Beth to the ER. She doesn't feel right." Jessie said, "Eric will be home soon, and we will be right there." Jim said, "Eric was at the office when his mom called, so he is aware. I told him that he should stay home until we find out what the problem is. If it's bad, I will notify you immediately."

After Jim left, Jessie whispered out loud, "What else could happen?" Then all of a sudden, Jessie's phone rang. "Hello, this is Patty."

Jessie's voice quivered as she answered, "Patty, I have been searching for you so long, and I have longed to hear your voice. I have so much to tell you, but my father-in-law just came over to tell me that he is taking my mother-in-law to the ER. Will you forgive me if I call you back later?"

"Of course," Patty answered. "You do what you need to do and call me any evening or weekend. I'm an elementary school teacher, so I am at school during the day, but I will answer there if you text me and I'm not in class." Jessie realized that's why Patty didn't answer the phone when she called earlier. "We've waited this long. Take care of what's going on, and when you're free, I'll be here."

Jessie was straining to hold back the tears. She said, "What a wonderful sister I have. I love you, Patty. I will talk to you very soon." Patty returned with, "I love you, sis. Talk to you soon."

Two hours later, Eric called Jessie. "Hi, honey. I just wanted you to know that Mom is okay. She had a bad urinary tract infection. They gave her some antibiotics, and they is coming home."

"Oh, Eric, I felt like we should have been there for them, but I'm glad it wasn't anything worse than that."

"We would have been there if Dad called us. I'm on my way home."

When Eric walked in the door, he went directly to a kitchen chair and plopped down, giving out a huff. "I don't know about you, but I am beat." Jessie said, "I know you are tired. I'll be glad when your school is over." Jessie said, "I talked to Patty this evening, but I told her I would call her back because I was waiting on news from your dad."

"I'm sorry, Jessie. I know you've been waiting a long time to hear from her. There's a lot happening all at once, but maybe it's a test of faith. I think the three of us are strong and unbeatable."

Jessie glared at him and asked, "The three of us? Do you mean the baby?"

Eric said, "You and me, and Jesus." Jessie smiled and said, "I'm so thankful for you."

Eric said, "I'm thankful for you, too, honey." Jessie said, "I wish everybody had a love like ours."

Eric smiled, "It is a blessing, but everyone has challenges in life. Money struggles, relationship struggles, and health issues. We need to remember where our help comes from." Jessie nodded in agreement. They both sat in the quiet for a moment, feeling thankful for what they had.

Jessie went to work the next morning with a lot on her mind. She said a little prayer for guidance and knew she had to keep her mind on her job. During her noon break, an inspiration came to her. She sat out in her car and swallowed half of a ham and cheese sandwich. She pulled her cell phone out of her pocket and called her dad. He recognized her name on his cell phone when he answered it. "Hello, Jessie." Jessie answered, "Hey, Dad, you sound great."

"I feel great. I think I am getting better every day."

"That's great, Dad. I wish I could be there for you every day, but maybe we can see each other soon. I wanted to tell you that I'm not sure when I will be back there because I am going to meet Patty and try to figure out what to do from there."

"Your mom would say, 'The Lord will lead you on the right path."

"Dad, you remembered. You are getting better."

"All in God's time. You go see your sister, and I hope I can see her before long."

"Don't worry, Dad, hopefully we will all be together before too long."

The next evening, Jessie could hardly wait to get home. She made some vegetable soup with the corn and green beans she had as leftovers in the refrigerator. She pulled out some canned diced tomatoes from the pantry and a can of purple hull peas from the cabinet. She diced up a couple of white potatoes, boiled them quickly, and added them to the soup. She made a couple of grilled cheese sandwiches and let the soup simmer a little bit while waiting for Eric to come home. The smells filled the kitchen, comforting and familiar. She walked into the kitchen and dialed Patty's number.

"Hello," Patty answered.

"Hey, Patty, it's Jessie. Labor Day weekend is coming up, and I wondered if you had any plans."

"No," she answered. "What do you have in mind?"

"I thought I could come and visit you and your family, since I have the weekend off."

Patty said, "That would be great!" They discussed the best route to take, and Patty said, "We'll be looking for you."

Patty's husband, Mark, walked up behind Patty and rolled his eyes, pressing his lips together. Patty asked, "Did you hear that conversation?" Mark said, "I believe you made different plans for our weekend."

Patty said, "I'm sorry, Mark, I know we had plans to go to the lake, but…" Mark interrupted, "It's okay. I know you've been wanting to see your sister. We'll go another time." Patty hugged her husband and said, "Thank you for understanding."

Jessie began sorting through her clothes, and Eric walked in behind her and put his arms around her. "Are you excited?"

She quickly answered, "Yes, but I wish you were going."

Eric said, "I'm available to go, but I don't know who would look after the kittens." Jessie said, "I was hoping you would want to go, so I asked your mom and dad if they could take care of them, and they said they would."

Eric said, "You are full of surprises, or mischief, not sure which." She tossed a pillow at him. They both laughed, then Jessie said, "You'd better get packed."

Eric said, "Jessie, we have two days to pack, and we are only staying two nights." Jessie said, "I want to be ready to go out the door when it's time to leave." Eric started laughing so hard as he plopped down backward on the bed. Jessie gave him a glance with her eyes partly closed. Eric turned on his side. "I don't think I've EVER seen you this excited."

"I was on our wedding day," she said as she continued to sort through her clothes in the closet.

"Oh, you got me with that one."

Friday morning came, and Jessie reminded Eric that they wouldn't have a lot of time to visit, so he'd better get up and get ready. Eric rose up and said, "Okay, I'm up."

The door opened, and there she was, Patty. A little older, sure, but unmistakably her. The same hazel eyes, the same beautiful smile that used to flash when they shared secrets under the bed covers at night. They embraced long and tight, the years melting off their shoulders like snow in the sun. The bond felt as if no time had passed at all. She told Jessie to come on in, and then she stood very still as she noticed a man standing by the car. Jessie turned around and said, "Oh, that's my husband Eric. He drove me here. I think he worries about me driving too far since I'm pregnant."

Patty loudly said, "That's great! Now Mark will have another man to talk to. Come in, Eric." As Eric reached the door, Patty hugged him and said, "I'm so glad to meet you finally." Mark was standing in the kitchen doorway. Patty introduced Eric to Mark. Jessie caught Mark by surprise as she walked over to hug him. Jessie said, "This is the best family reunion." Mark invited Eric into the den to talk and have a cup of freshly made coffee.

Patty and Jessie sat down at the kitchen table. The warmth of the kitchen felt like a safe haven for the sisters, despite the years apart. All of a sudden, Jessie started to cry. She tried to wipe her eyes quickly, and her nose began to run. Patty handed her a tissue. "Are you okay?" Patty asked.

Jessie said, "I am so happy that this is finally happening, and maybe being pregnant, I'm a little emotional."

Jessie said, "I accidentally found Grandpa's friend's phone number, and Grandpa was there, and that's how this search came to be real. I found the number in an address book at our old house. I haven't been there since we were children, but one of my clients reminded me that I might find what I was looking for at our house, where we grew up. It was a Jesus moment."

Then Jessie asked, "Did you have a good life growing up?"

A tear rolled down Patty's face as she said, "I loved my grandparents, and they were good to me, but even though I can barely remember what Mom looks like, I miss her. I remember her telling me bedtime stories from the Bible."

Jessie said, "I remember her standing in front of the bathroom mirror putting on her lipstick. I don't remember seeing her wear makeup, but she put lipstick on so perfectly. The cherry red lipstick made her smile even more beautiful."

Patty asked, "Have you ever heard anything about Daddy?" Before Jessie could answer, Patty asked, "Do you think he is still alive?"

Jessie opened her mouth and pushed out a deep breath of air. She said, "I'm not sure where to begin. I found Daddy before I found you. Actually, Eric found him through a friend of his. This may surprise you or shock you, so try not to get excited or upset."

"Oh gosh!" Patty said with a slightly shaky voice.

"It's not bad, Patty, just strange, I guess." Jessie's voice was kind of shaking slightly, unsure of how to begin. Patty asked, "What is it?"

Eric heard about his dad through a friend in the military. I called the phone number that he gave Eric. Daddy's wife answered."

Patty put her hand over her mouth and sucked in a deep breath. Her eyes widened as she waited for Jessie to continue, sensing the weight of what was to come. She remained silent, holding her breath, her mind racing.

Jessie's words tumbled out. "That's not the strange part. Our daddy had been in a car accident years ago, and was in the hospital where he met the woman he married. Her name is Kathy. Daddy had amnesia from the accident. He did not remember having a wife or children. It's like he started over. A blank slate."

Patty continued saying, "Oh my gosh, oh my gosh!" Her voice cracked as if trying to process the shock of it all.

Jessie reached across and gently placed the top of her hand on Patty's. She could feel the trembling beneath Patty's fingertips. "I went to visit Daddy, and he didn't remember me. It was like talking to a stranger. I left some pictures and my phone number with his wife. Kathy said he looked at those pictures a lot, and over time, he began to remember some things. Slowly, like the pieces of a broken puzzle falling back into place. The last time I visited him in his home in Alabama, he told me about some things he remembered from our childhood. Memories are slowly, and miraculously, coming back to him. It's like he's been in the dark all this time, and now, he's beginning to see the light again."

Jessie paused, watching Patty's face, waiting for her reaction. "I spoke with him on the phone a few days ago. He said he hopes to see you someday soon. He said he remembers the boys, but he doesn't remember where they went or where they are now, so I still have more work to do."

Patty nodded, her face a mixture of hope and sadness. "We have work to do. I want to help." Her voice was soft but determined.

Jessie squeezed her hand reassuringly. "With God's help, we will find everyone."

Patty hung her head, a sorrowful expression crossing her face. Jessie could see the struggle within her. "What's the matter?" she asked, concern edging her voice.

Patty's voice trembled. "I...I believe in God, but I don't understand much about Him. I've never been baptized, and I have this fear... a fear of going to hell."

Jessie's heart softened as she listened. "Have you read the Bible?"

"A little," Patty replied, her voice quiet but honest.

Jessie looked at her with a warm and loving smile, her eyes filled with understanding. "Just the fact that it bothers you is meaningful. It shows your heart. We have a loving God, Patty. You do not have to be baptized to go to Heaven, but it's a good idea when you find the church where you feel at home. I will help you through this. I'll be with you every step of the way."

Then, Jessie gasped as something came to mind. "I meant to tell you, I heard that our brother, Jeremiah, is a preacher at a church somewhere near Montgomery, Alabama. He's next on my list. We need to find him, too."

Patty's face lit up with excitement, but there was a feeling of sadness. "This is all so exciting, but I wish I could remember Mama. Or maybe have a picture of her. Something to hold on to, you know?"

Jessie's voice softened, "I know, Patty. I wish we had something too. But we're getting closer to finding answers, and I promise we will keep searching. One step at a time."

"It's getting late," Jessie continued, glancing at the clock. "I have more to tell you and show you. I don't want to keep your child awake, so we'd better go find a motel room and come back in the morning."

Patty shook her head quickly. "You don't need a motel room. We have a guest room, and I insist that you stay the night with us. I'll be anxious to hear more tomorrow. It's all so exciting, and I want to hear more about God, about everything. I need to know more. Please stay."

Jessie smiled, feeling a warmth in her chest. "You got it. I'll stay. And we'll talk more in the morning, I promise."

Eric slept in the next morning while Jessie got up to look for a cup of hot coffee. Patty was awake and busy making breakfast in the kitchen. Patty's daughter, Julie, was still asleep. Patty said to Jessie, "Good morning. I'm almost done making breakfast. Help yourself to a cup of fresh coffee. I just made it. After breakfast, I hope we can resume our conversation."

"Absolutely," Jessie said. "We have the whole day."

Within the hour, everyone had eaten breakfast, and Mark and Eric went to the den to talk and watch a little TV. Mark knew Patty needed time to talk to her sister, so he gathered up some toys and put Julie in a quilt on the floor in the den.

Patty asked, "Did you and Eric sleep well?" Jessie said, "Yes, we were very comfortable, which reminds me… Eric and I slept in my old bed at our old house recently. It was nice, but a little weird."

Patty said, "Wow! You and Eric have had some adventures."

Jessie said, "Well, it wasn't like a fun safari, but it has been interesting."

Patty reminded Jessie that she said she gave her dad some old pictures, and she asked, "Would you have any pictures with you on this visit?" Jessie said, "I do, but I have something even better, I think. I think I left it in the car."

Jessie went out to look in the car, and her heart sank as she closed the car door. She stood still for a moment, feeling an odd sense of loss. She went inside and said, "I'm so sorry, Patty. I must have left the things I had for you at home. Let me check with Eric." She entered the den with soft steps, trying not to disturb Julie. She had curled up on the blanket and dozed off. Jessie said in a whisper, "Eric, do you remember where I left the box I had for Patty?" Her voice trembled slightly, hoping she hadn't misplaced it. She bit her bottom lip in anticipation. She was afraid they had left it somewhere at home. Eric said, "I took everything out of the car last night. The box is on the little rocking chair in the room where we slept last night." Jessie put her hand to her chest and let out a deep breath of relief. "Thanks, Eric." She walked quickly to the bedroom, and it was right where Eric said it was. She bent over and lifted the box in her arms, carrying it to the kitchen and setting it on the table.

Patty said with a little excitement, "That isn't a box, it's a chest!" Jessie said, "I guess you are right. It was a miracle that I could hold onto it all these years, especially as a child." Jessie opened the box with gentle care. She said, "Believe it or not, I have only looked in this box once, just minutes after Mama gave it to me. She told me to keep it with me always. Dad's parents understood how important it was, and they made sure I carried it with me."

The first thing she pulled out was a picture of her mom giving Patty her birthday doll. Patty called her "Twinkles." Patty stared at the picture like it was her very own gold. A tear flowed down her cheek before she could wipe it off, but it wasn't just sadness; it was a mix… a feeling where one feels relieved. Jessie said, "It's okay to cry. It's good memories."

Then Jessie said, "Look, Patty!" Patty raised an eyebrow, curious. Jessie reached in and pulled out a cloth doll, a little faded now, with button eyes, and yellow yarn hair. Its dress was hand-stitched, with tiny, imperfect flowers on it, still visible along the hem.

Patty gasped, reaching out to touch it. "Is that?... It's her. The one Mama gave you on my last birthday before she…" Jessie's voice caught. She paused, swallowing the lump in her throat. "She told me to keep it safe. I always meant to find you and give it back to you." Patty held the doll with shaking hands, holding it like something sacred. Her eyes filled. "I thought she was gone forever."

"She never was," Jessie said, her hand covering her sister's. "Neither were we."

Two sisters, lost and found, piecing together one memory at a time, with a wooden chest, a doll, and a love that never faded.

Jessie rustled through some papers in the chest in hopes of finding something that might help Patty in her life. "Lord, help me," she whispered to herself. In a split second, she found her prayer was answered. She gathered a few papers with Patty's name on them. She reached out to give the papers to Patty. "What is this?"

Jessie answered, "I believe it is papers that you would love to have." Patty glanced over them for a few seconds. She said, "Oh, Jessie, it's my birth certificate, my old social security card, a note from Mama, and a picture of her and Daddy, with my name on the back of it. There's also a record of my childhood shots, a report card." She continued, "This means the world to me. I'm not sure what to do next."

Jessie said, "I suggest that you take good care of Twinkles and someday tell her story when you give it to your little girl." Patty reached over and hugged Jessie like she was never going to let go.

Jessie said, "I want to locate Jeremiah before I have my baby, so I will be working on that. I hope that soon in the future we can all get together with Dad and his wife, Cathy." Patty said, "I do okay as a teacher, and we have a small savings, but I'm not sure I can make many trips right now. I will be working on a way to travel, and I'm sure I can make the big trip to see Dad when we all get together."

"Oh my," Jessie said. Patty asked, "What is it?" Jessie said, "There was so much to tell you that I forgot to mention that Mama and Dad set up a trust fund for us. They had plans to put more in it, but…"

"I know," Patty said softly.

Jessie said, "You have four thousand dollars in a fund. When you come to Alabama, we will go to the bank, or the lawyer and figure it out together. We all have a little money in an account. God is amazing!"

Patty looked puzzled. "How did God do this?"

Jessie smiled. "Everything goes back to God. It will all make sense in time. In the meantime, read the Book of Matthew from your Bible, and we will talk about it when I see you again."

Patty laughed suddenly, like a light bulb came on in her head. She asked Jessie, "Do you remember the time Mama made some dresses for us out of old curtains? And I hated mine." Jessie laughed. Patty continued, "You traded with me. You always gave me the better one." Jessie said, "That's what big sisters do." Neither of them could keep from laughing.

The sun was beaming, putting a warmth in the early fall air. It was getting time to end the day. Tomorrow, Jessie and Eric will drive home. Patty wanted to know more and had a few more questions. She sat with Jessie on the living room couch, holding her little girl. She asked, "What is your life like?"

"Oh, where to begin?" Jessie thought for a moment. "I have a wonderful husband. We married right out of high school. We live with his parents in their guest house. We're saving money for a small ranch, or maybe a bigger one. I work as a physical therapy assistant, and Eric is going to school to become a physical therapist. We also recently adopted three kittens I found on the side of the road. It's been stressful at times, but Eric and I work through each challenge together. We've learned a lot about teamwork along the way. It's been exciting lately, especially finding Dad alive and well, and married to a good woman."

She continued, "Now, what about you? I know you have a handsome husband, a beautiful blond-headed daughter, and a nice home."

Patty said, "I'm an elementary teacher, which is stressful at times but very rewarding. Mark sells real estate. We're just trying to make it work, taking it day by day. We're saving money to pay off our vehicles and house."

Jessie remarked, "Well, ya'll do have a beautiful home. I love the blue siding and gray roof." Jessie continued, "We'll have to go home and get back to our lives for a little while, but I'll be making inquiries to find Jeremiah and hopefully find Dusty along the way. I'll keep you informed about what I learn, and you keep me updated on my little niece."

"Deal!" Patty said. Then she asked, while trying to hold back tears, "Jessie, we will keep in touch and see each other again, right?"

Jessie reached over and squeezed Patty's hand. "Of course, we'll see each other a lot and talk on the phone. I don't want to ever lose you again."

The next morning, Jessie and Eric wanted to get an early start so they could rest before going back to work and school the next day. The girls hugged each other, and the men shook hands. Jessie asked Eric if he had put the chest in the car. She knew there were items in it for Jeremiah and Dusty. Eric pointed to the back seat and reassured her that the chest was safe. Jessie gave Julie a kiss on the cheek. Julie reached out to Jessie as if she wanted to go with her. Jessie said, "Aww, let me hold her for a second." She spoke to Julie, "You be good for your mom and dad. We'll come back and see you as soon as we can." One last hug, and Jessie handed Julie back to Patty. Jessie looked back as they left the driveway and waved.

As they traveled down the road about four miles, Jessie was still silent. The weight of the past few days was heavy on her heart. Eric asked, "Are you sad?" Jessie said, "A little, but mostly more determined to bring all of my family together as quickly as I can, with God's help."

Another week went by. The weekend arrived. The weather had a cool breeze, enough to sway the leaves at the top of the trees. The changing leaves mirrored Jessie's own shifting emotions, hopeful yet uncertain. Jessie called her pastor that Saturday morning. As he answered the phone, Jessie said, "Brother Rick, this is Jessie. I need some help." Her pastor had been reading, and he removed his glasses and said, "How can I help, Jessie?"

Jessie said, "You know that I've been looking for my family for a long time, and I have been so blessed to find my dad, and last week I visited my sister. I understand that my brother Jeremiah is a preacher in a church near Montgomery. I don't know where to start looking."

"Do you know what denomination he preaches at?"

"Actually, I don't."

Pastor Rick said, "It might take some work and a little time, but I'll call around. I'll let you know what I find. In the meantime, you could put an ad in the Montgomery paper asking if anyone knows Jeremiah Davis."

Jessie said, "That's a great idea. Thank you so much." Pastor Rick answered, "My pleasure." Jessie looked up the number for the newspaper and asked about putting in an ad, possibly for three weeks. When she explained that she had not seen her brother since childhood, due to her mother's death, and it was imperative that she find her brother, the editor's heart was touched, and he offered to put it in the ads for no cost.

The ad read: Jeremiah Davis, your family needs to talk to you. Please notify Jessie. And he left her phone number at the end of the message.

After a week, Jessie was getting frustrated. She spoke to Eric, "Maybe he doesn't read the paper." Eric said, "Maybe you could put an ad on a local radio station, or a station that plays gospel." Jessie said, "That is brilliant!" She called two radio stations on Monday and told them her story. They agreed to put out the message, and there was no cost. Jessie told Eric, "I would be willing to pay, but God has touched people, and He is amazing!"

Another week went by, and still no word from her brother. "I just don't know what else to do," Jessie said to Eric. "I've done everything I can think of, but nothing's worked yet."

"BE PATIENT," Eric responded.

"It's hard," Jessie said.

"Life is hard, honey. Stick with your faith and keep praying."

A month went by, and no word. Jessie kept praying, sometimes with tears in her prayers. Eric hated to hear her cry. He tried to comfort her by telling her that it may take a little more time. "Montgomery is a big city," he said.

Weeks went by, then another month. Jessie called the radio stations and the newspaper and asked if they had heard from her brother. The reply was, "No ma'am. Not yet."

Jessie called Patty and told her that there was no news yet, but not to give up. Patty said, "I know you are doing everything you can."

Jessie called her dad and explained to him that she hadn't been able to reach Jeremiah. "This is a mystery," he said. Then he added, "Jessie, your mom and I believed in the Lord, and we know things happen in His time. We don't always understand His timing, but it is always on time. You must believe and have patience."

Jessie's face lit up as she said, "Dad, do you really remember that you and Mama taught me about the Bible and the Lord?"

"I remember a lot of things," he replied. "I remember that we had life insurance, and after your mom's funeral was paid for, there was money left in the account." Jessie said, "Dad, that is your money, but I will be glad to help you find it." He continued, "I remember the bank, and I will make a trip to go there and visit you and Eric when it is convenient for you."

"Dad, how much are you remembering?" Jessie asked, her voice tinged with hope.

"I think, pretty much, everything, or close to it. I've seen a therapist, and I've done some relaxation therapy, and it has helped me find my way. It all started with you, Jessie." Jessie remembered this time, that the Lord led her, and she gave credit to Him. Joe said, "I'm so proud of you."

"Thanks, Dad. That means a lot." She hesitated a few seconds, then said, "I hope Jeremiah turns up soon. Maybe I would do better to look for Dusty first."

Joe said, "Wait a minute, I gave both boys to my brother Keith and his wife, June. Let me think…" He was silent for a moment. Then he said, "They had a small farm in Tennessee. I don't have their number, but maybe you could call information and ask for Keith Davis." Jessie said, "That's a great idea. I'll let you know what I find out."

Jessie didn't waste any time. She called information. The phone beeped and said the number had been changed or disconnected. Frustration bubbled up, but Jessie quickly pushed it aside. This wasn't the end. This time, Jessie had an idea. She looked in the address book she found at the house. There was a phone number for their house and a cell phone number. She covered her cell phone with both her hands and said a quick prayer. "Please help me find him." She dialed the number. It rang twice, then an answer came at the other end.

"Hello?"

Jessie asked, "Is this Keith Davis?"

The reply came, "Yeah, this is Keith."

Jessie could hardly contain her excitement. "This is your great-niece, Jessie."

Keith responded, "Oh goodness, Jessie, you sound so grown up. How are you?"

Jessie said, "I'm fine, Uncle Keith. I have a story to tell you, and I need to ask you where I can find Jeremiah and Dusty. You see, after Mama died…" She continued with her story to her uncle and concluded with the question, "Can you help me find my brothers?"

"I'm not sure right now. Jeremiah travels a lot, but I will try to locate him." Said Keith.

Chapter 6
Searching for answers

A few months passed. Jessie kept working, and Eric kept going to school. Jessie called her dad every week, then Patty. There was never any new information, but she stuck to her promise of staying in touch.

One Saturday afternoon in November, Jessie received a call from Aunt June. She said, "Jessie, your Uncle Keith had a heart attack and passed away. I wanted you to know. Also, I received a letter from Jeremiah. I'll give you his address since he's hard to reach by phone. He's been in Africa, helping set up a church and getting doctors the equipment they need for the hospitals."

Jessie wasn't sure how to feel. Part of her was sad about her uncle's passing, but another part was glad to hear about her brother. It was almost too much to process all at once, the mix of emotions swirling around. She said, "Thank you for the info about Jeremiah. I'm really grateful. I'm so sorry about Uncle Keith."

After a pause, she asked, "When's the funeral?"

Aunt June replied, "Your uncle and I talked about funeral plans a long time ago. We traveled all over this country and to other countries. He had a full life, and as you know, we didn't have children. We were lucky to travel with Jeremiah and Dusty. Keith's funeral wishes were simple. He just wanted a small graveside service and to have *Amazing Grace* played because, even though we didn't have kids, we were blessed with the chance to see so much of the Lord's creation. We had a good life."

Aunt June's voice softened, a quiet sadness in her words. "Jeremiah loved those trips. He was eager to learn, so we homeschooled him. He did great in everything. Dusty, though, didn't care for the traveling. He'd always say school was a waste of time and would only do enough to get by. We never knew what was going on inside him. He didn't talk to us about it. Sometimes he'd get angry, and we didn't understand why. When he turned eighteen, he left. Jeremiah said Dusty talked about horses and rodeos a lot, but no one really knows where he is now. I heard once that he's out there riding broncos and bulls. It worries me, but I don't know how to reach him. I hope you can find him."

Aunt June added, "The funeral will be quick. You don't need to drive all the way here. Take care of yourself, and call me when you can."

Jessie's voice cracked as she said, "I know it's been a long time since I've seen you, but I love you. I'll be praying for you. I'm so grateful that you and Uncle Keith took such good care of the boys. I don't know what's caused Dusty's anger, but I know it's not your fault."

Aunt June's tone softened. "Thank you, Jessie. We love them both so much. We left everything to them in our will. Jeremiah knows about it. I love you, too. Please call me again soon."

"I will," Jessie promised, before hanging up.

Eric had spent the morning working for his dad, trying to catch up on some things. Around noon, he walked through the door. Jessie told him about her call with Aunt June.

Eric, trying to focus on getting lunch, asked, "Did you tell your dad and Patty yet?"

Jessie sighed. "No, but I will. I'm dreading telling them about Dusty, especially Dad." She felt the weight of it, how hard it would be to bring it up with him. "There's just so much going on, and I don't know how they're going to take it."

She made a tomato sandwich for Eric and handed him a glass of sweet tea, an Alabama favorite. They sat quietly for a moment, both lost in their thoughts.

An hour later, Jessie decided to call her dad. She took a deep breath before dialing. When he picked up, he asked how she was doing.

"I'm fine, and the baby's fine according to the doctor," Jessie replied. "But I need to tell you about a call I got today from Aunt June."

Joe paused. "Oh, how are they doing?"

Jessie's voice broke a little as she explained about Uncle Keith's passing. After a brief silence, her dad said, "I'm sorry to hear that. I remember Keith as a good man. I think he was fairly young, maybe in his early seventies."

Jessie went on to tell him about Dusty's behavior. Joe responded, "Well, I don't know what happened with him, but I hope we find out one day." There was a lot left unsaid, but Jessie knew her dad didn't have the answers.

"I hope so," Jessie replied quietly.

Later, Jessie called Patty. Patty answered, "A lot's happened in our family. It's kinda sad."

Jessie said, "It's sad at times, but I've come to realize that everyone has a story. Our family has its own, too."

Patty asked, "What do you mean?"

Jessie took a breath. "God gives us love and purpose, and when things happen, we can share our experiences and help others who are going through similar things."

Patty said, "I can't imagine anyone living like our family."

Jessie smiled softly. "Oh, you'd be surprised. People have lost their entire families to death. Some have been homeless. Others struggle with health issues for years. I could go on and on, but the point is, people need to hear these stories. It helps them understand they're not alone in their struggles."

Patty paused for a moment. "That's beautiful, Jessie."

That evening, Jessie sat down at the kitchen table with a small glass of tea and a pen in hand. She had a lot to say to her brother Jeremiah and tried to fit it all onto three pages. Eric looked over from the other side of the room.

"You've had a busy Saturday," he said.

Jessie smiled, her eyes focused on the paper. "Yes, but I feel like I've done a lot today. Now, I just have to wait for a response from Jeremiah."

Life went on, and Eric and Jessie were getting closer to having a baby. It was December, and Jessie had a little less than four months to go. She was getting tired more easily, and the cold winter weather didn't help with her motivation, but she was excited about Christmas.

Jessie took some money out of savings and bought small gifts for her whole family. She bought Patty a journal with a daily Bible reading for the year. It felt like the perfect gift, something that would bring peace and inspiration. She wasn't sure what to get Mark, so she hoped he would like a Walmart gift certificate. She purchased a teddy bear for Patty's daughter, Julie.

For her dad, she bought a silver pocket watch with a design of a dog on it, along with a photo album that contained pictures of the family. She included a note, encouraging him to add future pictures and child drawings to it, for Kathy bought a beautiful, flowered scarf and a pack of three ladies' handkerchiefs, each with a different, colorful flowered design.

Eric's gift had to be extra special. Jessie bought him a leather bag, a stethoscope with his name engraved on it, a blood pressure cuff, and a small picture frame. She couldn't wait to explain that the frame was for a picture of her and the baby, once Eric had his own desk. She giggled to herself as she thought about it.

For Eric's mom and dad, she bought a model car for Jim to assemble, hoping it would help him relax and enjoy a new hobby. She also bought some lotion for Beth that smelled strongly of roses. Jessie even sent Aunt June a card with an updated picture of herself and Eric, letting her know that she was in her thoughts.

"I know we have to be careful with money, but I wanted everyone to have a blessed holiday this year," Jessie said.

Eric smiled. "If everybody gets together, it will be a good one for sure."

On Christmas Eve, the entire family gathered, with the exception of Jeremiah and Dusty. Eric's parents invited Joe and Kathy to stay in their extra bedroom, while Patty, Mark, and Julie stayed in the guest house with them. Everyone gathered for Christmas dinner in the guest house. It was small and a little crowded, but no one seemed to mind. It was a joyful time of talking, eating, opening gifts, and making plans to continue the search for family as the New Year approached.

Joe sat quietly in the recliner near the heater. Jessie moved over and sat beside him on the straight chair. She asked, "What are you thinking about, Dad?"

Joe looked at her, his eyes welling up with tears. "We've come so far this year. I got to know the family I had left behind and forgotten."

Jessie smiled softly and said, "Don't think of it that way. Your family is together now, almost all of it. It will work out."

Joe nodded, his voice filled with emotion. "I'm grateful. And I'm so proud of you and the work you did getting everyone together."

Patty walked over, carrying Julie, and brought her over to see Joe. She placed Julie on his lap, and he wrapped his arm around her. "Life is good!" he said with a smile.

Jessie wiped a tear from her cheek and said, "I know, Dad. I miss her too, but she's in a great place. And we have those good memories. Don't forget, you hooked up with a great woman who loves you."

A few months passed, and early one morning at the end of March, Jessie and Eric were resting in bed. Eric's arm was around Jessie. Suddenly, Jessie spoke.

"Eric," she whispered.

With sleepiness in his voice, Eric asked, "What is it, honey?"

Jessie replied, "I'm pretty sure we're about to have a baby."

Eric blinked, his eyes widening. "Of course we are," he said. But then his eyes shot open. "Do you mean now?"

"Yes!" Jessie replied, laughing a little through her excitement.

He jumped out of bed, rushing to the closet to get his clothes. Jessie called out, "Slow down, boy! My contractions aren't heavy or close. My water broke, but we still have some time."

When they arrived at the hospital, an LPN came out to the car with a wheelchair. Jessie was wheeled into a room, and the doctor came in to assess the situation. After checking her, the doctor said it might be a few more hours before the baby would arrive.

Jessie told Eric, "Go call your parents and my dad. Hurry back!"

Eric saluted her with a grin. "Yes, ma'am!"

Jessie rolled her eyes and muttered, "Smart aleck."

When Eric returned from his phone calls, he sat in a chair beside Jessie's bed. Jessie said, "My mouth is so dry. I could really use some ice chips."

Eric smiled and left the room, returning shortly with a cup of ice chips for Jessie.

Three hours later, Eric was holding Jessie's hand as she pushed one final time. The nurse wrapped the baby in a blanket and said, "He's a handsome one."

Eric bent down to kiss Jessie and said, "We have a boy." Then, looking at the nurse, he added, "We have a boy!"

Jessie snickered, and the nurse smiled warmly. "Yes, you do."

As Jessie was assisted into a wheelchair to be moved to her room, a tall, slim man with brown hair and blue eyes walked over to her. He was dressed in dark blue jeans, a light blue dress shirt, and a dark blue sports jacket. Eric, unsure of the situation, clenched his fists, ready to defend Jessie and the baby if needed.

The man leaned over and gently said, "Jessie, it's me. Jeremiah."

Eric relaxed his fist, but Jessie's eyes locked on Jeremiah. With excitement in her voice, she gasped, "Jeremiah!"

She reached up to hug him, tears streaming down her face. "Where did you come from? How did you find me?"

Jeremiah gently held her hand between his. "Let's get you to your room, and I'll answer everything. By the way, what's your baby's name?"

Eric and Jessie hadn't decided on a name yet, but Eric suddenly had an idea. He leaned over and whispered it in Jessie's ear. She looked up at him, smiling. "It's perfect."

Turning to Jeremiah, Jessie said, "Jeremiah, this is your nephew, Joseph."

Jeremiah smiled. "You're right. It is perfect."

The nurse watched carefully as Jessie stood up from the wheelchair and slid into her bed. She said, "Oh, Jeremiah, you don't know how long I've waited to hear from you."

Jeremiah nodded. "Oh, I think I do. Apparently, someone, many months ago, put newspaper ads out asking me to call you. Then I heard the radio station mention my name. By the way, I notified both of them, told them I got the message, and was on my way. Apparently, their ratings went up, and the newspaper sold a lot of papers because people were wondering when I'd come home."

He smiled. "I also got a letter from you, and Aunt June left a message with the Red Cross about Uncle Keith. She also mentioned you'd been looking for me, so I finished up at the hospital, got a replacement for me, and caught a plane. Looks like I got here in time to see my nephew."

Jessie couldn't take her eyes off him. Eric let out a little fake cough. Jessie smiled and said, "This is my husband, Eric."

Jeremiah smiled and said, "So nice to meet you, Eric. You have a very handsome, healthy-looking son."

Eric nodded. "It's good to finally meet you."

Jessie yawned and said, "I have so much to tell you. How long can you stay?"

Jeremiah replied, "I'm not leaving anytime soon, honey. I want to spend time with you and your family."

Jessie's tears flowed again. "I'm so happy, and I hope this isn't just a dream."

The nurse carried the baby off to the nursery so Jessie could get some rest. Eric leaned over and kissed Jessie, and she closed her eyes.

Eric and Jeremiah walked to the waiting area and sat down. Jeremiah asked, "What do you two do?"

Eric answered, "I'm still in school, working to become a physical therapist. Jessie is a physical therapy assistant."

Jeremiah asked, "Where do you live?"

Eric said, "About ten miles east of here."

Jeremiah raised an eyebrow. "Wow, I've mostly been in Montgomery when I'm not traveling. It's strange that we all live in Alabama and haven't crossed paths."

Eric smiled. "I'm sure Jessie won't mind if I tell you about her journey to find the family."

Jeremiah's interest piqued. "I'm very interested."

Eric said, "It's been quite a journey, but we still haven't found Dusty."

Jeremiah's eyes lit up. "I think I can help with that. We can talk about it later."

Eric's heart raced. He knew Jessie would find this too good to be true, but this time, he was sure. It was real.

Eric added, "Through a friend in the military, I found your dad."

Jeremiah looked at him, surprised. "So, you've been on this journey as much as Jessie."

Jeremiah smiled. "It seems we've all been searching, in one way or another."

Eric humbly nodded. "Well, I helped a little."

Eric continued, "Your dad had an accident, lost his memory, and couldn't remember Mary or any of his children. He remarried a kind lady, but things were different for him. Jessie spoke to him face-to-face and left him some photos of the family, hoping it would help. He decided to give therapy a chance, and slowly, over time, he started to remember bits and pieces. He remembered all of you, but it was like there was a wall between him and the rest of the world. He couldn't figure out how to get in touch with any of you. One of Jessie's clients suggested that she visit the house where you grew up. We went there together and found one name. That was our start."

Jeremiah shook his head slowly. His eyes were clouded with regret. "I wish I could've been there for you both, through all of this. I should've known sooner."

Eric gave him a reassuring smile, putting a hand on his shoulder. "You're here now. That's what matters. You've made Jessie incredibly happy. She'll probably wake up tomorrow and wonder if it was all a dream, but it's real. It's happening." They both chuckled softly, the sound warming the room.

Eric added, "And Jessie also found Patty."

Jeremiah's eyebrows shot up in surprise. "Patty? I remember her. How is she?"

Eric's grin widened, the joy of the news bubbling over. "Jessie will be thrilled to tell you everything. Patty's doing well. She has a little girl named Julie, and her husband is Mark. They've settled in Georgia."

Jeremiah pressed his hand to his chest, a deep sigh escaping him. "Thank you, Lord. This is... this is more than I could have ever hoped for." He glanced over at Eric, his expression serious. "I was only four when Mama passed away, and the family was split up. Our aunt and uncle would remind me, every now and then, that I had another family. That there was hope I'd see you all again. I prayed for that reunion, countless times. And now, here you are. It feels like a miracle."

Two hours later, Jessie woke up with a start. The soft beeping of the machines around her and the quiet of the room made her feel disoriented. She pressed the nurse call button, her mind still foggy.

When the nurse arrived, Jessie asked for Eric. Her voice was weak, but there was a sense of urgency in her tone.

Eric walked in a moment later, his eyes searching her face. There was something different in her expression, a faint look of confusion. "Eric, is Jeremiah here, or did I dream it?" she asked, her voice uncertain.

Jeremiah had been standing just outside her door. He heard her question and nodded to Eric. Eric motioned for him to come in. Jeremiah stepped through the door, and Jessie's eyes softened as she recognized him. Her heart skipped a beat.

"I think it's Christmas," she whispered, a touch of awe in her voice. "This feels like a gift from God." Her hands trembled as she spoke, and the vulnerability in her eyes was clear.

Jeremiah smiled, his heart swelling at the sight of her. "I'm thankful to see you, too. Eric's told me bits and pieces about your journey. What a story you two have! I might just share it in my next sermon. It's something special."

Eric nodded. "Jessie, Jeremiah mentioned that he might be able to help us locate Dusty."

The mention of Dusty made Jessie's breath catch. She held her hand to her chest, her face full of concern. "Oh my goodness…" she murmured, her voice small. "Do you think he's okay?"

Before Jeremiah could answer, Jessie continued, almost desperately, "I heard he was angry, and no one knows why. Is he still angry? Does he still hate us?"

Jeremiah's face softened as he leaned in slightly, trying to reassure her. "I know he was angry when he left home. He didn't want to talk about it. He was like a storm, mad at the world. But I think he's just been lost, trying to find his way. The reason I might know where he is? He always loved the rodeo. Cattle roping, bronco busting, you name it. I kept an eye out for his name in rodeo lists and news. Sure enough, he's become a rodeo star."

Jessie's mind raced. "Hmm, that's so strange," she murmured, her thoughts working quickly to piece together the past.

"What's strange?" Jeremiah asked, his voice laced with curiosity.

Jessie took a deep breath and glanced over at him, a mysterious smile tugging at her lips. "I have something to show you when we get to the house," she said, her voice thick with anticipation.

The next morning, after being discharged from the hospital, Jessie and the baby made their way home, but they were not alone. Jeremiah followed them in his car, his heart full of excitement. What would they find when they reached the house?

When they pulled up to the little guesthouse, Jessie's eyes widened in shock. The yard was decorated with balloons, colorful flowers, and ribbons. Standing at the door were Jim and Beth, Joe's parents, waiting for them. Their faces were filled with emotion.

As Jessie walked closer, a sudden scream escaped her. Jeremiah, following close behind, looked around frantically.

"What's wrong?" he asked, his voice full of concern.

Behind the recliner stood Patty, holding her daughter, Julie, by the hand. Mark was standing behind them, his arms wrapped around Patty's waist protectively.

Jessie's heart raced. "Is it really...?" she whispered in awe.

Patty glanced up at them, polite but clearly unsure of who the man was. "Hello," she said softly, unsure of the overwhelming emotions swirling around the room.

Eric and Jessie exchanged a glance, both of them bursting into laughter at the same time. The laughter was warm, real, full of love and years of anticipation.

Patty blinked, completely confused. "What's so funny?" she asked, her voice a mixture of curiosity and concern.

Jessie laughed harder, tears beginning to spill down her cheeks. "Patty, this is one of the most unforgettable days of my life," she gasped between fits of laughter.

Eric, always quick with a joke, added, "Oh, good, a home for one of the kittens."

Patty's brow furrowed. "Huh?" she asked, looking at him with bewilderment.

Jessie wiped her eyes, still laughing, but her voice was filled with so much joy. "I'll tell you all about it later."

Jeremiah stepped forward, his voice quiet yet full of emotion. "You must be Patty. I'm your brother, Jeremiah."

Mark's eyes widened in disbelief as he instinctively reached out to support Patty, who seemed to falter slightly, overwhelmed. Her legs trembled, and tears began to fall freely.

Eric, watching the scene unfold, couldn't help but smile. "These are the only people I know who cry all the time," he joked, trying to break the emotional tension in the room.

Jessie laughed softly, wiping her own tears away. "Eric, we've had a lot of reasons to cry. But mostly? These are happy tears."

Patty's eyes narrowed, her face a mix of disbelief and wonder as she stared at Jeremiah. "Is it really you?" she asked, her voice shaky.

Jeremiah smiled, his tone teasing. "Last time I checked, it's still me."

Jessie rolled her eyes, laughing at his teasing. "Oh, funny," she said sarcastically.

Patty took a deep breath, gathering herself, then took a few steps toward Jeremiah. Without warning, she threw herself into his arms, holding him tightly. Her grip was strong, desperate even. "You're actually here," she whispered. "This is my brother."

Mark, still processing the moment, chuckled. "I figured that out," he said dryly.

Patty stepped back, wiping away her tears. She looked at her husband, then turned to Jessie, a wide smile breaking across her face. "You did it! You actually did it!"

Jessie's heart swelled with pride and love. "I had a little help along the way," she said with a smile. "And God was with us every step of the way."

Jeremiah nodded in agreement, his voice rich with emotion. "That's obvious."

Patty looked between the two of them, her eyes still sparkling with tears. "I don't understand it all, but I am so happy. More than I can express."

Jeremiah gave her a kind smile, but his eyes flickered to Jessie. There was something there, an unspoken question. Jessie met his gaze and nodded, understanding the weight of his inquiry. "We'll talk about it later. I need your help with something," she said, her tone serious but kind.

Jessie walked over to Patty with a softer smile on her face. "Would you like to hold Joseph?" she asked gently.

Patty's eyes widened, her face softening with awe. "Oh my!" she breathed as she reached out. "He's beautiful. He has your eyes, Eric."

Julie, the little girl, squeezed her way between Patty and the couch, her tiny hands reaching out toward Joseph. She touched his hand gently and looked up at her mother with a smile. "Baby," she said simply, her innocence filling the room with warmth.

Jessie walked over to Jim and Beth, reaching out to hold each of their hands. "I don't know what we would have done without you two, ever since we married and even before that, having your support," she said, her voice full of gratitude. "Your presence has meant everything to us, and I just wanted to let you know how much we appreciate both of you." "Joseph's middle name is James, after his grandpa," she added, pointing at Jim's chest with a smile.

Eric, watching the emotional moment, chuckled and said, "Now you even have my dad crying." Jessie, a little agitated but still sentimental, replied, "It's a special moment, Eric! Let's not ruin it."

That evening, after the meal, Jessie asked Jeremiah and Patty to join her at the kitchen table. The quiet of the night made the moment feel more serious, as if they were about to share something important. Jeremiah, always the curious one, asked, "Okay, what's on your mind, Jessie?" His voice was calm, ready to listen.

Jessie answered, "There's a lot on my mind, brother, but right now I just want to show you something important. Jeremiah, do you remember when I said earlier that it was strange Dusty was in the rodeo?"

"Yeah," he answered, still processing what she had said earlier.

Jessie continued, "Well, our mom left me in charge of a chest to keep safe until we were all together again. It's full of things that mean something to all of us, a way for her to keep us all connected, even when she couldn't be here anymore. Dusty was just a little baby, barely had a personality, but Mom, our mother, left a note with this beautiful brown, six-inch-long stallion figurine." She reached into the chest and pulled out the small, but intricately carved horse. "Do you think it's strange that she got him a horse figurine when he barely knew what horses were, and now, look at him, he's all about rodeo life?"

Jeremiah put his hand up to his chin, thinking deeply. After a few seconds, he said, "It does seem a bit strange, but maybe the Lord gave her the idea and inspiration. It has happened in history. Remember how God forewarned Noah, as stated in the KJV Hebrews 11:7, about the coming flood? And how Jesus spoke to His disciples in advance of the events to come, as mentioned in Isaiah? Maybe it's like that, God whispering to us, guiding us in ways we might not fully understand at first."

Patty, puzzled by the depth of the conversation, asked, "What are you saying? You think Mom had some kind of divine insight?"

Jeremiah nodded slowly. "I'm just saying it's possible. It's hard to explain any other way."

Patty looked at him, her expression filled with uncertainty. Jessie, sensing Patty's confusion, turned to Jeremiah and said, "Jeremiah, Patty has some spiritual and Biblical questions, and I believe you can help her while you're here." Her eyes softened as she looked at Patty, and she smiled warmly. "She has so much love in her heart; she just needs a little direction."

Jeremiah placed his hand gently over Patty's and said, "It'll be my pleasure to talk with you and answer as many of your questions as I can." Patty's cheeks turned bright pink, a mix of embarrassment and gratitude. Jeremiah noticed this and smiled softly. He said, "We all have questions about our Lord and our life. I wish everyone would seek these answers. No one knows everything, but we can help each other with love, patience, forgiveness, and charity."

Patty asked, "You mean giving money to people and charities, right?"

Jeremiah replied, "Of course, giving money is one way, but charity comes in many forms. We can give our time, our kindness, our understanding. Let's sit down after supper and talk about some of your questions. I think there are others who might have similar ones, too. I might even have a few questions myself. Would that be alright?"

Patty released a deep breath and nodded. "That will be great."

Jessie, quietly sitting beside Jeremiah, realized she hadn't shown him everything. "I have another surprise, perhaps you could call it another miracle," she said, her voice soft but filled with emotion. "Mother left this for you." With trembling hands, she pulled out an envelope and handed it to him.

Inside was his birth certificate, along with a few other personal papers, and a personal note from their mother.

Jeremiah looked at the papers, surprised but moved. "This is great," he whispered.

Patty, her curiosity piqued, added, "But there's something else."

Jeremiah sat silently as Jessie pulled out a Red King James Bible, its leather cover well-worn but carefully preserved. The weight of the Bible in his hands felt symbolic, like a bridge between the past and present. A bookmark was placed at the beginning of Romans, a passage Jeremiah read often. As he saw it, a wave of emotion hit him. He was speechless, his eyes welling up with tears. He held the Bible like it was a treasure that had been handed down through generations, knowing its value wasn't just in its pages but in the faith it represented.

Patty and Jessie sat quietly, watching his reaction. Jeremiah's eyes were red from the tears, but there was pride in his voice when he finally spoke, not for himself, but for the deep love he knew his mother had for him. "This is beautiful," he said, his voice full of reverence.

Then, turning to Patty, he said, "You see, all things in this world go back to God. He created this world, and He has His people. He's everywhere, and He knows everything, even the number of hairs on your head, as mentioned in Luke 12:7. He took care of Mama and led her in the right direction."

Patty, still processing, asked, "So, mama gave us gifts that were inspired by God?"

Jeremiah nodded excitedly, "That's it! Everything, even the smallest details, was part of God's plan." He paused, the weight of it all settling on him. "I believe she always knew what we would need, even before we did."

Patty thought for a moment, then said, "I think I get it, but I don't understand everything."

Jeremiah smiled softly, "That's okay. Nobody understands everything, but things will become clearer as you learn and grow." Then he said, "Jessie, I am so thankful you were able to hold on to this chest. It's a great last gift from our mom." Jessie was trying to swallow a hard lump in her throat. Her eyes were sparkling with emotion. "She reminded Jeremiah to read the letter to him when he had time." She said, "I don't know when Mama had the time, but she made a great effort to write to each of us what was in her heart. I was thinking that one day, when we are all together, we could share our letters from her."

Jeremiah said, "I think that would be nice and comforting."

The next morning, Patty and her family had to head back home and go back to work the next day. Jessie was holding baby Joseph in her arms while standing at the car to tell Patty and her family goodbye. She squeezed her son a little tighter, realizing how much her family meant to her. Eric stood by her, and Jeremiah stepped over close to Patty. She began to cry and hugged his neck. Jeremiah said, "Don't cry, we will see each other again."

Patty continued to wave as they drove down the road.

The next morning, after breakfast, Eric went back to school. Jeremiah said to Jessie, "I have enjoyed this visit so much. It has warmed my heart with love and blessings I would have never dreamed of. I always had a hope of seeing my family again one day, but my life in the ministry has kept me so busy. I don't think I have even stopped to smell the roses in a long while. The Lord chose the right one to do the work of locating family, and I believe He will continue to bless you, as He has so many people searching for answers in one way or another."

Jessie said, "You talk like you are leaving."

Jeremiah said, "Jessie, I have commitments, and I will leave in the morning, but we will keep in touch. I don't believe this reunion is over. I think there's much more to come."

Jessie and Jeremiah stayed up and talked until almost midnight, reminiscing and sharing moments from the past. The conversation felt like a gift, a chance to reconnect after so many years apart. The next morning, Jessie made breakfast, her hands busy as Eric shook Jeremiah's hand and said, "It's great to meet you, man. Come back soon."

Jeremiah smiled and replied, "Thanks, Eric. We'll get together before long." Eric waved and got in his car, driving off down the road.

Jeremiah went back inside and found Jessie wiping her wet cheeks, her emotions still raw from their goodbye. She said, "It seems like it took so long for us to get together, and now we are going our separate ways again." Her voice wavered, but there was a sense of peace in her words, too. The time they shared felt like a chapter closing, but she knew it wasn't the end. They walked out together to his car, their steps heavy with the bittersweet farewell.

Jeremiah said, "We're just going back to work, but we know how to get in touch with each other now, so I'll leave on a happy note." He opened the door to his car, then stepped back and said, "I forgot my kiss," and he leaned over to the baby in Jessie's arms and kissed him gently on the cheek.

As Jeremiah was about to open the car door, Jessie loudly said, "Jeremiah!" He looked back at her. She smiled softly and said, "I'll try hard to get everybody together for a big family get-together soon. We talked about Dusty, and remember, I may need your help to find him and talk to him."

"I'll do what I can and let you know if I hear anything," he said, his voice filled with determination to help her. Jessie shouted, "I love you!" Jeremiah waved and said, "I love you, too, sis."

Jessie had about twenty days left in her leave time. She knew she had a lot to do, but today she just wanted to spend the day with her baby. She had earned this quiet moment, and she was going to soak it in.

Jessie was all alone for the rest of the day. The house was still, the only sound being the occasional creak of the old floorboards. Jessie held her small baby in her arms. As she looked down at him, her heart swelled with emotion. "I wish you could have met Mama. She would have loved you so much." Her voice cracked as the weight of the moment hit her. She blinked her eyes a few quick times to keep the tears at bay. She looked back at Joseph and whispered, "You have a wonderful family that loves you, and before long, you will meet your other grandpa and grandma, and your Uncle Dusty. They are all waiting to meet you, little one, just like I am waiting for us all to be together."

The next morning, there was a knock on the door at 10 a.m. Jessie was dusting the furniture as little Joseph took a nap. She walked slowly to the door, a bit cautious since she didn't expect any visitors. As she answered the door, she put her hand to her mouth and gasped, "Daddy!" she said loudly. Her heart raced as she quickly opened the door and reached out to hug him.

Kathy locked the car doors and walked up to the door. Jessie hugged her tightly and said, "Come in! I am so happy to see you two." Her dad, smiling warmly, said, "Kathy and I wanted to see the baby and hear all about him. I wanted to come by and share that my memory is still progressing, bit by bit. I remembered our house and my friend Jerry." Jessie said, "The baby is asleep, but he'll probably be awake in about an hour. I hope you can stay."

Jessie's dad said, "We can stay until tomorrow because I have a therapy session on Monday morning." Jessie smiled and said, "I'll show you the baby, and then we can come back to the living room and catch up." "He looks wonderful," Kathy said, her voice soft with affection for the little one. Then she asked, "What is his name?"

Jessie beamed. "Eric and I named him after two very important men. His name is Joseph James." Joe swallowed hard, clearly moved by the significance of the name. Jessie added, "He has your name, Dad."

Joe's voice trembled with emotion. "I don't know what to say. I have my family, and now a grandson named after me." Jessie said, "Yep, it's been a special year. A year of new beginnings, and a reminder of the beauty of family."

Jessie began telling her dad and Kathy about the visit from Patty and her family, as well as Jeremiah. Joe said, "I wish I could have been here to see them."

Jessie said, "Don't worry, I am planning another get-together when the weather is warmer, God willing."

Joe asked, "Have you heard anything about Dusty?"

Jessie's smile faltered slightly. "Well, yes and no. We know he's a little famous with the rodeo, but we're not sure where he is now or even if he'll talk to us. But I won't give up."

About an hour and a half later, Joe sat down on the couch by Kathy and held his grandson. His eyes gleamed with pride as he gazed at the baby. Jessie took out her camera and captured the moment, knowing it would be one of those memories she would cherish forever.

The next morning was Sunday. Joe and Kathy went to church with Eric, Jessie, and Joseph. It felt like a community coming together, a circle of support and love that would always surround them. Mary introduced them to Pastor Rick, who was thrilled to meet them. He shook Joe's hand with a rapid, hearty shake and said, "This is a glorious day!" His voice was full of warmth, and Joe couldn't help but smile.

After the church service, Jessie and her dad stood outside at the end of the steps. Joe held the baby close, straining to hold back his tears. "Jessie, now that so much of my memory is back with me, I have so much…" His voice cracked, and he struggled to continue. Jessie interrupted gently, "I know, Dad. Things may be tough at times, but we can get through this. We are blessed with family and great friends, and I know there were people praying for us, people who don't even know us, but they heard about us."

Joe handed little Joseph back to Jessie, his heart full. He said, "We will see you soon. And by the way, Joseph is a little fidgety; I think he's wet." Jessie laughed, shaking her head, as she waved goodbye to her dad and Kathy. Eric walked out and threw up his hand to wave as they drove off.

Chapter 7
Finding Dusty

Three days later, Jessie got a surprise call. "Hello?" she answered, recognizing the voice immediately.

"Oh, hi, Dad," Jessie said, surprised but eager to hear what he had to say.

Joe replied, "Jessie, I wanted to tell you that I remembered what you said about Dusty being involved with the rodeo, and I decided to make some inquiries." Jessie kept silent, her heart racing, hoping to hear good news. "I know you're anxious to hear from your brother, and I want to know where my son is and if he's alright," Joe continued. "I thought, if he is famous, then someone should know him. I called some people who run a local arena where there are rodeos at times, as well as other horse shows and events. The lady I spoke to said that she had heard of Dusty but couldn't say which rodeo he was involved with. She suggested that I call the radio or TV stations. I took a shot and called a news channel, and after a while, I finally got connected with a man named Rodeo Bob. He told me that he knew Dusty. He said Dusty had been in Texas. Apparently, Dusty rides wild broncos on a regular basis, but on a dare, he entered the bull riding competition."

"Oh no!" Jessie exclaimed, a lump forming in her throat. Her voice quivered as she asked, "What happened?"

Her dad responded with a sigh, "Jessie, as you would imagine, he wasn't fully prepared for his first bull ride. The bull threw him off in the final three seconds, and the fall put him in the hospital. But it could have been worse." Jessie's heart sank.

"That sounds pretty bad," Jessie said softly, fear creeping into her voice.

Joe added, "The rodeo clown was on alert and ran out into the arena, distracting the bull long enough for some guys to pull Dusty out. I don't know how badly he is hurt, but I do know which hospital he's in."

"That's wonderful!" Jessie said with a small breath of relief. Her dad gave her the details, and they made plans to go together. Jessie had about a week left on her maternity leave, and she wasn't going to waste it.

When Eric came home, Jessie met him at the door with a big kiss.

Eric smiled and said, "This is nice." Then, looking concerned, he asked, "What happened?"

Jessie quickly explained the news about her brother. Eric nodded, looking worried. "I'll miss you," he said softly. "I guess we'd better find a babysitter."

Jessie shook her head. "No, I'll take her with me."

"Don't you think he's a little young?" Eric asked, furrowing his brow.

Jessie replied, "It's a sixteen-hour drive."

Eric shook his head. "No, I don't think it's a good idea."

"Eric, this is a great opportunity for me to find my last sibling," Jessie said, her voice filled with determination.

"I understand, honey. I think you should go, but I don't think it's a good idea to take a baby so shortly after birth. What if he gets sick?"

"What do you think I should do?" Jessie asked, her voice soft but searching for advice. Then she said, "You know, I'll only be gone about three days. I just want to see him and talk to him. He's in the hospital." Jessie paused, considering. "I think you're right, Eric. I don't need to take our baby to a hospital."

Eric chuckled. "Well, if he gets sick, that would be the place to be." Jessie took a few seconds to let that sink in, then she laughed. "Do you think you and your parents could take care of him while I'm gone?"

Eric smiled and said, "I think they'd be happy to take care of their only grandchild." Jessie called Jeremiah and told him of her plans to go to Texas and hoped to see Dusty. Jeremiah said, "It's kinda last-minute, but I can spare a few days."

Jessie responded, "Sorry about the last-minute warning, but I don't want to risk losing him again."

Jeremiah reassured her, "I'm with you."

Since Jeremiah, Jessie, and their dad all lived in Alabama, they met at the little townhouse to leave together for the airport. Jessie held her baby and kissed him a few times before they left. James said, "We raised a boy on our own and we'll take good care of this one."

Jessie shrugged her shoulders like a child who had done something wrong. "I feel so guilty leaving you and our son."

Eric hugged her. "Some people have to get back to work quickly and leave their newborns with a babysitter or daycare. You just have to make a brief trip, and you'll leave our baby in good hands. Besides, you can't let this opportunity pass." He looked at Jeremiah and Joe and said, "You two take care of her."

Joe nodded. "Don't worry, son. We'll look after her."

On the plane, Jessie sat in silence. Jeremiah looked over at her and said, "You haven't said a word in the last thirty minutes. We'll arrive there before long." Then he asked, "Are you okay?"

Jessie just looked back at him with saddened eyes. Her voice quivered as she answered, "I miss my baby, and I wonder if it's all worth it. Maybe Dusty doesn't want to see us." Joe spoke up gently, "I seem to remember Mary being very emotional after the birth of Jessie."

Jessie looked confused. "What are you talking about?"

"It's normal for a mother to be emotional after giving birth."

Jessie's eyes widened. "Oh my gosh!" She gasped. "Are you talking about postpartum depression, which I don't have!"

"It's okay, Jessie. It's been an emotional year," her dad remarked, trying to keep her calm.

"I feel like my baby needs me," Jessie said with conviction, her tone serious.

"Of course, he needs you, honey, but right now, he needs some time with his dad and grandparents, and you need to stay on the path. We won't be gone long," Joe reassured her.

Jessie sighed deeply. "I guess Kathy is missing you, too."

Joe nodded. "Yeah, but she understands and supports me." Then he asked, "I've been meaning to ask you, Jessie, how do you feel about me being married?"

Jessie looked directly into her dad's eyes and said, "Mom is gone, and I don't want you to be lonely. I know you can't help what happened to you and your memory of the past, but you're better now, and I'm happy for you and Kathy. I'll admit it's a little strange, but the past several years have been strange, almost unreal. But I have enough sense to know that no one has a perfect life."

Joe let out a sigh of relief and gratitude. "Have I told you lately that I'm so proud of you?"

Jessie let out a breath with a small laugh and said, "Yes, you have a few times, and it's nice to know."

The plane landed, and Jeremiah said, "I'll get us a rental car." Within the hour, they were on their way to a motel. Jeremiah drove like he knew his way around, and Jessie complemented him. "You drive very well on these busy roads, and you seem to know your way around."

Jeremiah smiled and said, "I do travel as a minister, and I've been here once before, but I did ask for directions while we were at the airport." Jessie laughed.

They unpacked and met for a late lunch. While at the lunch table, Jeremiah spoke up. "I need to tell you two something." Joe and Jessie gave him their attention, waiting for him to speak.

He proceeded with caution. "I should have said something earlier, but I could never find the right time." Jessie urged him, "Come on, Jeremiah, don't keep us in suspense."

Jeremiah sighed deeply. "Dusty and I haven't talked since he left home. But the day he left, he told me that he felt worthless. He said his dad must not have wanted him, and his mom left him before he even got to know her. He never wanted to travel with Aunt June and Uncle Keith. He wanted to be around animals, mainly horses. Aunt Jean bought him most everything he wanted, and he felt like she was trying to win him over or con him with new clothes, candy, boots, and souvenirs. He said he felt like a black sheep when he walked out the door and got into a taxi. I yelled for him to wait. I wanted to talk with him, but I never saw him again, except on TV from time to time."

Jeremiah paused. "I can't verify it, but I wonder if he's doing dangerous things because he doesn't care about himself anymore. That's one reason I'm glad you decided to come, Jessie. I think it's very important, and I'm glad I could come at this time."

Jessie's lips quivered, and her eyes began to tear up. Her dad's eyes were also filled with sadness as a tear rolled down his cheek. Jeremiah said, "I'm sorry if this hurts you. I felt that it was the right thing to do, to tell you both."

Jessie nodded slowly. "It's okay, Jeremiah. I needed to know." Joe said, "It's a good thing you said this. I needed to know too. It helps me tremendously to know what I need to do when I see Dusty." He reached over and gave a couple of fatherly pats on Jeremiah's shoulder.

Jeremiah felt the confirmation that he had done the right thing at the right time. Joe wiped his nose, stood up, and said, "We'd better get to the hospital and see our cowboy."

They walked side by side down the hall of the hospital, the sound of their footsteps echoing in the quiet corridor. Jeremiah stopped at the first desk he saw and told the receptionist, "We are looking for Dusty Davis's room."

She scrolled down the list of names, her fingers moving quickly across the screen. Jessie watched her with growing anticipation. **Her heart was racing, each second feeling like a lifetime.**

"Yes, sir. Mr. Davis is on the third floor, Room 319. Take the elevators down the hall on the left."

As they stepped out of the elevators, Jeremiah looked at Jessie and said, "Jessie, be calm and slow when you see him. He hasn't seen any of us in years, and it might shock him to see Dad."

Jessie nodded, swallowing hard. "Okay," she whispered, unsure of what to expect.

Jeremiah knocked on the door. From inside, Dusty's voice called out, "Come in."

As the door opened, Dusty recognized Jeremiah immediately. "Well, hello, bro. I haven't seen you in a long while."

Jeremiah reached out and grabbed Dusty's hand. "I've missed you, Dusty."

Dusty looked over at the person standing beside Jeremiah. "Who do you have with you?"

Jeremiah paused for a moment, then said, "It's a long story, but this is your oldest sister, Jessie. Jessie has been looking for all of the family for years, and recently, she found out where you were. So, we just caught a plane and rushed out to see you."

Dusty stared at the woman he didn't recognize. "I think you look familiar," he said, squinting, as if trying to piece together a memory.

Jeremiah smiled softly and said, "Dusty, this is our dad, Joe Davis. He's called Joe Smith."

Joe quickly wiped a tear that had slipped out onto his cheek, the emotion overwhelming him. **The moment was raw and real.** He walked over closer to the bed where Dusty was lying and said, "Hey, son."

Dusty gritted his teeth together and clenched his fist, disbelief flashing in his eyes. He looked straight at Jeremiah and asked, "Is this a joke?"

Jeremiah put his hand on Dusty's arm, his voice calm but firm. "This is not a joke. This is your dad and one of your sisters. Jessie found our other sister and her family in Georgia. Jessie and her husband, Eric, have worked tirelessly to find our family, and we are all thankful for the opportunity to find you."

Joe now stood beside Dusty and said, "I'm glad we found you, son. I…"

Jessie interrupted softly, trying to explain. "Dusty, we have so much to tell you, but I don't want to overwhelm you all in one day. But it's important that you know that Dad was in a bad accident when we were very young. He was hurt, and the accident caused him to have amnesia. He didn't remember his family, but over time, with therapy, he has most of his memory back."

Joe asked, "How bad are you hurt, son?"

Dusty looked down at his injuries, then back at his family. "I'll mend. I have a fractured left wrist and some bruising around my ribs, but I'll be up and about in no time."

Jessie asked, her voice filled with concern, "Do you plan to go back to bull riding?"

Dusty hung his head, his shoulders heavy. "I'm not sure right now. I know it's about time for me to get out of the rodeo business." He yawned, exhaustion settling in.

Jeremiah, noticing Dusty's fatigue, said, "I think you need some rest and time to soak all this in. We'll come back tomorrow morning after breakfast, if that's okay."

Dusty nodded. "I'll be here."

As they got in the car to head back to the motel, Jessie turned to Jeremiah and asked, "What was that all about?"

"What?" Jeremiah asked, pretending not to understand.

"You know what!" She snapped. "You wanted to go, and we hadn't been there but a few minutes, and then Dusty seemed a little distant."

Joe kept silent, listening carefully. Jeremiah sighed, "This was a lot for him to hear all at once. Maybe I should have seen him alone and prepared him. He is scared in more ways than one."

"What do you mean?" Jessie asked, puzzled.

Jeremiah explained, "A family walked into his room that he thought had abandoned him. I'm sure he has questions and concerns, but he'll have to break down that tough exterior of a bronco rider to feel the love that he needs. He also mentioned that he'll give up bronco riding, but he has to ride one more time. Before you ask why, Jessie, I believe this accident frightened him, and it could scar him emotionally if he doesn't prove to himself that he can do what he needs to do."

Jessie's eyes widened as the understanding clicked. "You mean if you fall off a horse, you need to get back on it?"

Jeremiah gave her a funny look, his eyes slightly squinted. "Yeah, that's what I mean."

Jessie said, "I want to show him what Mom left him in the chest."

Jeremiah nodded. "That's a good idea, Jessie. Just wait a little while, though, until we talk a little more and answer any questions he might have."

"Sure," Jessie replied quietly, lost in thought.

The next morning, when they went to Dusty's room, his bed was empty. Jessie looked around, confused. "Where did he go?"

A nurse walked by and heard Jessie's question. She stopped and told them that Dusty had gone to therapy and would be back in about twenty minutes. Jessie and Joe sat in chairs while Jeremiah sat on the side of Dusty's bed, lost in thought.

Dusty entered the room in a wheelchair, pushed by a nurse who assisted him back to bed. Then she raised the head of the bed so he could talk to his family more easily.

Dusty had a smile on his face, despite his exhaustion. Jeremiah said, "Do you feel better today?"

Before Dusty could answer, Jessie said, "I'm sorry we sprang this on you while you're trying to recover. I just didn't know where you would go after the hospital, and I didn't want to lose you again."

Dusty nodded, his smile still weak but genuine. "It's okay. I am fine. It was a lot to take in, but I'm glad to know that you thought enough of me to visit."

With a little frustration, Jessie let out a breath and said, firmly but softly, "Dusty, we love you and want to continue to see you wherever you live. We want to be a whole family."

Dusty scoffed sarcastically, "How can you love me? You don't even know me."

Jeremiah turned to Jessie and said, "Give it to him now, Jessie."

"Give me what?" Dusty asked, his brow furrowed in confusion.

Jessie reached into her backpack and pulled out the horse figurine their mom had left for Dusty. She handed it to him, watching his reaction carefully.

Jeremiah spoke softly, "Sometimes, people have love in their hearts that is unexplainable but genuine. That horse was given to you by our mama, who loved you and felt something about you before you ever knew it yourself. She gave it to Jessie to keep safe for you. She loved you, and we all love you."

Dusty looked at Jessie, his voice filled with uncertainty. "Is this true?"

Jessie smiled and said, "It is true."

Dusty was quiet as he looked the horse over. He humbled himself for a beautiful moment and said, "I have a small collection of horses on a shelf at my apartment, but this is my favorite." Jessie couldn't contain herself. She gently lay close to him and hugged him carefully, then kissed him on the cheek. **Tears of joy welled up in her eyes, but she held them back, enjoying the moment.**

Joe walked over and said, "I'm sorry about the years we've missed, but I hope we can enjoy a lot more time together."

Dusty had tears welling up in his eyes, but he couldn't speak. He just kept nodding his head up and down.

Dusty listened carefully to every word his family told him about their adventures in finding Patty and her family, about Dad's wife, Kathy, and Jessie's little baby. They all talked and laughed for hours. Dusty had let most of his anger go, but he was still mad at himself.

He told Jeremiah, "When I heal, I have to go back and ride that bronco, Thunder Bolt, one more time." He knew Jeremiah would understand.

Dusty had a secret plan that he could not tell his family right now, but he decided he would tell them at a later date. Jessie gave Dusty the letter their mom had written for him, along with some papers he might need. They exchanged addresses and phone numbers before they left Dusty at the hospital.

Jessie said, "I hope you recover soon. I wish I could stay longer, but I have to get back to my baby."

Dusty smiled and said, "I want to meet my nephew soon."

Jessie nodded. "Sounds good."

Dusty held onto the horse as they were leaving, looking down at it fondly. "Thanks for coming to see me. I'll be fine, and I'll see you all again soon. I have a family now."

Chapter 8
Dusty is in danger

Two weeks later, the rodeo clown who had helped Dusty stopped by to see him. He knocked lightly on the door and asked, "How are you doing?"

Dusty looked up from his recliner and smiled faintly. "I'm good. I'm going home today."

The clown, a friend named Ben, asked, "How are you getting home?"

Dusty shrugged slightly. "I'll call a cab or bus."

Ben hesitated, then said, "I'll take you home."

Dusty felt strange that someone cared enough to volunteer to give him a ride. For the first time in a long while, he was touched by someone's kindness. He wasn't sure what to do. He looked at Ben and said, "Thanks."

Dusty slowly got out of the hospital bed and packed the few items he had into a hospital plastic bag. One of the hospital volunteers brought him a clean T-shirt and a pair of sweatpants that had been donated, so he would have something to wear home. His clothes were still stained with dirt and blood from the rodeo, a painful reminder of the fall.

When the nurse came by with the discharge papers, she smiled kindly and spoke in a gentle voice. "Please sit in the wheelchair, and I'll take you downstairs to your friend's car."

Dusty felt warm and a little strange with all the kindness people were showing him. It all started when his family arrived earlier, and now this. It felt almost like he was being cared for again, as he mattered.

Ben parked in Dusty's parking area at the apartment. He quickly got out of his car and reached for Dusty's arm to help him. They walked slowly to the door, and Dusty went over to his recliner, moving with a slow but steady gait.

Ben watched him, then said, "I'll be going now." Then he asked, "Is there anything I can do for you before I go?"

Dusty shook his head. "No, but do I owe you something for all your trouble?"

Ben smiled, his tone warm. "No, no trouble. Call me if you need anything. I'll let the guys know you're home."

Dusty lifted his hand and waved. "Thanks."

"Sure," Ben answered as he closed the door behind him.

Dusty let out a deep sigh of relief. "Ahhh, home at last!" He lay back in his recliner and took a look around the apartment, soaking in the familiar surroundings. For the first time in a while, the place didn't feel so empty. His eyes wandered over to his horse collection, and then, all of a sudden, he shouted, "Oh no!"

He wasn't sure if he'd packed the horse that his mom had left him. He got up slowly, his body aching as he leaned over the side of the recliner. His heart was racing as he grabbed the bag from the floor beside him. He felt inside, hoping for the familiar shape of the figurine. He turned the bag upside down and dumped everything out. The horse was gone.

Dusty didn't realize how much the beautiful stallion meant to him until now. It wasn't just a toy, it was a piece of his past, something that connected him to his mother and his family. In desperate hope, he looked all around the bottom of the recliner, hoping it had just fallen out of his bag, but it was not to be found.

He sat back in his recliner, staring up as if looking toward Heaven. "I'm sorry, Mom. I lost the horse," he whispered, his voice full of regret. The weight of the loss was more than just material; it felt like losing a piece of his family again.

That evening, around six, there was a knock on his door. Dusty didn't want to see anybody, so he stayed silent, ignoring them. Another knock on the door.

Dusty sighed and eased over to the window, looking outside toward the door. He saw a slim, blond-haired young woman standing there. He watched her for a few seconds, and as she started to walk away, he could not contain his curiosity. Maybe it was the loneliness, or maybe just the need for human contact. He walked over to the door and saw her about to get in her car. She glanced up and saw him waving at her.

She shut the car door and walked back to his front door.

"Hi," she said when she reached the door.

Dusty blinked, still unsure of what was going on. "Hi, can I help you?"

"My name is Christy," she said, smiling a little. "I work at the hospital. I just got off work about forty-five minutes ago, but I rushed over."

Dusty nodded, beginning to recall her face. "Oh yeah, I remember seeing you come into my room and take me to therapy."

She nodded. "That's right. I noticed that you seemed to care about this..." She began to pull out the stallion that Dusty thought he had lost. Before she finished explaining, Dusty reached for the horse and, in his excitement, kissed this girl right on her lips.

He pulled back quickly, his eyes wide with shock. "Oh, I'm sorry."

Christy laughed softly. "It's okay. That was a nice greeting. A little unusual, but nice."

Dusty rubbed the back of his neck, embarrassed. "Come on in."

Christy planted her feet firmly on the sidewalk and didn't move. Dusty turned back toward her and asked, "Is something wrong?"

She hesitated, then answered, "I'm not sure it's appropriate for me to go into a man's house."

Dusty, surprised, said, "Oh." His face softened. "It's safe with me. I just want you to tell me where you found my horse."

Christy looked around, a little uncertain, but slowly walked inside. Dusty offered her a chair, and she sat down, still looking around.

"I wasn't sure if I should have come to your home, but as I said, you seemed to care about that horse when you brought it with you to the therapy room. I took a chance and looked up your address in the chart. I felt like I needed to bring it to you. I hope that's okay. I didn't mean to intrude."

Dusty smiled, feeling a little warmth in his chest. "You didn't intrude. I know now why they call nurses angels. You do the right thing." He paused and sighed, his tone turning more reflective. "This is not an ordinary horse. I think I was about two years old when my mother died. She left this with one of my sisters to give to me when I was older. It's a long story, but my family all got separated when we were very young, and my oldest sister found me a few weeks ago and brought it to me."

Then he asked, "Where did you find it?"

Christy smiled softly. "Housekeeping found it at the end of your bed, wrapped up in the sheet. She took it to the nurses' desk on the third floor, and I recognized it when I walked by."

Dusty smiled, relieved. "It's a wonderful story about your horse." His eyes softened as he looked at the figurine in his hands. "Thank you for bringing it back."

Christy stood up. "I'd better go now. My cat may be wondering where I am."

Dusty, looking a bit nervous but hopeful, asked, "Would you… uh… Would you like to go out to lunch with me tomorrow?"

Christy smiled, her eyes lighting up. "That would be nice, but I have to work tomorrow. I'm off Saturday."

Dusty's face brightened. "Great! Tell me where you live, and I'll see you about eleven-thirty."

Dusty held onto that horse like a little boy holding on to candy. His fingers closed around it with a sense of relief, as if it were his last connection to his past. He was so relieved to have it back, and now, he had a date. He thought out loud, "I wonder if Mom planned that too? Nah!" He placed the horse on the shelf with the others and said, "I'm going to name you Thunder Bolt."

Dusty's body healed, and two months later, he entered the rodeo with the same ambition to ride Thunder Bolt again. He had to prove to himself that he was tough enough and brave enough to win this competition. He had scars to remind him that he couldn't do this forever. Christy had never heard of Dusty because she never took an interest in the rodeo, but she found out about it and decided to witness this rodeo star people talked about. Her curiosity had finally gotten the best of her, and she wanted to see him in action.

She walked down to the gate where Dusty was getting ready for the bronco ride. She stood leaning over the rail. Dusty walked over to the pen where the horse was, and as he looked up, he caught a glimpse of Christy standing there. He walked over to her and asked, "What are you doing here?" They had been dating for a while, but this was the first time she had come to watch him compete.

She said casually, "Oh, I thought I'd see what this rodeo business is all about." Then she smiled and said loudly over the crowd's yells, "I wanted to see what you do, but being this close to that snorting horse is a little scary."

Dusty climbed the rail, reached over, and kissed her. He spoke close to her ear and said, "Don't worry. Piece of cake."

Dusty was mistaken. Another rider was chosen to ride Thunder Bolt. He heard the announcement over the intercom. His heart sank when he heard the words. "THERE HAS BEEN A CHANGE IN THE SCHEDULE. DUSTY DAVIS WILL BE RIDING HURRICANE."

Dusty told the guy getting the horse ready, "No one informed me of this change. I was supposed to ride Thunder Bolt."

One guy said, "Hold on, I'll find out what's going on."

The crowd began chanting, "Dusty! Dusty!" Dusty looked over the rails toward Christy. She looked concerned, her hands covering her mouth. She began to realize that this was a dangerous sport. Her stomach twisted with worry as she silently prayed, "Please God, don't let him get hurt. Please don't let him get hurt!"

Christy turned to the lady she was sitting by and asked, "Is that a bad horse?"

The lady, wearing a dark pink western shirt with black shiny outlines on it and a beige cowgirl hat, said, "Honey, that Hurricane is one of the meanest broncos you'll ever see. That cowboy had better hold on tight and jump off quick."

Christy whispered, "Don't do it, Dusty!" but Dusty couldn't hear her over the crowd. The gate opened, the horse bucked, and Dusty was holding on with all his might. The announcer counted off the seconds.

Dusty made it. He conquered his fear, but now his hand was stuck, and he couldn't release it. Another rider rode close and kept trying to get Dusty free. The crowd murmured. Christy's breath caught in her throat as she watched, unable to look away.

All of a sudden, Dusty broke free and jumped onto the rider's horse that came up beside him. The crowd roared in approval. Christy removed her hands from her eyes. It was over.

Dusty was sore from the twisting and turning, but he was fine. Dusty ran over to the stands where Christy sat. He held up his first-place trophy. Christy was forcing a smile as she clapped for him, her hands shaking slightly.

Dusty put his arms around Christy's shoulder. "That was the best ride of my life!"

Christy looked over into his eyes, concern still lingering. "Are you going to continue to ride these horses?"

Dusty and Christy walked over to a brown wooden picnic table, and Dusty asked Christy to have a seat. He looked at her, his expression softening. "You're trembling. Is something wrong?"

She said, "No, I'm fine."

Dusty said, "I can tell this frightened you. I've been doing this for a while, but I know I can't do it the rest of my life, so that is the last bronco I will ride."

Christy asked, "Are you sure?"

Dusty was quiet for a few seconds as he lowered his head, contemplating. There was an unsettling weight in his silence, a decision that weighed heavily on him.

Christy reached out and gently lifted his face by his chin. "Dusty, we've been together for a little while, and I like you a lot. As a matter of fact, I…" Was it too soon to tell him how she felt? Would it scare him off? She hesitated, but then decided to speak from her heart. "I care about you, and I hope we can always be honest with each other."

Dusty carefully chose his words. "I care about you, too, and I won't lie to you. I won't ride another bronco, but I do have one more ride. I don't want my family to know about it, so they won't know until the day it happens."

Christy asked, "Are you going to keep it a secret until then?"

"Yes, from my family. I'll tell you, but you must keep it secret from everybody so it won't have a chance to get back to my family." He asked, "Can you keep my secret?"

"I will," she answered, hoping she hadn't made a mistake.

Dusty proceeded to tell her his secret. "In three weeks, I'll ride a bull called DEATH THREAT. That will be my last ride in the rodeo."

Christy's eyes widened. "That sounds like a very dangerous name. Why do you feel a need to ride this bull? Everybody knows how good a champion you are."

Dusty took a deep breath, his expression turning serious. "Horses are majestic, wonderful animals. I want to have a horse ranch. I would like to rescue horses that are mistreated. I would also like to have a special area of the ranch to teach kids how to ride these beautiful animals. It's been a dream since childhood, and my mom reinforced the idea in my head and heart with the gift she saved for me. I didn't have my mom and dad growing up, and I guess I was bitter. I was jealous of kids walking around with their parents. I grew up, and through the years, I was angry at myself, I was angry at God, and I was angry with people in general. I didn't have much ambition, so I didn't care whether I lived or died. The rodeo was an experience that I enjoyed, but it was okay with me if I got killed. The same rodeo was an outlet that brought me to my family and closeness with the mother I never knew. That may not make much sense, but I know what I need to do, and I understand God has shown me love, and that it's okay to love."

It suddenly popped out of his mouth, like an unplanned explosion. He blurted out, "I love you, Christy!" He anxiously waited for her to say something.

"I love you, Dusty Davis," she replied, her voice trembling slightly with emotion.

They embraced the moment with a long, passionate kiss. The rodeo clown walked up and said, "Get a room, you two." They turned and looked at him, laughing out loud. Dusty had a smile from ear to ear.

He continued his story to Christy. "You see, there's a big purse for the winner of the bull ride, and I would have enough with my savings to buy you a ring and also buy that ranch, or at least put a great down payment on it."

Christy frowned, her voice concerned. "You don't have to put yourself in danger. I have savings, and I will continue to work. We can make it work without the bull ride."

Dusty looked directly into Christy's sparkling blue eyes. "I need to do this. If I don't win, I will not do it again."

Christy's voice trembled. "I don't want you to do it, but I will be there for you if you're determined to do it."

A week later, Jeremiah called Dusty. He said, "Hey, I saw you on the TV last week. Congratulations on the win. You're really good. It looked a little scary for a minute, but you pulled it off."

Dusty didn't like keeping this secret from Jeremiah, but he feared that if the news got to his family, some of them might put pressure on him to back out of his last rodeo ride, so he just replied, "Thanks." The phone call was brief. Jeremiah said, "I just wanted to call and congratulate you, and I hope you're feeling well."

Dusty said, "I'm good. Thanks for calling."

Jeremiah always had a keen sense about things when they didn't seem exactly right. He could hear the uncertainty in Dusty's voice. All he knew to do was pray about it.

March finally arrived. Jeremiah had called his connection in the rodeo circuit and learned about Dusty's plan to ride the bull. He called all of the family beforehand and explained what Dusty was going to do. Jessie asked, "Why is he doing this again?"

Jeremiah said, "Dusty may not have wanted us to know or worry, but I think we all need to be there to support him. The rodeo is in Louisiana. I can drive my camper for the weekend, and we can all go."

Eric was very interested. "I have some homework, but I can study on the bus."

Eric and Jessie decided to take Baby Joseph. Patty, Mark, and little Julie said they would come. Dad and Kathy are coming. Jeremiah checked off his list. That's everybody.

No one knew about Christy yet.

The camper was packed, and everyone met at Joe's house. Jeremiah said to the family in the camper, "This is going to be an interesting trip, and it might be a little cramped. It's about a six-hour trip, so it might be tiring. I hope everyone is on their best behavior."

Jessie smiled and teased, "You of all people don't need to be so negative."

"Let's go!" Patty said with excitement. "I want to see my other brother."

Jeremiah cranked the camper that Friday morning, and they were on their way.

Saturday, March 22nd – The day of the rodeo. Jeremiah parked the camper with some RVs and plugged it in at the designated spot for campers. The main event was scheduled to start at five PM. Eric wanted to watch the calf roping, and Jessie wanted to see the barrel races. Jeremiah said, "Try to be discreet and don't let Dusty see you until later. We don't want to make him nervous."

Little Julie squealed with excitement when the cowgirls rode their horses around the arena carrying flags.

Patty said, "It's beautiful. I can see why Dusty loves the horses and the western atmosphere."

Jeremiah said, "It is beautiful, but don't forget that Dusty has a dangerous ride coming up. It might be a little scary, so keep calm."

The family moved as close as they could to the event dirt floor. The cowboys walked out and waved their hats at the crowd as the announcer introduced the lineup. He announced, "Dusty Davis, the all-around champion." Dusty stepped forward and waved his hat.

The family began to shout, "Go, Dusty! Yay, Dusty!"

Christy was sitting nearby and heard their shouts. She moved a little closer to them, and Jessie noticed her walking toward them. Christy sat near Jessie. She asked, "Do ya'll know Dusty?"

The crowd was getting louder. Jessie shouted to Christy, "He's my brother! We all came to support him." She then asked, "What's your name?"

She smiled and said, "I'm Christy."

Jessie smiled back. "Nice to meet you."

Christy said, "Oh no!"

Jessie asked, "What?"

Christy hesitated, then said, "Um, that's great. It's nice to meet you." She thought to herself, "Geez, he's going to think I told his family."

The cowboys all took their turn on the bulls. One made the ride in seven seconds before he was thrown. Jessie asked Jeremiah, "How long do they have to stay on the bull?"

"Eight seconds," he answered.

Jessie said, "That doesn't sound too bad."

Eric laughed. "It's a lot harder than you think, honey."

Dusty walked over to the pen holding the bull, Death Threat. He looked up into the stands for Christy. He spotted her. He waved at her. She tried to smile, but her teeth were clenched in nervousness. She pointed to her side to Jessie and his entire family, and then put her hands up in the air, palms up, to let him know she didn't know about it. Her heart raced, knowing Dusty hadn't wanted his family to know.

Dusty started walking toward the stands where his family was when the announcement came over the speakers.

"LADIES AND GENTLEMEN, THE MAIN EVENT WITH DUSTY RIDING DEATH THREAT, THE MEANEST BULL IN THE COUNTRY. HE HAS PUT FOUR COWBOYS IN THE HOSPITAL. CAN DUSTY BEAT THIS BULL? THIS RIDE IS NOT FOR THE WEAK AT HEART. IF HE CAN STAY ON THIS BULL FOR EIGHT SECONDS, HE WILL BE WORLD CHAMPION AND WIN FIVE MILLION DOLLARS."

Jessie whispered, "Now I am scared."

"Too late now," Jeremiah said. "He knows we are all here. He will give it everything he's got to impress his family."

Dusty climbed onto the bull and tightened his grip. He motioned for the gate to open. The bull jumped high in the air, which would have thrown a less experienced cowboy to the ground. The count was on. Dusty fought to stay on as the bull twisted and bucked.

The eight seconds seemed like minutes to Jessie. She asked, "Can't they count faster?" Her body was tensed, the fear crawling up her spine. Not as tense as Christy's, who had her head bowed in prayer. Christy's silent prayer echoed in her mind, "Please, God, don't let him get hurt."

The horn rang out. Dusty had ridden the bull for the full eight seconds, but now he was trying to get off. The bull was still jumping and snorting. Dusty took a big sideways leap and landed hard on the ground. The breath was knocked out of him, and he was stunned for a second.

The bull ran to the other end of the arena, lowered its head, and charged at Dusty. The clowns rushed in, distracting the bull. Patty screamed. Dusty moved like lightning, rolling out of the way before the bull could get its balance and turn around again. Dusty ran to the gate and jumped over it, but not before the bull nicked his leg. Blood was trickling down his pant leg.

The medic came out quickly, and Dusty was taken over to the side of the arena to a tent. The crowd waited with anticipation, murmuring anxiously. Christy was rubbing her hands together, her face full of worry. Joe had a concerned look on his face. Jeremiah was praying. Eric and Mark were quiet. Baby Joseph began to cry. Jessie held him close and rubbed his back until he closed his eyes.

Five minutes passed. Then five more minutes. Dusty's family sat in silence, holding their breath, waiting for any news.

Finally, Dusty hobbled out onto the dirt arena, waving his hat. The announcer shouted, "LADIES AND GENTLEMEN, THE NEW WORLD CHAMPION, DUSTY DAVIS!" The crowd erupted in cheers, screaming and clapping.

Dusty walked over to the stands, and his family thought he was coming to talk to them. But they stood still in shock as Dusty pulled himself up on the rails and leaned over to kiss his girl, Christy.

Jessie whispered, "I was sitting by that girl, and I had no clue."

Jeremiah smiled knowingly. "That sounds like Dusty to keep things to himself. He had two secrets."

The family strolled over to Dusty, and they all began to hug him. Joe said, "Congratulations, son," as he glanced over at Christy. "On everything."

Christy asked, "How bad is your leg?"

Dusty smiled. "It's just a scratch."

"Bull!" said Jeremiah, and everybody stopped and laughed.

Dusty asked Christy, "Did you call my family?"

Christy looked at him with a smile. "Dusty, I didn't even know your family, much less how to reach them."

"Oh, sorry, baby," Dusty said, laughing.

He turned to Jeremiah. Jeremiah said, "Yeah, it's my fault. I felt like there was something strange in your voice when we talked last on the phone, so I found out where you were going to be and brought the whole bunch." He quickly changed the subject. "By the way, this is your sister Patty, her husband Mark, and your niece, Julie."

Dusty reached down and held Julie's hand in his with a gentle handshake. "Hello, Julie." Julie giggled. He shook Mark's hand and hugged Patty.

Jessie walked over and said, "This is my husband, Eric, and your nephew, Joseph." He shook Eric's hand, then Dusty reached his hand down to Joseph and held his little hand. "This is the best night of my life so far, except for one thing I need to do."

Jessie frowned, "I hope you're not going to ride another bull."

Dusty smiled, shaking his head. "Yes, I am."

Jessie looked at him, her eyes wide. "What?"

"Just kidding, Jessie. My days of bull riding are over." He asked Eric to hand him his denim jacket. "I want to marry the love of my life," he said, reaching into the jacket pocket and pulling out a golden ring with a shiny, large diamond on it. He bent down on one knee and asked, "Would you marry me, Christy?"

Her immediate response was, "Yes, yes, yes!"

Jeremiah said, "What are you going to do with all that prize money?"

Dusty said, "I'll come back here and tell you all about it tomorrow morning. I need to take Christy home and talk to her for a few minutes."

Everybody hugged Christy and said, "Welcome to the family."

When they arrived at the motel where Christy was staying, Dusty said, "I'm sorry your family wasn't here. Are you disappointed?"

Christy smiled softly. "Well, it would have been nice, but we can see them in a day or two. They've told me that they aren't crazy about your rodeo activities anyway, but they think you're a great guy. They will be so happy you are moving on to safer things to do with your life."

Dusty said, "Our life."

Dusty looked at the ground for a second and kicked a tiny stone. Christy asked, "What is it, Dusty?"

Dusty paused, his expression pensive. "I told you the plans I have for the future, but I never asked what you wanted. Maybe you don't like horses." He awaited her reply, feeling a little vulnerable.

She smiled warmly, understanding his concern. "Dusty, I do like horses. I've never thought about wild broncos or mean bulls, but I love animals. Maybe we could have some dogs and a cat."

Dusty smiled and hugged her tightly, as he would never let go. "Whatever you want. I love dogs and cats too. I never thought I could find anybody like you in a million years." He held her a little longer, savoring the feeling of being understood.

Christy said softly, "I'm happy too."

Dusty pulled back slightly and looked at her. "I'll see you tomorrow about eleven, and we can go out to eat at that new restaurant and talk about our future plans."

Christy nodded, her smile bright. "I will be here, but I have to go back to Texas after that. My neighbor has been feeding my cat. She'll wonder when I'm coming back."

Dusty nodded, understanding. "I know, me too."

The next morning, Dusty didn't feel very good. His body ached, and his head was foggy. He felt weak, and his skin was hot to the touch. Something didn't feel right. He got in his car and drove to the arena area, where his family was parked in the camper.

He knocked on the camper door, and when Jeremiah answered, Dusty passed out forward into his arms.

Jeremiah's eyes widened in alarm. He quickly picked him up and carried him to the bed Dusty had slept in. Jeremiah grabbed his cell phone and called an ambulance. His voice cracked slightly with worry. "Wake up, everybody!" Jessie looked up and asked, "What is it?"

Jeremiah's face was filled with concern. "Dusty has passed out. Something is wrong!"

"I'll call an ambulance," Eric said, moving toward the phone.

"I did that," Jeremiah replied urgently.

The ambulance arrived about seven minutes later. The EMTs quickly entered, assessing Dusty's condition. One EMT asked, "What happened?"

Jeremiah explained, "I don't know. He just passed out when he came to the door." One of the EMTs began taking Dusty's blood pressure. Dusty began to wake up, groaning. "My leg hurts," he moaned, his voice hoarse.

Jeremiah nodded, "I explained to them about the bull stabbing him in the leg the night before." The EMT cut Dusty's pants with scissors and examined the wound. "His leg is infected, and he has a fever. We need to get him to the hospital."

They lifted him onto a stretcher and rushed him to the ambulance. Jessie asked, "What's going to happen?"

Jeremiah, still worried, said, "I don't know, but I need to get the camper unhooked. We'll go to the hospital and find out."

"Why are these things happening?" Patty asked, her voice full of emotion. "Our family was divided up, and there's been one thing after another. We are all together now, and Dusty is hurt badly."

Joe looked guilty. "This is my fault. I should have gotten out of the service when your mom died and kept you and the children together."

Jeremiah raised his voice, trying to comfort everyone. "There is no blame here. Everybody on this earth has challenges. Some get hurt, and some die, but we have a God who is watching over us and will not let us down. He is faithful. We will live, or we will go to Heaven, where there are no troubles at all. Meantime, we must be patient, faithful, and thankful for what we have. We have our family together now, including new additions. We also have a story to tell, and it just might help others with troubles. That's our purpose here."

Jessie nodded, wiping away a tear. "You're right."

They arrived at the hospital forty-five minutes later and found Dusty sitting up in bed, a little groggy but awake. The nurse said, "I will go get the doctor to answer your questions."

Fifteen minutes later, the doctor walked in. "Sorry to keep you waiting. I was discussing options for a patient. Now, Mr. Davis was dehydrated and had an infection in his leg injury. We have fluids going in with IV, as well as an antibiotic for the infection. He should be fine, but we will keep him overnight just to monitor his condition. If his fever is gone, he can go home in the morning."

The family sighed with relief. They all thanked the doctor.

Jeremiah said, "It will be lunchtime soon, and we need to be on our way home." Then he asked Dusty, "Do you have a way to your motel?"

Dusty's eyes widened. "Oh my…"

Jeremiah raised an eyebrow. "What is it?"

Dusty said, "I need to call Christy. I was supposed to meet her this morning before she goes back to Texas."

Joe handed him his cell phone.

When Dusty hung up, he said, "Christy was worried, but she's on her way. She'll stay with me until I get out of here." He handed the phone back to Joe and said, "Thanks, Dad." The words were slow but heartfelt, and for the first time, Dusty had said "Dad" with such sincerity.

Joe's eyes welled up, but he turned so it wouldn't show. It was a moment that would forever change their relationship.

They all hugged Dusty, and Jessie said, "Dusty, I hope you are available to come to our house on Easter. It's very important, and please bring Christy." Dusty didn't give an answer but smiled and waved as they went out the door.

Chapter 9
Exploring the past

Easter came and went. There was no family get-together. Jessie sat in a solemn state of mind on the step of the small concrete porch. Joseph was taking a nap. Eric came out and sat down beside Jessie. He sat quietly, waiting for Jessie to say what was on her mind. He knew her so very well.

In a moment, while she kept her solid posture, looking out toward a small patch of cedar trees, she said, "I was hoping that the family could honor Mom's wishes and meet together for Easter. It is so disappointing that no one bothered to come."

Eric spoke with gentleness as he said, "Easter is special, and it was special to your mom, but families have their own time together on that special day. A lot has happened this year, as well as in the past years, but maybe we could let everyone know in advance about the meeting next year for Easter."

Eric then added, "I just had an epiphany. I think now is the time to find a place of our own, maybe that land we were talking about. We could have our families over, and there would be plenty of room for everyone."

"Oh, Eric, that would be wonderful! But do you think we could do it in a year?" Jessie asked.

Eric said, "I don't know, but we could try. If it doesn't work out, we'd certainly be prepared for next Easter. In the meantime, we'll keep working on it and figure out a plan."

Jessie smiled. "Wow, your mind is on fast-forward today."

Eric asked, "Why don't we get everybody together at the house where you grew up? There are rooms for everyone, and they could even come on different days if needed."

Jessie asked, "What do you mean?"

"We could plan to stay a few days, two or three, and the others can come on Friday, Saturday, or Sunday, whichever is convenient. You and your siblings can sort through things and take some memories with you, and maybe your dad would like to come. It won't be Easter, but maybe it'll be a fun get-together."

Jessie said, "We sure know how to make use of our weekends, don't we?"

Eric said, "Yep." And they smiled at each other as she leaned over onto Eric's shoulder.

Jessie called everyone that evening to tell them of her future plans. Joe said, "I don't know if it'll be good memories for me, but I'll see what I can do and check with Kathy."

Jeremiah said, "I'm going out of state for a few weeks, but I should be back by then."

Patty said, "I'd be glad to come. I'm not sure if Mark can get off yet."

Dusty said, "I don't remember anything about that house, but I think I'd like to see it and show it to Christy."

Jessie told Eric, "It looks like my family might or might not come."

"Huh?" Eric asked.

"Never mind," Jessie said, "I'll enjoy exploring the old house."

Five weeks later, Eric and Jessie drove to the old house. Jessie had the key in her backpack, and one was hidden under a brick on the side of the house in case any of the family needed to come by sometime. They walked in, and Jessie laid her backpack on the kitchen table, setting up Dusty's old playpen for Joseph. She wiped it out with a wet cloth and placed Joseph in the pen with his Snoopy blanket. Joseph was content for a few minutes, then he began to cry a little. Jessie said, "Oh, I guess he's hungry." She gave him some baby food and a bottle of milk she had in the cooler.

In a short time, Joseph let out a small burp and closed his eyes in a restful sleep.

The family started driving up, one after another. Jessie had a smile that looked like it was glued on her face. It felt so good to have everyone returning to the house. They all returned after years away from their original home. Dusty said, "Christy said to tell everyone hello. She had to work this weekend." Jessie said, "Tell her we miss her." Patty said, "This is awesome, but a little dirty and dusty." Jessie said, "I suggest that we do a little cleaning while we are here, and we can explore as we work. It will be fun. Dad, you and Kathy can start in the kitchen if you like, or wherever you think you'd like to start."

"Guess we'll start in the living room," Dusty said, already pulling off his jacket.

Dust floated like ghosts in the afternoon light. The furniture was covered in sheets. Jessie's father smiled faintly, eyes distant. "Hasn't changed a bit."

Jessie wandered upstairs. Her old bedroom was the same as the night she and Eric spent the night. She smiled, remembering. The memories flooded back in waves.

Something tugged at her, though, a memory of her mom brushing her hair in her parents' bedroom. Humming. Laughing.

She walked down the hall into the master bedroom. It was quiet there. The closet still smelled of cedar and lavender. Then she saw it: a small cedar chest tucked beneath the window bench, partly hidden by an old blanket.

She knelt.

The latch was simple. No lock. Inside were old scarves, a jewelry box, and beneath it all, a leather-bound notebook.

Her breath caught.

The first page read:

"To Jessie, when you are older. Love, Mom."

She sat back on her heels, the notebook clutched to her chest. Her throat tightened. Her mom had been writing letters to Jessie after her diagnosis, knowing she wouldn't live to see her grow up. Each entry was a milestone she wished to share: first heartbreak, graduation, finding her passion, etc. It was something Jessie wasn't ready to share with anyone else yet, but it was a treasure she would keep to herself for now.

Then Jessie noticed a small, unfinished quilt with patches from Jessie's baby clothes and her mother's own garments. A note tucked inside said, "I was going to give you this when you turned 16." Jessie lifted the quilt to her face and rubbed it along her cheek, feeling the warmth of her mother's love still alive in each stitch. She began to dream of the times she had with her mother, talking about sewing, cooking, and life ahead. A few tears dropped from her face to the floor.

Eric walked in. He saw Jessie with the quilt clutched tightly in her hands and tears falling from her face. He thought she might want to be alone for a while. He quietly walked away.

Joseph woke up and cried out. Eric yelled out, "I got him!" so Jessie could have her moments alone. Jessie noticed that there was something under the quilt she had picked up. It was a small golden music box. Jessie wound the turn key and was surprised that it still played "Amazing Grace." Jessie used to hum the song when she came home from church service, remembering the first verse and singing it over and over again.

Beside the music box was a large family Bible with the family names in it. Some of the names she recognized, and some she had never heard of. The Bible seemed to hold the history of her family, a legacy of stories waiting to be discovered.

Patty said loudly, "Oh my gosh!"

Jessie jumped up and ran to the hallway where Patty stood. "What is it?"

Patty said, "It's a basement in the hallway."

Their dad walked over and said, "I vaguely remember that. It seems like your mom put her imitation flowers and canned vegetables down there." He opened the door and lowered the ladder that stood against the basement wall. It was dark. The light switch didn't work. He said, "I need a light bulb." Jessie started looking through drawers. She found a pack of 100-watt bulbs. Joe said, "It'll be a miracle if any of these work." The first bulb he put in was dim, but it worked. Mark held onto Julie as Patty stepped slowly down the ladder. Dusty followed her.

Dad was right. There were several shelves of vegetables that had been canned. There were some flower vases and imitation flowers. Patty said, "They are beautiful."

Jessie smiled as she looked at the flowers. She thought to herself how much her mom would have loved the idea of sharing them with everyone.

Jessie was looking down the basement opening and heard Patty. She said, "You have flowers and pretty curtains in your house, Patty. You should take as many of Mom's as you want. I know she would have wanted you to have them." Her dad said, "She's right, Patty. She always wrapped you in the prettiest blanket and put flowered curtains in your room. You didn't like cartoon characters like Winnie the Pooh, even though he was very popular with the kids. You were always picking flowers, and sometimes weeds that you also thought were pretty. Please take what you want."

"Thanks, Dad."

Dusty found some books that caught him by surprise. He said, "There are books here about horses, rodeos, and western books." He looked at his dad and asked, "Who read these?" Joe said, "I did. I was also in the rodeo once." He had Dusty's attention. "I roped calves at a young age of fifteen. I was pretty good. I won several awards. That's strange that I can remember that now." Then he said, "You can have those books, son."

Dusty said, "I couldn't take your memories away."

Joe smiled and said, "Dusty, they are still my memories, but I want you to have them. It would mean a lot to me."

"Take them with you, and when I come to visit you, we can look at them. I want you to have them."

Patty said, "Hey, there are some full wine bottles here." She asked, "Did you and Mom drink?"

Joe said, "I think so, but I'm sure it was for special occasions or maybe with a meal. It seems like we drank a little with dinner at times."

Patty said, "I guess it was romantic." Jessie noticed that Kathy was listening as she was standing close by. She asked, "Don't you think you had better come up and get some bags or boxes for the things you want?"

Dusty said, "Yeah, that's a good idea."

Patty looked over near one of the shelves and saw tall candles of different colors. She said, "I guess you and Mom had some pretty romantic nights."

Jessie said, "Patty, I need to show you something. Come up here, please."

"Okay, on my way."

Patty walked over to Jessie and asked, "What do you want to show me?" Jessie grabbed Patty's arms and pulled her to the kitchen. She said, "Kathy was listening to every word you said to Dad."

"So what?" She thought for a second and said, "Ohhh."

Jessie said, "It's okay, but we need to let her know that she is a wanted part of our family."

Patty looked surprised, then nodded. "You're right, Jessie. I didn't think about it like that."

"Thanks for understanding," Jessie said.

Eric and Mark left to pick up some food at a nearby fast-food place. They returned to find everyone at the kitchen table talking. Joe was telling Dusty about holding on to the money he won from some investments. Patty was talking to Jessie about the flower arrangements she found; many of them were faded, but the vases were in great shape. Jessie said, "Maybe you can make some flower arrangements for Dusty's wedding." Dusty's face turned slightly pink. Patty asked, "Why are you blushing, Dusty?"

Dusty said, "I'm not. You just surprised me."

Jessie laughed and teased, "You're blushing! Who knows, maybe there will be a wedding in your future soon."

"Let's eat!" Eric said, "And Jeremiah, would you say the blessing?" He said, "Of course, we have a lot to be thankful for."

After their lunch, Joe decided to explore his and Mary's bedroom a little more. He reached up for a box that was on the top of the closet. Joe grunted as he lowered it to the bed. It was heavier than he thought it would be. He opened the box with caution. As he pulled out a tuxedo, a silk cummerbund, a white shirt, and a black bow tie, he noticed a long white dress with lace that covered a bride's arms, and fragile lace that covered the white dress. Joe felt strange as the memory of the marriage to his beautiful bride, Mary, hit him. For the first time in years, he felt the loss, and sadness filled his eyes. He held the dress in his arms. Kathy walked in and said, "Joe," Joe coughed a fake cough and laid the dress back in the box, not taking time to fold it. Kathy walked over to Joe, "You are shaking." She said with a concerned look.

Joe quickly wiped his eyes. "I'm alright, Kathy. It's just… memories. I didn't realize how much I missed her until I saw this."

Kathy noticed the dress that was in the box and the tuxedo. She asked, "Did this belong to you and Mary?"

Joe said, "Yeah."

Kathy said, "Joe, I must admit, this has been a tough trip for me, harder than I thought it would be. I don't have any children, and I can't compete with their love for their mother. I wouldn't want to, but I hope you can come to love me as much as you loved her someday, but I don't want you to lose your memories of Mary. She was part of your life."

Joe said, "Kathy, Mary is a special part of my past. I miss her and the memories we had, but you are my present, and I love you more than I can say. This has been an emotional trip for me, too, but I am glad you are here with me. I believe my kids like you a lot."

Jessie and Patty stood by the door and said simultaneously, "We do!" Jessie said, "We are very happy that you love our dad and appreciate it that you have been willing to help him through this time in his life. You are a special lady." Jessie and Patty walked over and hugged Kathy. A tear dropped from Kathy's face. A happy tear.

Kathy smiled softly. "Thank you, both. I needed to hear that."

Jessie said, "Dad, there are more drawers to go through." Then she asked, "Do you want us to go through them?"

Kathy said, "Thanks for the offer, but I think your dad needs to go through these personal things, don't you?" Jessie said, "You're right."

As Joe looked in the bedroom closet, he noticed a box on the far left side of the closet on the floor. It was a metal box. He picked it up and brought it to the kitchen. He shouted, "Hey, kids, come in here. You too, Kathy."

Jessie asked, "What is it?"

Joe said, "I found an important box."

Patty asked, "What's in it?"

Her dad looked at her and said, "I am about to show you." He lifted out some papers.

"This is the life insurance policy. I never received the money after Mary passed away. These are accounts your mom and I set up for your kids. Jessie was the oldest, and we put $10,000 in an account for her. There is $4,000 for Patty, $4,000 for Jeremiah, and $2,000 for Dusty. We were still saving for Dusty, as well as Patty and Jeremiah. It's not a lot, but maybe it will be useful."

Patty laughed as she said, "To everyone but Dusty. He has too much money already." Then everybody started laughing.

Dusty said, "It's the thought that counts; besides, I don't know if anyone can have TOO much money." The laughter toned down but then started all over again.

Joe found an envelope under the bank papers. "Oh, wow!" he said.

"Now what did you find?" Jessie asked.

"Treasure!" He exclaimed. "I believe this is a time capsule that Mary and I buried when Dusty was born."

"What's in it?" Patty asked.

He said, "I'm not sure. We will have to dig it up."

They all felt excited as they started to head outside, eager to discover what was in the capsule. It was something they had all been curious about for years.

They all started to walk outside when the neighbor, Jerry, was standing at the door about to knock. He said, "I saw a lot of vehicles in the driveway and thought I'd better check it out." He looked at all the faces and noticed Joe standing there. He reached over and put both his hands out to cover Joe's hand in a handshake. He shook his hand up and down vigorously as he said, "Hey Joe, it's been a long time!"

"It's good to see you, too, Jerry. Come sit down and have a cup of coffee. We can talk."

He looked over at the kids and asked, "Do you mind if we go out later to look for the capsule?"

Dusty said, "Sure, Dad. I need to call Christy anyway."

Patty said, "Mark and I need to set up a sleeping area for Julie."

Eric said to Jessie, "Let's go find a place for everybody to sleep tonight." Jessie turned to Eric and said, "This house is pretty big, but it doesn't seem as big as it used to be."

Eric reminded Jessie that she used to be a smaller person when she was a little girl. Jessie said, "We can find some boxes or bags for the guys to carry stuff home in. In a way, it seems like we are trying to carry home some useful things, and some memories, and in another way, it seems like we are stealing from our own house."

Eric said, "I thought you were cleaning out the house."

Jessie said, "Oh, Eric. You are funny, but you are right. It will take a while to clean this old house. I wonder what Dad will do with it when it is cleaned out."

Eric said, "He'll do the right thing."

Joe and Jerry finished a second cup of coffee, and Jerry said, "I'd better get back to the house. Thanks for the coffee and the fascinating story about your family."

Patty came in, and Joe was sitting at the table in a relaxed state, rehashing the past few minutes with his friend, Jerry. Patty said, "I don't mean to interrupt you, but I was wondering when we would dig up the treasure you talked about."

Joe said, "We can do that now. Call everybody in here."

Jessie carried Joseph in her arms as they went toward the door. Joe had the paper with instructions on where to find the treasure. He led them all to the back of the house. The old stone that he and Mary found was still there where they put it. He counted off twenty paces from that stone. The small pile of gravel was still there at the end of the path, although a few stones were scattered.

He said, "Dusty, bring me a shovel from the little storage building. I don't remember where it is. You may have to look around."

A minute later, Dusty came running back. He said, "I got it!"

Patty said, "This is exciting!"

Joe smiled to himself, feeling a little nervous as he dug deeper. He had a feeling about what the treasure was, but wasn't sure how everyone would react.

Joe had dug about a foot down and heard a thud. He said, "I think I found it."

Joe got down on his knees and wiped the remaining dirt away, lifting up the metal box. He set it on top of the ground beside the hole he had dug. Joe just looked at it for a moment, lost in thought. The others stared at the box without saying a word. Joe didn't move.

Jessie spoke up, "Dad, is everything okay?"

Joe snapped out of his trance and said, "Yes, it's okay. Before I open it, I want you to know that it is not a fancy treasure with lots of money, but something your mom and I spent some time putting together for each of you." He opened the box, and there were envelopes wrapped in tin foil in hopes of keeping them clean and readable. He handed one to Jessie, then one to Patty, then to Jeremiah, and the last one to Dusty.

Each envelope was carefully wrapped, and as they opened them, the family felt an odd mixture of excitement and nostalgia.

Biblical notes and a silver dollar were in each of the envelopes. At the beginning of each paper was a note saying:

"We wanted to give you something to make sure that you were never penniless. We were going to leave a penny, but you never know about inflation."

They all read that beginning, and there were a few seconds of quiet. Then Jeremiah broke out laughing. Joe said, "That is what is supposed to happen. Mary wanted to start out with something to make each of you laugh or smile. She said that life is too short to be serious all the time. The Bible verses were written in the hope of guiding you in your life. It was and is important to know that you are never alone and you are loved."

Jeremiah said, "This is truly a treasure. Thanks, Dad," then he looked upward toward heaven and said, "Thanks, Mom, and thank you, Jesus."

Jeremiah glanced over and noticed that Patty was sniffing and crying. He put his arm around her and smiled. She said, "It's not what I would have imagined, but it is beautiful."

Jeremiah took this moment to say, "Sometimes the saying 'STOP AND SMELL THE ROSES' means different things to different people. Maybe we needed to stop and take time with family, but it is important that even though we enjoy that time, we need to help others who don't have the joy in their family, or sometimes they don't have any family."

Patty asked, "I have always heard to put family first."

Jeremiah said, "I have heard that too. God's family, the church, is not any one religion or church group of people. God's family is all over this planet." He then asked Patty, "What if you didn't have Mark, or Julie, or this family?" as he waved his arm around to family members.

Patty said, "I wouldn't want to think about it."

Jeremiah said, "Exactly! We are blessed, and God wants us to bless others."

"How?" Patty asked.

Jeremiah said, "Quite simply, with kindness, forgiveness, and love toward one another."

Patty looked a little confused. Jeremiah said, "I'll give you an example: If a family member backed into your car, maybe you would forgive them, or if a friend pulled out in front of you on the road, you might forgive them, but what if these things happened with a stranger? Could you forgive as easily?"

Joe said, "I think we have learned a lot on this trip and I, for one, am thankful."

Jessie had a moment with her dad, and she asked, "What will happen to this house when we get it cleaned out?"

Joe said, "I'm not sure yet, but I am in no rush to do anything with it. For now, it will be a place that all of you can come to when you feel like it."

The family shared a quiet moment, feeling closer than ever. The house, once a symbol of the past, was now a place of new memories waiting to be made.

Everyone made plans together to come back at times, check on the house, and spend the night from time to time.

Chapter 10
Unexpected surprises

Jessie asked Eric's parents if they would be interested in babysitting Joseph. She said, "Don't feel obligated because I understand if you can't. I think I may have a sitter in mind if you can't. If you do decide you can, we will pay you."

Beth looked at Jim, and they both smiled. Beth said, "Let me think about it." Jessie said, "Okay." As Jessie turned, Beth said, "I've thought about it. We'll do it!" with excitement in her voice. Beth said, "I am home every day, other than running errands like groceries and such, but I can take him with me."

Jessie said, "Thank you, that will be great. I am normally home on weekends, but Eric and I need to do something this Saturday. Would you be able to babysit for about three hours?"

Jim said, "I think we can do that." Eric had hinted around a few weeks earlier that he and Jessie needed to get a place of their own before too long, so Jim had an idea that that was what they might be doing.

That Saturday after Eric and Jessie left, Jim thought it might be a good idea to tell Beth about the idea of them leaving when they find a place. Beth said, "Oh no. I hope it is not far away!"

Jim said, "I don't think they will move today, but we will see what happens."

A few hours later, Eric and Jessie returned. Jessie went over to pick up Joseph. Beth had a saddened look on her face. Jessie asked, "Is something wrong?"

Beth said, "I just hope you, Eric, and Joseph are always near."

Jessie said, "Eric must have told you that we were looking for a new place to live. We have loved being here and appreciate all you have done for us, but we would like to have a place of our own with land, horses, a dog or two, and maybe some chickens. We were going to sit down and talk to you both when we got closer to finding a place, and besides, you need your guest house back."

Beth said, "There's no rush, but I understand. I just hope I still see Joseph often."

"Of course. We still need you to babysit," Jessie said with a gentle and loving smile.

Six weeks later, Eric and Jessie found the home of their dreams. There was an old 1940s white house with four bedrooms and one bathroom. The house was a fixer-upper, and it sat on forty-five acres. There was a little red barn that had several boards missing from the side and the musty smell of old hay on the floor. It was twenty miles from Eric's parent's house, and it would be on the way to work for them to stop by and drop off Joseph.

Eric looked at Jessie and asked, "It needs some work. Are you sure you like it?"

Jessie said, "I love it!"

Eric smiled, feeling relieved that Jessie was excited about it. They knew it would take time and effort, but they were both ready for the challenge.

Eric said, "I'd like to show it to my dad and get his opinion on it. He is better than I at figuring finances."

Jessie asked, "What if he doesn't like it?"

Eric said, "It is still our decision, and we will pray about it."

That evening, Eric went to the house and told his dad that he needed to talk to him. Jim told him to have a seat, and he asked, "What's on your mind?"

Eric explained about the place he and Jessie found and asked him if he would stop by and look at it. He said, "It's a fixer-upper, but it's nice and within our range."

Jim said, "Sure, I'd like to see it. I can go tomorrow afternoon after church service."

Around one Sunday afternoon, Jessie and Eric were standing with Jim on the porch of the house. Jessie was anxious to hear what Jim would say.

Jim stood still as he took another look at the area. He said, "This house and barn need a good bit of work, but it is very doable. I think it is a good investment IF you have the time and money to put into it. I think it could be ready for you to move in within eight months to a year, maybe sooner if you have help."

Eric asked, "Are you offering to help?"

Jim said, "Well, I've hammered a few nails in my day." Then he asked, "What about school and school work?"

Eric said, "It will not be easy, but I've come too far to let it go."

Jim said, "You know we have some family, like my brother and Jessie's family, like Mark, Dusty, and Jeremiah, that might be willing to give some of their time. There are also friends at church. I remember that Beth and I came to the call for help with our neighbors and church family. Maybe they would have a little spare time. You have options for assistance."

Jessie felt hesitant. "I'm not sure we should ask people to come help us. They probably have their own things to do."

Eric gently smiled at her, "Jessie, remember what your brother Jeremiah said when we were at your old house? He said, 'Our purpose on this earth is to serve the Lord by helping others. That is serving others and serving God. And when the opportunity arises, we will help our neighbors.'"

Jessie let out a heavy breath and said, "Okay, let's do this."

Eric used the inheritance his granddad left him, and Jessie used the money her mom and dad left her, and they put a large down payment on the land, house, and barn. They worked on it most every weekend. Jessie cleaned the house and put up new curtains. Eric and his dad made repairs to the house, restoring shelves and cabinets. Jeremiah and Dusty stopped by several times to help build an extra bathroom for the house. They bought some furniture little by little, and one year later, it wasn't new or perfect, but it was theirs with about ten more payments.

Jessie often found herself reflecting on how much they had accomplished. The house had transformed from a run-down fixer-upper to a home they could finally call their own. The work had been hard, but each improvement made the place feel more like home.

Patty and Mark drove to Alabama at the end of the year. Patty told Jessie, "I am so sorry that we haven't been able to come out and help you with your house, but things have been so busy with us. Mark got sick and..." Jessie interrupted, "It's okay. I understand. We had a lot of help, and I know you three have a busy life."

Patty said, "We are here now. Is there anything we can do to help? We can stay for a couple of days." Jessie said, "That's great! You can help me shop for some new bed linen and towels. I need to get a bed for Joseph soon, and I need to decorate his bedroom."

Patty was eager to know more about Joseph's room. She had always been close to Jessie and was excited about the changes in her life.

Patty asked, "How are you going to decorate Joseph's room?"

Jessie was eager to talk about that. She said, "He is just two, and I don't want him to grow up and have cartoon characters on his wall. I'll let him decide in a few years, but for now, I will just paint it blue, maybe put a few horse designs on it. I think he'd like that."

Patty nodded and smiled, "That sounds perfect for him. I'm sure he'll love it as he gets older. It'll be a nice space for him to grow into."

Eric showed Mark the barn and said, "We hope to have some horses soon, and I need to finish the chicken house." Mark said, "I can help with that."

That evening, Eric sat down on the loveseat he and Jessie had recently purchased. He said, "The Lord has been amazing, sending us so much help, I didn't realize we could have. Mark helped me with the chicken house today; now we need to start saving for the chickens and other animals."

Jessie reminded Eric about her savings. "Eric, I have been saving a few dollars ever since we got married, thanks to your parents letting us live in their guest house. I think I have about six or seven thousand."

Eric said, "That's great, but I think you had better hold onto that just in case. My dad taught me at a young age that I always need a backup."

Jessie asked, "What if I spend a little and get a few chickens and a rooster? We could save on eggs and share with your parents."

Eric said, "That sounds like a good investment."

Jessie was preparing the evening meal on Thursday and keeping a close eye on Joseph. He was walking and trying to climb on every piece of furniture. Her phone rang. It was Dusty. Jessie said, "Oh my gosh, it's good to hear your voice, Dusty. I miss you."

Dusty said, "I miss you too."

Jessie asked, "How is Christy?"

"She's great. I wanted to tell you that I finally talked her into working part-time so we could have more time together. I took Dad's advice and made some investments, and that worked out well for me, so Christy and I are ready to get married. Can ya'll come for the wedding on November 5th? It's a Saturday, at 2 pm."

Jessie said, "I wouldn't miss it for the world. I'm so happy for you and Christy. I was beginning to think one of you had changed your mind."

"Well, we have been busy this year, and I bought that ranch we wanted. We got a few horses, and I even got an area set up to train horses and teach kids how to ride, and especially how to treat horses with respect."

Jessie said, "Wow! I didn't realize you were so busy. I am so proud of you." She asked, "Are you going to call dad?"

"Sure. I'm inviting the whole family. I just called you first," he told her.

"Well, thank you. I'll be there with bells on."

Dusty said, "Please don't wear any bells. We have a few cows, and they might come running."

Jessie said, "Oh, that's funny."

Dusty said, "By the way, I am coming by to see ya this weekend. Can you put me up, or do I need to get a motel room?"

Jessie smarted off, "You know we have plenty of room. You will be staying with us." Then she asked, "I'm glad you are coming, but what's the occasion?"

Dusty said, "I have something to show you."

Jessie asked, "What is it?"

"I'll show you after I get there."

She said, "Dusty!" Dusty said, "Gotta go. See ya Friday evening about six." And he hung up, leaving Jessie in suspense.

Dusty arrived at five pm and stopped by the local furniture store he had talked to on the phone. He had ordered a surprise for Jessie and Eric. He asked the man to deliver it as close to six thirty as he could. At six pm, he drove up to Jessie's home. Jessie was preparing dinner, and when she heard him drive up, she ran out the door to meet him and give him a big hug.

"Wow! That's a nice greeting."

Jessie said, "I might start crying when I tell you about my thoughts, but I will anyway. It's not been that long since I didn't know where you were, and then we found you in a hospital, and now we call and visit. The thoughts go racing through my mind like wind through a tunnel. It's just all amazing for me."

Dusty said, "It has been an amazing journey. Your visit to me in the hospital started me on a new path in my life. Before that day, I didn't care if I lived or died. I haven't told anyone that except Christy."

Jessie said, "Oh, Dusty, I wish I had known so I could have been there for you."

Dusty said, "Don't you see? It all turned out the way it was supposed to be. The timing was perfect."

Jessie said, "And you are a millionaire."

Dusty said, "Not quite, but I have been blessed, as Jeremiah would say."

Jessie said, "I have dinner on the stove. Let's go in." As they started walking toward the house, a big white moving truck pulled up. It had the logo of the local furniture shop on it. Jessie said, "I wonder who that is?"

Dusty yelled out, "Bring it in!" Then he said, "Show me where Joseph's bedroom is."

Jessie was completely confused, but went along with it. She had no idea what Dusty was up to, but the look on his face told her this was going to be a big surprise.

She led Dusty to Joseph's bedroom. The room was painted sky blue, and there was a mattress on the floor. Dusty picked up the mattress and leaned it against the wall. The men from the truck came in with a standard-size bed frame and box springs, and a firm mattress. The men put the bed together and stayed an extra five minutes, placing sheets with horse designs on the bed and a pillow with the same design. The men handed Dusty another set of bed linen with blue sky and cloud designs. Then they went back out to their truck and left.

Eric was smiling but speechless. Jessie asked, "Why did you do this?" Eric said, "That sounded a little rude, but I'm sure she didn't mean it that way."

Dusty chose not to respond to that. He said, "I didn't get you a gift for your baby shower, so this is it, better late than never."

Jessie jumped over and hugged Dusty so tight he almost lost his breath. She said, "Thank you, Dusty. It's perfect." Eric reached over and shook his hand and said, "Thanks, Dusty."

Dusty said, "You're welcome. Just a little something from me and Christy me, and Patty, sort of."

Jessie asked, "What do you mean, sort of?"

"Well, when she and Mark came to visit you recently, I had asked her to find out discreetly what you needed in your house, especially for Joseph. I think she did a good job finding out."

Eric said, "Your family is full of surprises."

Dusty said, "Actually, I think we all owe you two for taking the time to bring us all together. I'm surprised you didn't hire a detective."

Jessie said, "I would have hired a detective if I thought I had the money. And by the way, I must give the credit to God for the things we learned as we went through this journey."

Dusty nodded slowly, absorbing Jessie's words. "I'm starting to see things more clearly about God, and Christy is a believer, so I'm sure I will understand things better in time."

After dinner, Jessie called Patty. She answered the phone, "Hello." Jessie said, "You, my sister, are a stinker."

Patty asked, "Oh, did Dusty come see you?"

"You know he did," Jessie responded. Then she said, "The bed is wonderful! Eric loves it too."

"I'm glad," Patty said.

Jessie could hear something in Patty's voice, a slight hesitation that caught her attention. She asked, "Are you feeling okay?"

Patty said, "I'm okay. I think I just have the blahs. I feel more tired than usual." Jessie said, "I have been feeling more tired lately, too."

Jessie asked, "You don't think we…"

Patty asked, "What?"

Jessie said, "Maybe it's the weather change, but I think I should see a doctor, and maybe you should too."

Patty said, "It will pass."

Jessie said, "It might not."

Patty started to ask, "What are you talking…" Then she continued, "You don't think?"

Jessie said, "See the doctor and call me back when you know."

Patty said slowly, "Okay."

By the end of the week, Patty felt somewhat better, but she did as Jessie asked her to do. That evening, she called Jessie. Jessie answered, "Hello." Patty didn't even say "hello" first. She just said, "Jessie, I am pregnant!"

Jessie said, "This is great!"

Patty asked, "How is this great?" Jessie said, "I'm pregnant too." Eric walked in and asked, "What?"

"Patty, I've got to go and talk to Eric. I'll call you back tomorrow. Congratulations, I love you."

Patty said, "I…" Jessie had hung up.

Jessie said, "I didn't mean to tell you that way, Eric."

Eric asked, "How long have you known?" Jessie said. "I just found out today. I haven't felt as good as usual, so I went to see the doctor. He did a pregnancy test, and it looks like we are going to have another baby."

Eric stood still in a daze for a moment. A million thoughts raced through his mind.

Jessie was a little unnerved by Eric's silence. She asked, "Are you mad?"

Eric came to himself and walked over to Jessie. He said, "Of course, I'm not mad, I'm happy." And he kissed her on the cheek.

She said, "Eric, you don't seem happy to me."

Eric said, "I really am. I guess it hasn't sunk in completely. I'm glad we already have a bigger house." Then he laughed and said, "We are going to have another baby!" This time, he sounded more excited. Jessie let out the breath she didn't realize she had been holding inside.

She said, "Eric, Patty is pregnant too. We will both have our babies around the same time." Eric said, "Hmmm, that's interesting."

Jessie smiled at the thought of the two families growing together. "It's going to be amazing, Eric. We'll have cousins so close in age, and I think Joseph is going to be such a good big brother."

Mark came in from work and found Patty sitting on the couch. She said, "I want to talk to you."

He asked, "Did I do something wrong?" Patty started laughing. She said, "It depends on whether you think getting me pregnant again is wrong."

Mark asked, "Really?"

"Yep."

Mark said, "Wow," and kissed Patty. "We may have to get a bigger house someday soon."

Patty said, "I think everybody in my family has money but us, but somehow we will make it. Jeremiah has told me on several occasions to have faith."

Mark said, "Patty, we are not deprived. We have a savings account, the four thousand dollars your dad gave us, and our paychecks."

Patty said, "I guess I didn't think of those things. That makes me feel better. Oh, by the way, Jessie is pregnant again, too."

Mark said, "You and your family are full of surprises. I wonder what your sister will do next."

Later that evening, Dusty called and told Patty about his wedding plans. Patty said, "We will be glad to come, but I may look a little overweight then."

Dusty asked, "What?"

Patty said, "I'm pregnant, and guess what? Jessie is pregnant too. You're going to be an uncle again."

Dusty said, "I hope that's not catching in this family. I want to marry Christy and have a little time before that happens."

Patty laughed and said, "You won't have to worry about that right away, but I hope you don't wait too long. Time has a way of sneaking up on us."

Dusty chuckled and agreed, "I'll keep that in mind, Patty. We'll see what the future holds."

Dusty called Jeremiah. Jeremiah said, "It's good to hear from you."

Dusty said, "Christy and I were talking, and we both agreed to ask you if you would marry us on the fifth of November, if you are free that day."

Jeremiah said, "I would be honored to do that. I'm writing it on my calendar now."

Dusty said, "This has been a crazy year or so. And this last spring has been different than any I've ever known."

Jeremiah replied, "I would call it blessed."

Dusty said, "Yeah, blessed. It's strange how things have changed, but in such a good way."

Jeremiah paused for a moment and then added, "You've come a long way, Dusty. I'm proud of you."

Dusty smiled, feeling a warmth in his chest. "Thanks, Jeremiah. That means a lot to me."

Chapter 11
More searching

Jessie woke up early on Thursday morning with an idea. She woke Eric and said, "Eric, I think we should go to South Alabama tomorrow and enjoy a relaxing day at the beach. The weather's not too hot. I can pack some food, and we can either stay in a motel or just come back home."

Eric replied, "That sounds great. It's kind of short notice, but I guess we can do it. We'd definitely have to stay in a motel overnight, though, because I can't see driving five hours, spending time on the beach, and then turning around to come back. There'd be no time to relax as you mentioned."

"You're right," Jessie said.

Eric added, "I think I just got conned into spending a day at the beach."

"Not at all," Jessie laughed. "I just wanted to get away from the house for a little while."

Eric replied, "We could always go to the park for that."

Jessie gave him a look, eyes almost squinted in frustration. "Okay," Eric sighed. "You know I have the day off from school because my teacher's out of town, so we might as well go too." He muttered under his breath, "I wonder what adventures we'll get into this time."

Jessie barely heard him. "What did you say?" she asked.

"I hope it's a great adventure," Eric replied with a grin.

Jessie said, "Let's get an early start tomorrow."

Eric agreed. "Okay."

Then Jessie had another thought. "Eric, Jeremiah lives on the way. Maybe he'd like to come with us. He might even help with Joseph, so we can enjoy the ocean together."

Eric chuckled. "Well, it's not a honeymoon or anything, but sure, call him and ask."

Jessie called Jeremiah, inviting him to join them. To her surprise, he agreed and even offered, "You three can stay at my house for the night. I have an extra room."

She turned to Eric and told him about the invitation. Eric nodded. "Okay." Jessie smiled at him, knowing he'd be happy to save a few dollars.

Jeremiah said, "Come to my house first, and we'll go to the beach together." Jessie replied, "We should be there around eleven a.m."

They arrived at the beach, and Eric said, "This is nice!" Then he asked Jessie, "What made you think of coming to the beach?"

"I don't know exactly. Maybe it was a chance to relax in the sand and the sun before the baby comes," Jessie replied with a smile.

Eric and Jeremiah carefully laid a quilt on the sand. Jessie set out the cooler of food. She handed little Joseph an orange plastic bucket with a plastic shovel to play with. Joseph laughed as he beat the shovel on the bucket.

Eric said, "Joseph is going to beat that bucket to death."

Jeremiah laughed and said, "Looks like he's going to be a drummer."

Jessie said, "Now there's a thought. We could bring him to stay with you if he decides to play the drums."

Jeremiah nodded. "Good. I could use some musical talent in the church."

Jessie smirked. "You always have an answer, don't you?"

Jeremiah smiled and nodded.

Jessie had brought sandwiches with mayo, ham, and sliced tomatoes, all packed separately. Everyone knows what happens if tomatoes are put on sandwiches for too long, soggy bread. Nobody likes soggy sandwiches.

Just as Eric took a bite of his sandwich, a boy about seven walked by, fast-paced, crying and calling out, "Jimmy! Jimmy!"

Jessie called out to him, "Wait!" The boy turned around, confused. Jessie asked, "Why are you crying?" Her heart went out to him as the boy wiped his tears with the back of his hand.

His mother came running up to him. "I'm so sorry, Daniel," she said, catching her breath.

Jessie, still sitting on the quilt next to Joseph, asked, "Is something wrong?"

Daniel's mother explained, "I let Daniel's dog off the leash for just a moment to untangle it, and the dog ran off. We haven't been able to catch up with him."

Daniel sniffed and said, "We can't find him."

His mother tried to comfort him. "I'm so sorry, Daniel. He's gone, and we have to go home."

Daniel loudly protested, "Nooo!"

Jeremiah knelt in front of Daniel and asked, "Do you know about Daniel in the Bible?"

Daniel stopped crying for a moment and nodded. "Yes, sir. I know about the story."

Jeremiah smiled gently. "Well, the name Daniel means 'God is my judge.' Daniel was known for his faith, wisdom, and courage. Remember how he was thrown into the lion's den to be killed? But the Lord closed the mouths of the lions, and Daniel was found safe. Do you think God could be looking out for your dog, just like He looked after Daniel?"

Daniel's eyes started to dry, and he said quietly, "I think so."

Daniel's mother took his hand. "Thank you," she said to Jeremiah.

As they began to walk away, Jessie called out, "Wait!"

Eric gave Jeremiah a knowing look. "I knew it. Jessie always finds a way to get involved."

Jeremiah put his hand to his mouth to stifle his laughter.

Jessie turned back to Daniel's mother. "If you give me your phone number and address, we'll look for your dog while we're here. If we find him, we'll let you know."

Daniel's mother hesitated, unsure. "I don't know…"

But Daniel pleaded, "Please, Mom!"

There was something about Jessie and the guys that made her feel she could trust them. She relented. "Okay." She gave Jessie the information. "We live just about five miles from here."

Daniel didn't want to give up. He looked up at his mom and asked, "Can't we stay just a little longer?"

She sighed, feeling conflicted. "I'm sorry, son, but we have to go home. I have an important job interview in the morning, and there's a lot to do."

Daniel looked up at Jessie with a hopeful face. "I hope you find him. His name is Jimmy. I named him after my grandpa, and he has a white spot on his back leg."

Jessie smiled warmly. "We'll be on the lookout for him."

Daniel smiled a little. "Thank you," he said as he waved goodbye.

When they were out of earshot, Eric shook his head. "Jessie, I hope you didn't get that boy's hopes up."

"I can't help it, Eric," Jessie said, frustrated. Then, she asked him, "What if it were one of our children who were heartbroken?"

Jeremiah said, "Those two need help."

Eric sighed. "Okay. What do you want to do?" To Eric's surprise, she said, "I want to sit at the edge of the ocean and let Joseph play in the shallow water."

Eric scratched his head. "Well, that sounds like a good idea. I'm still not sure what you're thinking, though."

Jeremiah said, "The Lord will let us know when the time is right if He wants us to do something." Eric wasn't sure what was going on, but he decided to go for a swim. Jeremiah went out in the waves and swam like a fish. Joseph laughed and splashed around. This was his first trip to the beach, and he was having a great time until he started rubbing his eyes. He began to whimper. Jessie quickly picked him up and carried him back to the quilt, gently wiping his eyes.

Eric came back to the quilt a few minutes later and asked, "Is everything okay with Joseph?"

Jessie said, "Yeah, the saltwater started to burn his eyes, but he's okay now." Eric had a blank look on his face. He was still wondering if something was on Jessie's mind, but didn't dare ask.

Jeremiah came out of the water and walked over to the quilt. He stood at the edge of the quilt as he dried his hair. "That was great! I haven't been in the ocean lately, maybe a few years ago," he said. He looked across the road and added, "That's a nice area over there with those green pine and red cedar trees."

Suddenly, Jessie sat up straight. Her eyes were focused on the trees Jeremiah had mentioned. Eric glanced at her. She looked like she was in a trance. Eric said, "Uh-oh, I know that look."

Jessie said, "Jeremiah, I need you to go across the road with me to look in those woods."

Jeremiah raised an eyebrow but nodded. "Okay."

Jessie said, "I have an idea. Eric, I need you to keep an eye on Joseph."

Eric said, "Okay, I can do that." He started to ask, "What are you going to…?" Then he stopped himself, "Never mind. You're going to look for that boy's dog, aren't you?"

Jessie said, "Yep, I'm going to look for the dog, Eric."

"Okay. Be careful."

"Jeremiah is with me. I'll be okay."

Jeremiah said, "This could be fun, but I'm not sure what we'll do if we find him."

Jessie said, "One thing at a time. Let's look for the dog first." Jeremiah pointed to a walking trail.

After half an hour, Jessie said, "I hoped we could find him, but I guess we'd better head back. Eric might be worried."

Jessie was feeling sad, and the trail was beginning to look long and dim. Jeremiah said a silent prayer for the dog. Jessie stood as the trail was about to end. She became more specific in her prayer, asking for help to find the dog.

Jeremiah put his arm around Jessie, waiting and expecting her to shed a tear or two. But suddenly, her keen hearing picked up a faint whimpering in the distance. She shot off the trail into the woods, not watching where she was going. All she thought about was locating the sound and hoping it was the dog.

Jessie stopped and listened. All was quiet. She called out, "Jimmy!" No sound. She called out again, louder this time, "Jimmy!" A soft whimper was heard. She walked a little further and caught a glimpse of something shiny. It was the tag on the dog's collar that caught her attention as a ray of late afternoon sun broke through the trees. Jessie yelled as loud as she could, "Jeremiah, come here quickly!"

Jeremiah was more attentive to the off-trail path he was on, so he could find his way back. He saw Jessie sitting on the ground beside a black lab. She never considered that it might be afraid of her and bite. Instead, she rubbed the dog's head and spoke softly. She eased down to his leg and was thrilled to see a white patch of fur on his back leg. The dog placed his head gently in Jessie's lap.

Jessie said, "Jeremiah, this is Jimmy," wiping away tears. Jeremiah smiled and said, "Now she cries. Must be happy tears."

Jessie ignored his comment. She gently lifted the dog's legs, which were stuck between some branches. "I wonder how he got here," she said.

Jeremiah said, "He was probably chasing a rabbit or something."

Jessie said, "Jeremiah, please carry him back to the quilt."

Jeremiah, a tall, muscular man at five feet eleven, had spent several years building structures in Africa and helping people rebuild their homes. His work had given him a dark tan that the rest of the family didn't have. He carefully picked up the dog while quietly giving thanks to the Lord for this gift. This was a happy moment.

Jeremiah caught Jessie smiling as he lay the dog down on the quilt. She asked, "Why are you smiling?"

He grinned. "My sister, the searcher."

Eric, still in disbelief, said, "I don't believe it. You guys found the dog."

Jeremiah said, "Jessie did."

Jessie remembered her prayer and said, "With God's guidance."

Eric asked, "What now?"

Jessie said, "If we hurry, we might be able to find a vet and get him checked out."

Jeremiah said, "I think I know where a vet's office is." He placed the dog in the back seat of his car, and Jessie sat beside him, with Joseph in his car seat. It was crowded, but they made it. The vet examined the dog and said, "It's just a sprain. He needs to rest, and he should be fine in about a week."

Jeremiah told the vet the story of finding the dog, and it touched him. He didn't even charge them for the visit.

Jeremiah said, "It's getting late, but it's not quite dark. Let's take Jimmy home to the boy who needs him. I hope his mom can afford to feed him."

Jessie said, "Stop at the nearest store!"

Eric asked, "Are we going to feed the dog?"

Jessie said, "We can afford a bag of dog food and some treats."

To Jessie's surprise, Eric said, "Yes, we can, and maybe we can find a new leash, too."

Twenty minutes later, they arrived at a white house with a blue roof, the number 205 on the mailbox. Jeremiah carried the dog to the house, and Jessie knocked on the door. Daniel answered and screamed, "Jimmy! You found him!"

Daniel's mom heard the shouting and ran to the door. Her eyes watered. Jessie was carrying Joseph in her arms. Eric came in behind Jeremiah, carrying the dog food and treats. The new dark blue leash, with colored bone designs, was attached to the dog's collar.

Daniel's mom said, "I don't know how to thank you."

Jeremiah said, "Just remember to give thanks and praise to God."

Jeremiah looked at Daniel and said, "Sometimes we don't get what we want in life, but God knows what we need. Always trust Him."

Jessie said, "The vet said Jimmy's leg is sprained. We found him in the woods across from the beach. He just needs to rest for about a week."

They started walking back to the car. Daniel and his mom waved and shouted again, "Thank you!" They all turned and waved back.

Jessie looked at the guys and asked, "Didn't that make you feel good?"

Eric said to Jessie, "I think I understand a little about how you feel when you follow through to help your family, as well as others, even a dog. It's a good feeling. I'm still not sure how you did it."

Jeremiah said, "Let's think about this. Jessie had a family that was lost, and one member was hurting mentally. But that young lady," He pointed to Jessie, had made up her mind, with God's help, to reunite them no matter what it takes. Human or animal, she doesn't give up. That sounds like a child of God."

The next morning, after breakfast, Eric and Jessie loaded the car and told Jeremiah goodbye. Jessie said, "It was a wonderful trip! I hope we see you again soon. I'd love to hear you preach sometime soon."

Jeremiah replied, "I have to go out of the country for a little while, but I'll be back around the end of October. Dusty and Christy's wedding will be at his ranch on November 5th. Maybe you can visit and attend services at least by Thanksgiving. I'll have completed my work in Africa, and I'll be around for a while."

Jessie said, "That would be great!" Then she asked, "How do you know you won't be leaving the country again?"

Jeremiah said, "The church collects and saves money to send different people to other areas if someone wants to go. It may be another state, or it could be another country. I'll be home for a while unless the Lord calls me."

Jessie said, "How do you know if the Lord wants you to go somewhere?"

Jeremiah paused, thinking carefully. "That's a good question. I've learned to trust the feelings that come from within, sometimes it feels like a nudge, something I can't ignore. When it's the Lord, I know because it's more than just a passing thought, it's something I can feel deep inside me, guiding me. Sometimes opportunities are handed to me. You were handed an opportunity to help a little boy find his dog, his companion. For some reason, his dad wasn't around, and he needed that dog."

Eric nodded but stayed quiet for a moment. Finally, he said, "We'd better go. We enjoyed it, but I knew something would happen."

Jeremiah smiled, "That's a gift too, Eric."

When they arrived home, Jessie moved at a fast pace, like she had somewhere to be. Her mind was racing with thoughts of what to do next. She gave Joseph a bath, making sure he was relaxed before she put him to bed. Then, without hesitation, she grabbed her notebook and pen and started to write.

Eric, noticing how quickly she was moving, asked, "What are you up to now?"

Jessie paused for a moment, her pen hovering above the paper. She said, "I have an idea."

Eric reached over, kissing her softly. "Life with you has never been boring."

Jessie smiled, a little sheepish, "Thanks, I guess."

Jessie completed her list, the to-dos stacking up, but her mind was already moving ahead. She looked forward to making phone calls, but for now, she had to get back to work and balance the needs of daily life.

The day of Dusty's wedding arrived. The barn had been swept out, the horses were grazing peacefully in the pasture, and metal chairs were arranged for the guests. There was a sweet smell of hay in the air that blended perfectly with the rustic feel of the venue. The atmosphere was lively, yet serene, a reflection of Dusty and Christy's love.

It was a small family wedding with a few close friends from Christy's workplace. Dusty, dressed in a beige western shirt with a brown yoke featuring intricate rope designs, dark blue jeans, and a leather western belt, was clearly in awe of the moment. As Christy stepped into the barn, his eyes widened, and his mouth dropped open in surprise. "Wow," he whispered as he looked at his bride.

Christy wore a knee-length, aqua blue chiffon dress with brown western designs and a wide light brown belt. They both wore western hats and boots. As Christy walked closer to the small white open gate where Dusty stood, he whispered, "You look beautiful."

She smiled warmly and replied, "You look very handsome."

Jeremiah leaned in close, "You both look good, now let's get you married!"

The audience chuckled quietly, and the ceremony proceeded. Dusty and Christy exchanged vows, and there were smiles all around. Jeremiah, standing at the altar, said, "I now pronounce you husband and wife! Kiss your bride!"

Cheers erupted as the reception began. There was food, cake, slow dancing, and even square dancing. Dusty, with a proud smile, assisted his bride into an old-time buggy led by a white American Standardbred horse. Christy threw her bouquet, and much to the amusement of everyone, it landed in Jeremiah's hands. He hesitated for a moment before tossing it to a lady from Christy's workplace.

Jessie ran over to the buggy, calling out, "I love you two!"

Dusty smiled. "I have to tell you something," he said, voice serious but gentle.

Jessie raised an eyebrow, "What is it?" as the buggy began to move.

Eric looked at Jessie and asked, "Is everything okay?"

Jessie nodded but was still curious about what Dusty had meant. "Yeah, but Dusty said he had to tell me something, and I wanted to tell him something, but they drove away."

Eric smiled reassuringly. "It'll keep. They'll be back soon."

A week later, Dusty called Jessie from his Texas home. "I'm thinking about opening a Western store in Alabama. I'm doing a little more research on it, but if you know of anyone who would be dedicated to running it, you could let me know. I'd like for you to do it, but I know you love your job."

Jessie paused, considering the offer. "That sounds great. Would you be coming out east here to get it started?"

Dusty responded, "Oh yeah, I'd probably be out once a month to check on things, but as I said, I'm still thinking about it."

Jessie smiled and said, "I'll be praying for you, and for guidance on what to do."

Dusty chuckled. "I never considered praying about it."

Jessie replied softly, "It's always a good thing to pray, especially when making a decision." She continued, "Speaking of which, I wanted to ask if you and Christy could come out for Thanksgiving."

Dusty's voice softened. "I'm sorry, we promised Christy's parents we'd go to their house."

Jessie smiled. "Perfect! Can you come and go to church service with us next Sunday, before Thanksgiving? I'm trying to get the whole family there to surprise and support Jeremiah. He's supposed to be preaching that day."

Dusty's voice grew more serious. "I'll talk to Christy, and I'll let you know. That's just a week away."

"Please try," Jessie begged. Her voice was filled with emotion, more than Dusty had heard from her before.

"I will try," Dusty promised.

Sunday morning arrived, and everyone met in Montgomery, Alabama, at a local motel. Jessie had arranged for everyone to meet there and follow her and Eric to church. They arrived and found enough seats to sit together toward the back right side. Jessie, holding Joseph, was proud to walk in with Eric, Patty, Mark, Julie, Joe, Kathy, Aunt June (who had helped raise the boys with her husband, Keith), Naomi and Richard (who raised Jessie), and Rick and JoAnn (who had raised Patty).

They sat together on two pews, their faces lit up with love and excitement. Ten minutes later, Dusty and Christy walked in, hand in hand. That's when Jeremiah noticed his family sitting there near the back. His heart swelled with pride as he saw them all there to support him.

Jeremiah stood up from his chair behind the pulpit and addressed the audience. "I'm so glad to see you all here today. It's a beautiful day. I want to start by telling you a little about my life and what God has done for me. You've known me a long time, but I don't believe I've ever told you where I came from."

Jeremiah paused, a wave of emotion washing over him. He continued, "When I was about four, my mother passed away. Some of you know that about me, because you've asked about my parents. I always said I didn't know where my dad was. All I knew was that he was in the military. I don't really remember much about the last time I saw him. It was over twenty years ago. I haven't known if he was dead or alive. I do have a younger brother and two older sisters, and we were raised by other family members, and we were all separated for many years."

He took a breath and continued, "Something happened in my life a few years ago that only God could have been a part of."

The audience grew silent, hanging on every word.

Before her death, my mother had taken the time to write letters to all of us, her children. She also left a few priceless sentimental gifts, things she knew would help us remember her and keep her close even after she was gone. These things were to be delivered to us by my oldest sister once we were old enough to understand their significance. He asked the audience, "Keep in mind, I was only around four years old. Would you like to know what she left me?"

The audience nodded, some saying "Yes!" loudly.

Jeremiah held up the Bible his mother had given him. The Bible was old, worn, its pages a little yellowed with age. It was clear that it had been loved, just like the words inside. The audience began to clap.

He asked, "How did she know that this is exactly what I needed?"

The weight of that question hung in the air, and the audience was silent for a moment, reflecting on their own experiences.

Jeremiah continued, "My younger brother was in the rodeo for a few years, and he had a deep love for horses. He was around one and a half when she passed. What do you think she left him?"

The answer was clear to him. "A beautiful stallion horse toy that he treasures still today." He smiled to himself, remembering the toy fondly. "How do I know? Well, here's the rest of the story. My oldest sister, who is as beautiful on the inside as she is on the outside, had a vision in her mind of what it would be like to find our family again. She had no idea how to start, but she couldn't afford a private detective, so she started looking on her own."

Jeremiah paused, taking a deep breath before continuing. "She searched for a long time, with the help of her husband, Eric. While she was searching for us, she also helped people she met along the way. She didn't just focus on herself, she cared about others, even strangers. She went so far as to search in the woods to help a boy find his dog. I know that because she ordered me to carry the wounded dog to safety." The audience broke out in laughter.

Jeremiah smiled warmly. "My sister's name is Jessie. In her search, she found our father, who had been in a terrible accident and lost his memory. He didn't even remember he had children. It was a surprise to his wife, Kathy, but she has been incredibly loving and supportive throughout this whole journey."

Jeremiah's voice softened. "Jessie reminded him of his family and left pictures for him. Over time, with therapy and patience, Dad remembered his children and the wife he had lost to cancer." He paused again, and some in the audience were wiping tears from their faces.

Jeremiah's eyes scanned the room before he asked, "Who could have been involved in this?" A child shouted from the back, "Jesus!"

Jeremiah smiled with a nod. "Thank you, I can see you've been taught well."

He continued, "My sister, Jessie, did not quit until she found every single member of our family, including the ones who raised us. She kept going, even when things seemed impossible, and she never gave up."

Jeremiah's tone grew more serious. "Where did her strength come from? How did she do this? Other than the fact that she's amazing, she knew about the love of our God. Our mother taught

179

her about the Lord and how He would be her guide, her strength. And that strength remained with her, even in the darkest moments."

Jeremiah's eyes lit up as he remembered something. "I also have a sister that Jessie found in Georgia. I thought that was pretty amazing. When I returned from Africa, I learned that a newspaper had placed ads for me, and a radio station had done the same. It took a while, but Jessie found me. I'm so proud of her."

He then asked, "I'd like the people in those rows three from the back to stand up, please. You know who you are."

As they stood, the crowd looked around, whispering to one another. Some were already starting to figure it out. Jeremiah said, "I'd like to introduce my sister, Jessie, and her husband, Eric, and my baby nephew Joseph. My sister, Patty, and her husband Mark. My baby brother Dusty, and his wife Christy, my father, Joseph, "

Before he finished, the entire audience rose in a standing ovation. Everyone clapped, and some were crying. The energy in the room was electric with emotion.

The clapping continued for a long while, but when everyone sat down, Jeremiah said, "There are other family members who are just as important, like the ones who raised us." More clapping followed.

When it became quieter, Jeremiah's voice grew serious again. "This was a surprise for me to see my family here today." He smiled warmly, then asked, "Can I assume that Jessie put this surprise together?"

Eric's voice rang out clearly from the back, "Yes, you can!" The room erupted in laughter.

Jeremiah grinned, "I am so happy to see them, and I'm happy to see all of you. Who brought us all together?" He answered himself, "I believe we are here to worship our Lord. Sometimes we can see clearly what He has done for us. Other times, we have to stop and look around to see what He has done for us. While we are searching for our own answers, we need to be thankful, forgiving, and always remember to ask the Lord for His guidance."

Jeremiah's voice softened. "Jessie had struggles along the way. Things didn't always go as planned. But she got what she needed."

After the service ended, people came by to shake Jeremiah's hand and meet his family. Almost everyone mentioned what a great service it was. The atmosphere was warm and filled with love. Patty, who had been sitting quietly, was in tears. Jeremiah embraced her tightly, and she looked up at him. "I've been through it, but I didn't understand until now. I was searching for answers, but now I understand. It's amazing."

Some people lingered a little while to talk with Jeremiah and his family. His dad walked over to him, his voice cracking slightly as he put his arms around Jeremiah's neck. "I'm so very proud of you, son. The man you've become... Your mother would be proud."

Jessie, standing nearby, added with a smile, "I need one more thing."

Jeremiah, still moved by the moment, looked at her. "That means a lot, Dad."

Suddenly, a woman ran out in tears, overwhelmed by the emotion of the moment. Jessie turned to Jeremiah and said, "Mom wanted everybody to get together on Easter, because it was her favorite day of the year. That hasn't happened yet, so that needs to happen next Easter."

Jeremiah laughed, "That's months away, sis."

Jessie nodded firmly. "Yep, you have plenty of time, put it on your calendar."

Jeremiah chuckled. "Okay, I'll do that." He paused for a moment, then gathered the whole family together and said, "We'll go to my house for a late lunch. I had planned to barbecue today, so if you won't starve for an hour, we'll grill out."

Chapter 12
Jessie's healing

In the following weeks, Jeremiah had his hands full with visits and phone calls from people at church, as well as others who had heard about his family. Many of the children at church wanted to know more about Jesus. Jeremiah enjoyed telling them about the miracles in the Bible and those that were happening today. It fascinated the children when he told them that they were a miracle at their birth. He reminded them how each of them was made unique and special by God.

Many young adults also had questions. It touched Jeremiah's heart when a lady in her twenties came to him and asked, "Will the Lord give me the money to take good care of my children?" Her voice trembled slightly, revealing the weight of her concerns. Jeremiah prayed for help and wisdom, and he received the answers he needed. Still, his heart hurt to see so many struggling, going through such a difficult time, knowing that he couldn't always offer the solution they were hoping for.

One young man was angry when he came to Jeremiah after church and said, "Your family is rich, but how can I help my family, because we don't have the money that yours does?" His voice was full of frustration, and he seemed on the verge of tears.

That was an easy one for Jeremiah to address. He said, "We didn't have a lot of money. We worked hard for what we received. My younger brother put his life in danger to get the money to take care of his future wife, and now he has to be careful and research ways to invest that money so he doesn't lose it, money that he almost died for." Jeremiah paused, looking the young man in the eyes. "We are not wealthy, but we are rich in blessings. We have bills to pay just like anyone else, and there are times when we worry about making ends meet."

He continued, "Wealthy people have problems too. Sometimes it's the family trying to take their money. Sometimes it's death in the family. Sometimes it's disabilities from birth or some accident. No one on this earth has a perfect life, and that's why we depend on our God. It's easy to look at others and think they have everything, but the truth is, everyone has their own battles."

That following Sunday, Jeremiah felt a strong need to talk about the love of God to the congregation. He stepped up to the pulpit, his heart heavy yet full of purpose. He said, "There are things that happen in life that we don't understand, like why do babies die? Why do young people die? Why is there so much hate? Why do people's homes burn or get taken away in a tornado or hurricane? Why didn't the treatment work for some with cancer or other diseases? Why can't we have the money we need? Why do some people have money while others have to watch every penny to survive? And why are there so many bullies in our lives?"

Jeremiah paused, his eyes scanning the congregation, before continuing. "I want to start by telling you that no one is promised a perfect life. If we had the perfect life, there would be no devil, and we wouldn't feel the need for our Lord. The Lord has a love for His children that no one can fully understand. He sees His children through every situation in their lives."

He then asked, "Did you ever look back and ask yourself, 'How did I get through that?'" Jeremiah paused as a few heads nodded in agreement. "There are bullies in our lives that teach us that we have to stand up and defend ourselves. I'm not talking about revenge, just fighting for what is right. Christians have to fight sometimes. People get mad because their family member went to war or got hurt, or was killed in the military. There aren't many people who want their children in the military, but most of the time, it's a choice that the person made to go in and serve their country. It's a decision that comes with sacrifice, and the sacrifice should be honored."

He looked around at the congregation and asked, "How many people think they will live forever on earth?" There was silence in the room. "I don't see any hands, so we understand that we will not live forever. And as much as it hurts to lose a loved one in death, we have to accept it because we all die, unless we are here when Christ comes. Then, we will be called up to be with Him."

Jeremiah said, "I personally am not a wealthy person, but the Lord has provided. There were times I wanted some extra money to go on a trip, or I wanted spending money. My sister, Patty, taught me how to pick up cans on the side of the road and turn them in for money. I don't agree with littering our beautiful country with trash and cans, but if they're out there, I will be glad to pick them up. It is a humbling, but grateful experience. It reminds me that every little bit helps, and sometimes you have to work for what you want, even if it's not glamorous."

He smiled as he continued, "My sister, Jessie, taught me to take every coin change I have every day and put it in a container. I was surprised, actually shocked, when I discovered I had collected fifty dollars at the end of the month. Sometimes we may need to take on a second job for a few months or a year to pay off a bill or two. I work for this church, but eventually, I will need a job during the week, at least for a while. The Lord provides opportunity."

Jeremiah's voice became more passionate as he continued, "Now when our loved one passes away, the Lord knows where they are, and He knows the feelings of the ones left behind to mourn the loss. Maybe the baby that died would have had a horrible life or a disease growing up, and the Lord brought it home before it got bad. When rescuers die, they have left behind an example of love that honors God. He gives us joy in life, but don't ever forget that we are here to serve Him."

Jeremiah continued teaching with biblical scripture and an excitement in his voice that kept the attention of the audience, both young and not so young. His words were powerful, his message clear, and everyone could feel the passion behind his words.

That afternoon, Jessie called Dusty and said, "I have an idea about someone to run your store. I was thinking about Jeremiah. He has been traveling a lot, but he said he'll be sticking around now."

Dusty replied, "That's a great idea, Jessie, but I'm not sure if western wear would be a big seller in the big city."

Jessie responded confidently, "Actually, I checked it out, and there are numerous farms and ranches near Montgomery. Some ranches are for sale right now."

Dusty said, "Thanks, I'll certainly check into it. And if Jeremiah is available, I will be glad to hire him." Dusty talked about the prospect of having a business in Alabama. Christy, ever the voice of reason, said, "I think it will be a great opportunity for us, but I think we should pray about it and make a decision when we feel it is right."

Dusty said, "Okay."

After hanging up, Jeremiah immediately went to his knees, giving thanks to the Lord. Not only did he have a job that would allow him to continue his work with the church, but he could also hire people who came to him with financial struggles. It felt like a weight had been lifted from his shoulders, and he thought to himself, "The Lord works in mysterious ways."

Jeremiah called Jessie and asked, "Guess what?"

Jessie, always ready for a surprise, responded, "What?"

Jeremiah's excitement was clear in his voice. "Dusty is building a store in Montgomery, and he wants me to manage it!"

"That's great!" Jessie said, her voice filled with happiness for him. Then she asked, "Are you going to do it?"

Jeremiah's smile was evident even through the phone. "Yes, I am. He gave me an offer I can't refuse."

"That's wonderful, Jeremiah. I'm so happy for you."

Jeremiah chuckled softly. "Thanks, but by the way, I know you instigated this."

Jessie feigned innocence. "What are you talking about?"

Jeremiah laughed. "You're sneaky, but you have so much love in your heart, always looking out for other people. Just think, this wouldn't be happening if you hadn't taken the time to look for the family. You have a good connection with God, whether you realize it or not."

Jessie's heart swelled with emotion. "Thank you."

A few days later, Jessie started feeling sick. She noticed blood clots when she went to the bathroom. A wave of concern washed over her, and she immediately called Eric's mom, Beth, asking if she could take her to the emergency room. Beth hurried out the door without hesitation. When they arrived at the ER, Beth helped Jessie in. Jessie doubled over in pain and felt faint. A nurse quickly grabbed a wheelchair and whisked Jessie to the back.

Beth called the school to leave a message for Eric, and shortly after, Eric arrived, breathless and concerned. He rushed back to the room where Jessie was. He found her crying, her face pale and filled with pain.

"Jessie, are you okay?" Eric asked, his voice shaking.

Through the tears and coughing, Jessie managed to say, "Eric, I lost the baby." She sobbed in his arms, the weight of the loss crushing her heart.

The doctor walked in and gently spoke to them. "This is not your fault, Jessie. We don't know the exact reason, but this does happen sometimes. I'm so sorry."

Eric looked up, his voice thick with emotion. "Is Jessie okay?"

The doctor reassured him, "She will need a D&C to clean things out and some rest for a few days. But physically, I believe she is in good health."

Two days later, Jessie went home, exhausted and emotionally drained. She lay on the sofa, wrapped in her favorite quilt. Eric gently placed it over her, trying his best to comfort her. Jessie cried at times, wondering why this had happened. She struggled with feelings of guilt, though she knew deep down it wasn't her fault.

Eric called Patty, Dusty, and Jeremiah to inform them of the news. Jeremiah, ever the thoughtful brother, immediately asked, "Is Jessie okay?"

Eric replied, "She seems to be okay, but she cries at times."

Jeremiah, with his compassionate heart, said, "If it's okay with you, I will come by tomorrow to see her."

"You are always welcome," Eric said, his voice full of gratitude.

The next morning, Jeremiah arrived at 10 am. He walked over to the sofa where Jessie was lying. Without saying a word, he sat down beside her, his presence offering comfort. He just put his arms around her, and she started to cry again. Jeremiah continued to hold her, offering silent support.

Jessie said through her tears, "I don't understand, Jeremiah. I felt fine, and I didn't do anything strenuous. I tried to take care of myself and the baby. I feel like it was a little girl."

Jeremiah gently replied, "You need to stop right now, blaming yourself. This is not your fault. This happens more often to women than you think. I don't have all the answers, but there was something wrong with the baby, and the Lord knew about it and took her home to take care of her."

"Oh, I know it's not God's fault," Jessie said softly, "He has always been there for me, and He has a purpose for taking my baby. I'm thankful the baby didn't stay around and suffer, but it still hurts so much." Her tears flowed again as she spoke the words that were breaking her heart.

Jeremiah squeezed her hand and reached into his jacket pocket, pulling out a chocolate candy bar. "You know, this helps with your challenges," he said, his voice filled with warmth and lightness.

Jessie looked at him with a surprised expression. Her crying stopped for a moment, and she laughed softly. She took the candy from his hand, opened it, snapped off a bite, and put it in her mouth. Then she broke off another piece and reached up to offer it to

Jeremiah. They both laughed, a brief but much-needed moment of levity.

"I don't mean to cry so much," Jessie said with a smile.

Jeremiah nodded. "It's okay to cry, honey. It was devastating. It will take time, but don't forget to let Eric know you love him. It was his loss too."

Jessie looked at him gratefully. "You're right. I'm so glad you came."

Jeremiah gave her a warm hug. "Me too. I left you some food and more chocolate on the table. I'm going to get a hug from Joseph and head back home."

"Thank you so much, Jeremiah. You're such a great brother."

"I know." He laughed lightly. "You're a wonderful sister."

Later that day, Beth and Jim came to visit and spent time with Joseph, and comforted Jessie and Eric as best as they could. Beth sat down with Jessie at the kitchen table. She could see that Jessie was still sad but not crying as much.

Beth asked gently, "Are you feeling better?"

Jessie nodded. "I'm better. I just feel a little guilty, but I know it's not my fault. I feel like I let Eric down."

Beth gave her a comforting look. "I understand those feelings. We lost our first baby before Eric. I was devastated. It wasn't my fault. It just happened."

Jessie's eyes widened. "Eric never told me that."

Beth smiled softly, "I'm not sure that we ever told him. These things happen more than you would think. Babies are sometimes stillborn, even after nine long months."

Jessie wiped a tear away. "Things could have been worse. I will pray hard for those who have lost their babies and children. It is a comfort to know that the little ones belong to God and are well taken care of in their heavenly home."

Jeremiah, during his sermon that Sunday, shared with the congregation what had happened to Jessie and asked for prayers for her. After the service, a young lady came up to Jeremiah and asked, "Why do you think this would happen to your sister? She's such a good person."

Jeremiah smiled gently. "Jessie is a good person. She understands the love of the Lord. She will continue to serve Him, and He will continue to bless her. Death is hard to understand sometimes, but it's a comfort to know we can trust in God. He knows exactly what to do."

Later that week, Joe and Kathy came to visit Jessie and Eric, spending time with Little Joseph. Joe said, "I'm sorry you and Eric had to go through this tough time, but it will get easier in time." Kathy made tea for everyone and offered to make dinner. She brought pecan pie, homemade lasagna, and a fresh salad, offering comfort with both food and her presence.

Eric smiled, feeling comforted. "This is a feast."

Meanwhile, Dusty had come out to Alabama and asked Jeremiah to meet him at a building he discovered online. Jeremiah arrived and looked around in awe. "This is amazing!"

Dusty grinned. "Let's call the owner and discuss the price and take a look inside."

"Good idea," Jeremiah said.

The owner wanted two hundred thousand for the building and parking lot. Jeremiah rubbed his chin, considering the offer. He was sure Dusty had the money, but two hundred thousand seemed like an awful lot. He glanced at Dusty, unsure of what his next move would be. Dusty turned to the side and winked at him. Jeremiah wasn't sure what that meant, but he decided to stay silent and let Dusty handle the negotiation.

Dusty stood his ground and said, "This place has been for sale a long time, so I'm guessing it hasn't been easy to find a buyer. The building itself is decent, but it needs a few repairs. I can give you eighty thousand today, but two hundred thousand is too steep for me."

The man stood back, thinking for a moment. He seemed to weigh his options before he spoke. Finally, he looked back at Dusty and said, "I could be persuaded to accept ninety thousand."

Dusty smiled and reached out his hand. "Deal!" he said, his voice full of satisfaction.

"Do you know a notary or handy lawyer to help us write this up?" Dusty asked.

The man nodded. "We can write this up and head down the road to the bank. There's a notary there."

Dusty said, "We'll follow you there."

As they got in the car, Jeremiah shook his head in amazement. "Wow! You just saved over a hundred thousand dollars."

Dusty chuckled and leaned back in his seat. "I've learned a few things from my financial advisor."

That evening, Dusty stayed at Jeremiah's house, and they spent hours discussing the store and the things they needed to get started. Dusty said, "We'll need to make a few repairs first. And I want a hitching post over to the side of the building."

Jeremiah smiled. "That'll be cool, as they said in the sixties."

Dusty grinned. "After the repairs, I'll start ordering the items we need to get things up and running. I'll come in to help get things started, then I need you to take over because I have some work to do in Texas."

Jeremiah raised an eyebrow. "What kind of work will you be doing?"

Dusty explained, "I have an arena where I use horses to teach children and adults how to ride and take care of horses. It's something I've always loved doing."

Jeremiah nodded. "That's a good way to make money."

Dusty's expression grew more thoughtful. "I probably won't make a lot of money with that, but it's important to me that I can help people using this opportunity. I guess your church sermons and the family talks have rubbed off on me about giving back. I'll only charge a small amount for the lessons, maybe ten dollars per person."

Jeremiah smiled warmly. "God bless you."

Dusty chuckled. "Your pay will increase significantly once things start rolling. Maybe, you'll even get rich from this."

Jeremiah laughed softly. "I'm not looking to get rich, just need to be able to pay my bills and put a little away for emergencies."

Dusty's face softened as he reflected on their journey. "Do you ever think about how much our lives have changed since Jessie started her journey to bring our family together?"

Jeremiah's voice grew serious. "Yeah, I think about it a lot. We've had challenges, and it seemed like we were all searching for answers in our lives, but we find more answers when we try to help each other, and others. I feel so blessed."

Meanwhile, Jessie had healed and was making plans for the holidays. She had spoken to her siblings, and everyone but her dad had already made plans. Jessie understood the challenges of balancing family time, but this year, she wanted everyone to come to her house for Easter. She called each of them and said, "I know you all have your families, but this year, I need everyone here for Easter. And bring the letters Mom wrote for you. It's important for us to be together, especially this year."

Dusty hesitated on the phone. "I don't even know if I have it anymore."

Jessie, always optimistic, replied, "You probably put it somewhere around the horse Mom gave you. See if you can find it. If not, just come anyway. It will be a great Easter."

Jessie also knew that Kathy, her mother-in-law, didn't have any immediate family nearby except for a few cousins who lived out of state. So, Jessie made sure that she, Eric, and Joseph would visit Kathy, or they would make arrangements for Kathy to visit them. Jessie was determined that no one would feel left out or alone.

A few days later, Jessie had a quiet moment to reflect. As Easter drew closer, she thought back on how far they had all come. She had spent so much time focusing on the family being together and healing, but she couldn't help but be grateful for the progress they'd all made. There had been so much loss, yet so much love. She knew this Easter would be a chance to celebrate what they had and what they had overcome.

Jeremiah, on the other hand, had not forgotten about Jessie's strength and the love that had guided them all. The store venture with Dusty was just another step in a new chapter of their lives, but it would not have been possible without the foundation Jessie had built through her faith, her strength, and her commitment to their family.

Chapter 13
Jeremiah's new adventure

The winter months were tough on Jessie and her entire family. Dusty was getting his business in Montgomery started, and Jeremiah was learning about western equipment like saddles, bridles, and western apparel. It was all new to Jeremiah, and at times, it felt overwhelming, but he was catching on. It wasn't always easy dealing with the public, especially the more difficult customers, but Jeremiah practiced patience and persistence, knowing it was a skill he would need.

Patty had some exciting news: she was having a baby boy! She was cautious and didn't stay on her feet as much at school. Instead, she made a point to sit at her desk as often as possible.

Business was slow for Mark, but he found part-time work at a local gym. He enjoyed it and was grateful for the opportunity, especially since he got to work out for free. He found that helping others stay fit and healthy also helped him stay focused and motivated.

Jessie continued her work with patients in need of therapy. One day, she met a nurse named Truly, who was wearing a wooden cross around her neck. Jessie complimented her on the necklace, and the two began talking. It didn't take long for them to realize they had a lot in common, both of them had been shaped by their faith and family experiences. Jessie shared the story of her family's reunion, and Truly shared her own family struggles. Truly's family had come apart, each person going their separate ways. Some members refused to speak to her, leaving her with a lot of unresolved pain.

Despite this, both women loved the Lord deeply, and they bonded over the ways He had influenced their lives in miraculous ways. Truly and Jessie became fast friends, finding comfort and strength in their shared faith.

Joe's therapist informed him that he was now well enough to end therapy. Kathy, always thoughtful, encouraged Joe to start working on small projects at home. She suggested building furniture, like small tables, to keep him busy outside of his part-time maintenance job for a local apartment complex. Kathy had also returned to work at the hospital and still had her nursing license, which kept her busy and fulfilled.

Jeremiah visited Jessie as often as he could. Their conversations were always uplifting, and they both found comfort in talking about the blessings they had received. One day, during one of their visits, Jeremiah expressed his deep gratitude for their family being reunited and getting along so well. Jessie shared her own thoughts about her job.

She said, "Jeremiah, sometimes people start to open up to me while we're doing therapy. I know people have difficulties in life, but I didn't realize how many people are suffering. Sometimes I come home crying for them, and sometimes I cry with them at work. I know it's unprofessional, but it just happens."

Jeremiah nodded with understanding. "You have some special gifts, strong faith, love for your neighbor, and the ability to listen. Professionalism includes faith and the courage to deal with what comes in your path. Like the winds through the trees, we do not always know which direction we will go each day."

Now that man had it rough.

"That's beautiful," Jessie said, touched by his words.

Jeremiah smiled. "It's true." He paused, then asked, "What's going on with your friend Truly?"

Jessie smiled, her eyes sparkling with affection for her new friend. "She has a gift. She told me it's unique, maybe strange at times, but it can only come from God."

Jeremiah raised an eyebrow. "What is it?"

Jessie laughed. "Well, people will stop and talk to her about their life struggles, just if she says hello to them at Walmart or other places."

Jeremiah chuckled. "That happens to people sometimes when they're about to burst to talk to somebody. It's a gift to be trusted as a listener, and sometimes to have the wisdom to help them find the answer they're searching for. I'm glad you have a friend like Truly, and she's blessed to have a friend like you. You'll have stories to tell for a long time."

Jessie paused for a moment, then suddenly said, "Jeremiah!"

"What is it?" he asked, surprised by her sudden excitement.

Jessie's face lit up with a spark of inspiration. "You're a preacher! You have stories to tell. Why don't you write a book to tell your stories? It could help answer questions people have. You can even tell our story."

Jeremiah blinked, taken aback. "Huh?"

Jessie snapped back, "You would be perfect for writing a book, or several books! Patty is a teacher, and she might be able to help you with grammar or punctuation marks. My friend Truly has written several books, and some have even been published. I know she would help if you need her."

Jeremiah rubbed his chin, considering her idea. "Well, I don't know…"

Jessie, sensing his hesitation, said, "I know you can do it. You should do it!"

Jeremiah smiled at his sister. "You've been a great encouragement to me. I'll give it some serious thought. But with my job at the store, Bible study, preaching, and other obligations like visiting the sick and homebound, I'm not sure when I'll find the time."

Jessie grinned. "It sounds like you have a lot of stories there already!"

Jeremiah laughed. "Okay, Jessie, I'll give it a try, but it might take a while." He kissed her on the cheek. "I need to get home now. It's been enjoyable seeing you, as always."

Jessie smiled warmly. "Just start an outline and see what happens. I love you. Drive safe."

"I love you, Jessie."

As Jeremiah got in his car and drove away, he muttered to himself, "What have I gotten myself into?" He chuckled out loud at his own uncertainty. Then, on a more serious note, he whispered, "What do you want me to do, Lord?"

Before reaching his home, Jeremiah made a quick stop at the store to grab a sandwich and a drink. He hadn't eaten all afternoon and was starting to feel the effects of his hunger. As he walked out, he noticed a thin man sitting on the side of the store, wrapped in an old coat. Something about the man caught his attention. He walked over and asked, "Are you okay?"

The man looked up at him, his eyes weary. "I'm okay, thanks."

Jeremiah still had a strange feeling, a tug at his heart. "Do you have a place to stay out of the cold?"

"Not tonight," the man replied, "but I'll be okay."

Jeremiah felt a mixture of concern and frustration. "How can you be okay if you're sitting in the cold and don't have a place to stay?"

The man's answer surprised him. "The Lord has always taken care of me, even when I get myself in a mess."

Jeremiah sat down beside him, handing the man his sandwich and drink. The man took it eagerly, as if he hadn't eaten all day. "My name is Jeremiah," he said softly. "What happened to you?"

The man looked at Jeremiah with a sad smile. "My name is George. I lost my job about three months ago. My wife passed away last year, and I guess I got depressed and kind of sick. I was fired, and I couldn't make my house payment, so I had to leave. Kind people like you offer me food from time to time, and I get by. When I think of giving up, I remember that the Lord has been providing for me. There's a purpose for this, and He'll show me the way. I think of the story of Job in the Bible."

Jeremiah snickered under his breath, "Yes, he did have it rough."

Jeremiah looked at George, his heart aching for him. "Come home with me. I may be able to help you."

George's eyes filled with tears, and he wiped them away quickly, squinting as he tried to stop the tears from flowing. He asked softly, "Are you sure?"

Jeremiah smiled warmly, "Absolutely."

George said, "I have a special feeling about you, and I feel sure I can trust you."

Jeremiah smiled warmly, his heart full of compassion. "I was thinking the same about you." Then they both smiled as Jeremiah offered his arm and helped lift George off the ground.

George looked down at the sandwich in Jeremiah's hand and asked, "What about your sandwich? You gave yours to me."

Jeremiah chuckled. "Yeah, I didn't really need it. I have bread and sandwich stuff at home." George understood the unspoken kindness in Jeremiah's gesture. He silently thanked God, his heart filled with gratitude.

Jeremiah showed George to the bed where he would sleep. He brought George some towels and a washcloth and pointed toward the bathroom. "I'll have breakfast for us when you wake up," he said. "Then we'll talk." As Jeremiah walked to his own room, he realized that he hadn't given George privacy. He eased back to shut the door gently, and as he did, he caught a glimpse of George on his knees by the bed, praying silently. Jeremiah knew without a doubt that he had done the right thing.

The next morning, while they ate breakfast, Jeremiah spoke up. "I'd like to take you shopping for some clothes."

George hesitated. "I need some clothes, but I don't know how I can repay you. I can wash the ones I have on."

Jeremiah smiled reassuringly. "I have to make a phone call, if you'll excuse me. I'll be right back. Enjoy your breakfast."

Jeremiah stepped outside and dialed Dusty's number. He explained what had happened and said, "Dusty, I'd like to give George a job. He needs help."

Dusty was silent for a moment, considering. Then he replied, "You're in charge of the store. If you feel led to give him a job, it's your decision. I trust you."

Jeremiah felt a sense of relief and responsibility. It was comforting to know that Dusty trusted him.

Jeremiah returned to George, who was still eating his breakfast. "Do you like Western clothes?" Jeremiah asked casually.

George smiled weakly. "I like western clothes, but I know they're more expensive than regular clothes."

Jeremiah, with a warm grin, said, "You can have this shirt, underwear, and sweats until we get you some nicer clothes. After you get cleaned up, I want to show you something."

Jeremiah had a glow about him that was brighter than even the joy of a happy pregnant woman. His spirit felt renewed, and his faith seemed to radiate from him. He felt the presence of the Lord strongly that morning, and it showed in everything he did. George was not as tall as Jeremiah, so the sweatpants were a little long. He looked down at his feet, then back up at Jeremiah, both of them bursting out into laughter at the sight.

Jeremiah grinned. "Come on, we'll fix this."

A few minutes later, they arrived at the store, now proudly called "Dusty's Western Wear." George looked up at the store in awe. "This is a nice place. I like the statue of the horse by the hitching post. It almost looks real, like it's about thirteen or fourteen hands."

Jeremiah raised an eyebrow. "Do you know much about Western stuff?"

George nodded with a quiet smile. "Yeah, I grew up on a farm. We had horses, cows, pigs, and chickens."

Jeremiah nodded, feeling an immediate connection. "George, I run this place, and I need someone like you to help me with it."

George hesitated. "I appreciate all you've done for me, but I don't know how much charity I can take. I don't know how to repay you for all you've already done for me."

Jeremiah's expression softened. "George, this is not charity. I need help with this store. All I need you to do is fill out the application for tax purposes. It's already been approved by the owner. Will you help me, George?"

George looked down, a little embarrassed. "I need to find a place to stay."

Jeremiah offered a kind smile. "You can stay with me until you're able to get the place you want. Just put my address as your present home and your old address as the last home."

George raised an eyebrow at the request. "That seems a little strange, but I have a job now, so I'll do what you say."

Jeremiah had an ulterior motive for asking for George's old address. He made a quick call to check on the property. He spoke with the bank manager, explaining George's situation. "The bank was going to auction it off," the manager said, "but I understand your concern. We can give you a week to clean out his things."

Jeremiah breathed a sigh of relief. "Thank you," he said gratefully.

Later that afternoon, Jeremiah called Dusty again. "I hired the man. He's living with me for now until he can get back on his feet. But Dusty, I think I may need a small loan to rent a storage room for about four months and rent a truck to pick up his things. I want to do this discreetly so I don't embarrass him."

Dusty hesitated for a moment before asking, "How would you feel if someone came into your house and moved your stuff and gave it to you later?"

Jeremiah, feeling conflicted, answered honestly, "I guess I would feel weird about it, but I've got to help him."

Dusty, always practical, replied, "I'll be happy to donate the money to help George. But I think you should tell him what you're doing. He needs to have that independence. He needs to pick out the things he needs the most. You can rent a U-Haul fairly priced and get it all done in one day."

Jeremiah smiled, relieved by Dusty's wisdom. "Thanks, Dusty. I owe you."

Dusty's voice lightened with a grin. "No problem. Just have a steak ready when I come by later next month."

Jeremiah laughed, "You got it."

Jeremiah went back to the store and found George. He sat down and explained what he had done. "I've made arrangements for us to get your things out of the house. We can do this discreetly. I want you to pick out what you need, and I'll be there to help."

George's eyes filled with tears as he looked at Jeremiah. "I was looking for answers, praying every day, hoping I would see my wife's picture again and my kids."

Jeremiah gently asked, "Why didn't you call your children and tell them you needed help?"

George sighed deeply, his voice filled with regret. "I didn't want to burden them. I was ashamed that I let myself get into this situation. I thought they might be mad at me for losing the house and the pictures, the memories. I guess you're regretting helping me now."

Jeremiah shook his head, his heart full of compassion. "Of course not, George. Things will go as planned, and when you're ready, you'll call your children and explain what happened."

Jeremiah smiled reassuringly. "George, we only have one week to get your things. We can try to get everything you need in one day. Let's plan to go tomorrow morning, bright and early, so we have enough time to get everything."

George's face lit up with hope. He took a big breath, feeling a sense of relief for the first time in a long while. "I'm sure we can get everything I need in one day. I just don't know where to store it."

Jeremiah nodded. "I'll call today and get a storage room as soon as you tell me what size we need."

George said, "You've done so much for me, I feel like I need to pay you something."

Jeremiah smiled gently, his heart warm with compassion. "George, I explained your situation to the owner of Dusty's, and he donated four months for the cost of the storage room. We also need to look for a car that you would like."

George started to speak, "I don't know what to…"

Jeremiah cut him off with a reassuring tone. "George, before you say anything, I want you to know that the owner understands. There was a time in his life when he was down, almost ready to give up. We serve a God who tells us to help each other in Matthew 25 (KJV), and somewhere down the line, you can serve Him by helping someone else."

George understood and nodded. He didn't speak, but the tears welled up in his eyes. He was overwhelmed by the kindness and generosity that had been shown to him.

The next day, Jeremiah and George rented a U-Haul and began moving George's belongings. The work was finished by one in the afternoon, and George felt a sense of relief and satisfaction. He looked at Jeremiah and said, "I had better get back to work so I can earn the money for my new place in four months."

Jeremiah smiled. "We can start Monday morning, working hard. I need to earn my pay too. Today, though, we'll have lunch and then unload your belongings. On Sunday, you can go to church with me, and we'll take a day of rest. We can ride to work together, so finding a vehicle for you can wait a little while. I know this is a lot to take in, but it will all come in time."

George nodded, his voice filled with gratitude. "It is a lot. In a way, it's like I'm starting over, but starting over is a new chance to do things right."

Jeremiah's eyes brightened. "I like your attitude, George."

It was now April 3rd, and George was walking through the store, whistling and smiling as he greeted customers. It was such a sight to see George so happy. Jeremiah couldn't help but smile too, feeling a warmth in his heart. He walked over to George and asked, "Are things good, George?"

George beamed. "Yes, sir. Things are good. Today is my birthday. I'm fifty-two, and I have a job. I've found a small house with payments I can afford, so I'm good."

Jeremiah's smile faded slightly. "George, I need to talk to you for a minute." Those words always made a boss's conversation uncomfortable, and George's smile faded a bit as he became uneasy.

Jeremiah led him into the store lounge. The moment they walked in, the employees shouted, "Happy Birthday, George!" There were flowers on the table, and balloons dangled from the ceiling. George had not had recognition for his birthday since his wife passed away. He was overcome with emotion. His smile stretched wide across his face as he stood there in shock.

"Thank you so much. This is a wonderful surprise. It's the best surprise I've ever had, other than my wife accepting my proposal," George managed to say through his joyful tears.

Dusty walked into the lounge, chuckling. "Hey, I like a party!" He walked over and stood beside Jeremiah.

Jeremiah smiled, feeling a deep sense of pride in the team he had helped create. "George, this is Dusty Davis. He owns this store."

Dusty extended his hand to George. "Glad to meet you, George. Happy Birthday."

Dusty then motioned for Jeremiah to step outside the door, his face shifting to a more serious expression. George, still stunned by the attention, felt a bit uncomfortable but continued to mingle with the others, enjoying the cake and punch.

Jeremiah asked, "Is everything okay?"

Dusty's expression was somber. "I'm not sure. Patty is supposed to have her baby today, but Mark called and said there are some complications."

Jeremiah's heart sank. "Oh no. I'll be praying and head out to Georgia to check on her immediately."

Dusty nodded. "I need to look at some paperwork, then I'll go with you."

Jeremiah replied, "I'm glad to have the company."

He turned to George. "Is everything okay?"

George looked at him with concern. "Is everything okay?"

Jeremiah's face softened. "I'm not sure, George. Dusty and I need to make a trip to Georgia to check on our sister. She's in the hospital."

George looked puzzled. "Is Dusty your brother?"

Jeremiah smiled. "Yeah. Didn't I mention that?"

George shook his head. "No, you didn't."

"I hope your sister is okay," George said quietly.

Jeremiah nodded, his heart heavy. "Thanks, George. I'll get Ben to carry you home after work. He can pick you up in the morning and take you home. I shouldn't be gone too long."

Dusty walked back and spoke to George. "I've heard good things about you, George. We're glad to have you aboard. Maybe we can talk more when we get back."

Jeremiah explained things to Ben, asking him to take care of George. Then Dusty and Jeremiah left, heading to Georgia.

Jeremiah and Dusty made it to the hospital in record time. Dusty grinned. "I'm surprised you didn't get a speeding ticket, bro."

Jeremiah laughed, his voice tense. "I was praying as hard as I was driving."

They walked into Patty's room and found her holding a healthy baby boy. Dusty asked, "Is everything good?"

Mark looked relieved. "I'm sorry I didn't call you back. I didn't think you would have time to come. The baby was breech, and Patty was in a lot of pain, but the doctor figured it out and had to do a C-section to get him out. They're both okay now."

Jeremiah sighed with relief. "Where is everybody? I figured the whole family would come running."

Mark answered, "Joe and Kathy are in the cafeteria with Julie. Jessie had a full schedule at work, but she had her cell phone in her pocket. Oh my gosh, I need to call her. Excuse me."

Patty was tired and groggy, but still managed a smile. Dusty and Jeremiah stood by her bed, and she reached out her hand. Jeremiah held it gently. "I'm sorry Mark worried you, but I'm glad to see you both."

Dusty gave her a warm smile. "You look good."

Patty laughed softly. "I'm a mess, but we have a beautiful boy. His name is Robert Jeremiah."

Dusty raised an eyebrow. "That's a first. You've made Jeremiah speechless."

Patty smiled. "We'll probably call him Bobby, but he will know all about his uncles." She looked at Jeremiah, her eyes filled with love. "I love you."

Jeremiah kissed her forehead. "I love you."

Dusty did the same. "We'll go see Dad, Kathy, and Julie before we head back to Alabama."

On their way back to the store, Dusty turned to Jeremiah. "Is there a steak at your house? I'm hungry."

Jeremiah grinned. "No, but I know a great steakhouse near the store. We'll pick up George and go eat a late supper."

As they drove, Jeremiah updated Dusty on George's progress. "He's been doing great at the store. He's very attentive to the customers, and sales have started to increase."

Dusty nodded thoughtfully. "That's great news, but make sure you let George do more for himself. He needs his independence."

Dusty continued, "You could check the book and, if we can spare it, you might want to give him a small raise. Maybe that will help."

Jeremiah smiled, feeling grateful for Dusty's wisdom. "Thanks, Dusty. Maybe he can get a car soon. I know it's hard starting over with payments like a house, car, and insurance, but he has a great start, thanks to you and the Lord's blessings."

The next day, Jeremiah called Jessie to tell her about the recent events. He updated her on George's progress, about how his life had changed, and how he had turned things around. "My life has changed, too," Jeremiah added.

Jessie's voice brightened. "Do you remember me telling you that you needed to write a book?"

Jeremiah laughed, "Yeah."

Jessie's tone was a little sarcastic. "If you had been writing a book, it would be full by now."

Jeremiah grinned. "Well, I've kept a journal, as you suggested."

Jessie's voice softened. "That's a start."

George found Jeremiah at the back of the store. "I'm ready to move into my little house," he said, his voice filled with a mix of excitement and uncertainty. "It needs some work, but that'll keep me busy for a while. I also need a ride to find a small car, if you have time. I'm sure you'll be glad to have your house back."

Jeremiah looked at him with a soft smile. "Actually, I'll miss having you around, George. It'll be lonely when you leave."

Then, as if it had just come to him, Jeremiah added, "Your next check will show an increase in your pay. You've been doing a great job."

George's eyes brightened with gratitude. "Thank you, Jeremiah. I've really enjoyed living at your house and getting to meet some of your family. I appreciate everything you've done for me. I just wish I knew how to thank you in a better way. But I need to get started on my own now. Starting fresh is exciting, but I'm also a little nervous."

Jeremiah paused, sensing there was more George wanted to say. "Why are you nervous?" he asked gently.

George hung his head for a moment before replying. "I remember what I went through being without money or a place to live. I just don't want to lose everything again."

Jeremiah put a hand on George's shoulder and spoke with conviction. "I might suggest that after you get your car, you call your children. I bet they've been wondering if you're alive and well."

George hesitated. "I don't know…"

Jeremiah smiled. "And you won't know until you try. Have faith."

George found a used Honda with only twenty thousand miles on it. When he drove it to his new home, he remembered Jeremiah's advice and decided to make the call. His hands shook as he picked up the phone, staring at the number he knew by heart. He put the phone back down for a moment, taking a deep breath to calm his nerves. His eyes landed on the picture from his old home, his daughter, Sara, smiling back at him.

He took another deep breath and dialed her number, hoping it hadn't changed. A lady's voice answered, "Hello."

George's heart raced. "Sara, this is your dad."

The voice on the other end cracked with emotion. "Daddy, is it really you?"

Tears welled up in his eyes as he answered, "Yes, honey, it's me."

She asked, her voice full of longing, "Where have you been?" Before he could answer, she asked again, "Are you okay?"

George started to cry but fought to remain strong. "I'm all right. I have so much to tell you." He paused, taking a shaky breath before asking, "I was wondering if you could come to my house in Montgomery so we could talk?"

She was silent for a moment, then replied with a soft smile in her voice. "Yes, I'll come see you this Saturday. My husband has work this weekend, but I'll come. Your grandsons will want to see you. They ask about you all the time. After we talk, we'll all get together as a family."

The next day, George went to work at the store. When Jeremiah walked over to him, George couldn't help but share the good news. "I called my daughter. She seems happy to come visit me this Saturday."

Jeremiah beamed with joy. "That's great, George. The Lord works in mysterious ways. Always trust in Him, even if things aren't going the way you think they should."

George nodded, his face reflecting a new understanding. "I will. I understand that now."

Jeremiah placed his arm around George's shoulder and gave him a manly hug. George felt a warmth and brotherhood in that embrace, something he hadn't experienced in years.

An employee standing nearby observed this moment and commented, "That's an unusual man. He's not afraid to show he cares about people."

The other employee, nodding, smiled and replied, "Yep, he's a godly man. He's good to all of us here. He's helped more people than you can imagine, and his brother is good to us too."

Chapter 14
Reading the letters of a mother's love

It was getting close to Easter. Jessie had called all of her family earlier to remind them of the Easter get-together. She explained the importance of the day and asked everyone to bring the letters that their mother had written before her death.

Dusty and Christy arrived first. Dusty grinned as he got out of the car. "I love Alabama, but I've made too many trips here lately."

Christy, with a warm smile, nudged Dusty. "Two trips in a month isn't too bad, except for me missing you."

Dusty chuckled and pulled her close. "Aww, that's sweet, baby."

Jessie smiled at the couple. "That is sweet. I needed to get everyone together for Easter, at least this one time. It was Mom's favorite day, because she always said, 'The best day in the world was the day Jesus arose,' because it made it possible for us to go to Heaven someday. She wanted us all to remember that."

Just as Jessie finished speaking, Joe and Kathy drove up. As Jessie went out to meet them, Mark, Patty, and their children, Bobby and Julie, pulled into the drive. Jessie walked with all of them into the house and toward the living room. She had set up Joseph's playpen by the wall so Bobby would have a place to lie down, but after thinking about it, she decided it would be quieter and more comfortable to put him on her bed since he was still an infant.

An hour later, Jeremiah drove up. Jessie went out to greet him with a smile. "You're the last to arrive, brother."

Jeremiah grinned, rolling his eyes. "Traffic wasn't cooperating with me."

Jessie laughed. "It's okay. I'm just glad everybody decided to come." The front side door of Jeremiah's car opened. Out stepped a tall, slim woman with long brown hair, layered in waves. She wore blue jeans, a turquoise western-type shirt, and brown leather sandals, as Jeremiah had suggested.

Jessie stood, waiting for her to walk up to the front of the car. "Hello."

Jeremiah smiled, his eyes glinting with mischief. "This is Rebecca. Most people call her Becky. She's a good friend."

Jessie quickly extended her hand. "Good to meet you, Becky. I'm Jeremiah's sister, Jessie."

Becky smiled warmly. "I've heard so much about you. I'm so glad to finally meet you."

Jessie smiled back but couldn't help but glare at Jeremiah. She hadn't heard anything about Becky before.

Jessie gave Becky directions to the bathroom, and Jeremiah waited outside. The warm Easter day had everyone gathering outside, with chairs set up on the deck. Jessie stood close to Jeremiah, her voice lowered. "I've never heard of Becky before."

Jeremiah shrugged, a bit sheepish. "I knew everybody had a mate, so I decided to bring a friend."

Eric had already started the grill and was putting the burgers on to cook. Patty walked over to Jeremiah, a curious look on her face. "I'm surprised you missed your church service."

Mark, overhearing, raised an eyebrow. "Patty, why would you say that?"

Patty shrugged, feeling embarrassed. "I didn't mean anything by it."

Jeremiah smiled to diffuse the tension. "It's okay. A lot of people had family plans today, so we had an early sunrise service. I don't usually like to get up that early, but I'm glad I did. There were a lot of people there, and it was so beautiful in more ways than one."

Jessie walked over to them, beaming. "I'm so very thankful you all came. I know it wasn't easy. Mark and Patty have a new baby, Jeremiah had to get up early…" There was a ripple of laughter. "And

Dusty and Christy had a long way to travel, so thank you all for coming today." She paused, her eyes softening. "It seems like just yesterday when Eric and I got married, and shortly after that, we started on a journey to find my other family, my original family."

She gestured to everyone around her. "Our family has been extended in such a blessed way with Dad's wife Kathy, and Joseph, Julie, Bobby, and new friends like Becky." Jessie's voice caught slightly, but she pressed on, her heart full. "I don't know about you, but there have been some tough times, some weird times, some crazy times. But as Jeremiah says often, 'WE ARE BLESSED!'"

Jeremiah, his voice strong, added, "AMEN!"

Jessie smiled at him before continuing. "We'll enjoy my husband's cooking, I know I will, and then we'll tell stories from our lives and maybe read some letters from our mom."

Becky came over to Eric and said, "The meal was delicious."

Everyone joined in thanking Eric for the great food. Jessie had set a table with a red-checked tablecloth, and on top of it were baked beans, potato salad, and a plate of burgers, sausages, and hot dogs Eric had grilled. Bobby had woken up a bit fussy, but Patty quickly took him inside, changed his diaper, and fed him. Shortly after, Bobby went back to sleep. The ladies pitched in to help clean up, and the mood was relaxed and warm.

It was time to reminisce and share stories. Jessie, standing up, asked, "Does anyone want to share a story or read their letter from mom?" There was a long silence before she spoke again. "This is a special time. We celebrate Jesus coming out of the grave and celebrate my mother, who appreciated and loved this day and what it represented."

Jessie turned to her father. "Dad, didn't you have a letter from Mom?"

Joe looked at her, unsure. "I'm not sure about reading it, Jessie."

Kathy squeezed Joe's hand gently, encouraging him. "Go ahead, Joe. It's beautiful."

Joe nodded, a tear slipping down his cheek as he pulled the letter from his pocket. He began to read:

"My Dearest Joe,

I have loved you every minute we have known each other. You have been my love and my rock. I have been sick for just a little while, but there is certainly no earthly way for me to get better. But I don't want you to be sad. I have a Heavenly Father who will carry me home. I hope you can find happiness with a mate who loves you and also loves the Lord. I don't want you to be lonely. We had a brief time together, but it was good, and we had four beautiful children."

Joe wiped away a few tears as he finished reading. He took a deep breath, his voice shaking. "Joe, enjoy your children and enjoy your life. I'll see you again, someday. With all my love, Mary."

There wasn't a dry eye in the crowd. Jessie hugged her dad tightly, her voice thick with emotion. "I know that was personal, but it meant so much." Then she turned to Kathy and hugged her too. "Thank you for loving our dad."

Jessie looked around at everyone and asked, "Dusty, would you like to say whatever's on your mind or read your letter?"

Dusty hesitated for a moment. "I didn't bring the letter Mom wrote to me, but I'll say that she was a remarkable lady, even though I don't remember her. Sometimes I think I can remember her face as she held me in her lap while sitting in the rocker." He paused, his voice thickening. "She had written in her letter that, as a baby, I would stare at horse pictures on the wall. I had a plastic book of horses that Uncle Keith brought for me, and Mom said I looked at it most every day. She thought it might be my favorite toy. She left me a six-inch stallion, and I thought it was awesome."

Dusty smiled, his eyes distant with memory. "She put Jessie in charge of bringing the family together, and the timing was perfect for me. Jessie came into my life when I had no desire to live anymore. The horse she brought made me feel something inside, and that horse eventually brought me my beautiful bride, who found it where I left it, in the hospital."

Christy turned to Dusty, wrapping her arms around him as tears ran down her face. Dusty tried to hold back his tears, but a few slipped down his cheek.

Jessie wiped her eyes, her voice trembling. "This is so beautiful, but I'm wondering if I can take any more. Maybe it was a bad idea to share such personal memories."

Jeremiah spoke softly but firmly, "It's too late now. Let's hear from you, Jessie."

Jessie unfolded her other letter from her mom that was sealed in an envelope. She began to read:

"My Sweet Jessie,

You are the oldest and bear the biggest responsibility. You have been a remarkable daughter and so helpful to me. I'm so sorry that I didn't get to watch you grow up, take pictures of you in your prom dress, and hold your hand at your wedding, but I'm betting that you married a wonderful man and have wonderful children. I know the Lord is looking out for you. He will guide you and give you the strength you need. I need you to look after your sister and brothers, as well as your dad. Your dad will probably remarry, so support him and be kind to his wife. I will always be your mother, but you will be blessed with other people in your life. You are a good caregiver to me, your sister, and your brothers. You are a good caregiver to the dog and other animals. Don't change, Jessie. Stay true to yourself. Others will love you for who you are.

My sweet girl, I love you.

MOM"

Jessie held the letter down, her eyes glistening with tears as she looked into the faces of her family. She tried to smile but couldn't quite hold it back. It was hard not to cry. It helped when Dusty broke the silence.

"Well, that explains a lot!" Dusty chuckled, looking around at the family. "Jessie looks out for us, but she can get a little bossy at times."

Laughter broke out, and Jessie couldn't help but laugh too, her heart lightened by the warmth in the room.

Patty, who had been sitting quietly, mustered up her courage and stood. The room grew silent as all eyes turned to her. She took a deep breath. "I believe I was seven when Mom passed away. She made a few dresses for me and Jessie that looked alike, because I wanted us to be twins. Mom's letter to me is in a frame at home in my bedroom. I read it most every day."

Patty's voice cracked, but she continued. "She tells me to be good to my brothers and always keep in touch with Jessie. When Jessie found me for the first time, she brought me a doll Mom had saved for me. It was my favorite doll, and I called her Twinkles. I never, in a million years, dreamed of seeing Twinkles again. Mom said in my letter that I would be a good teacher and a good mother because I took such good care of Twinkles and talked to her all the time, teaching her the ABCs and how to be a good girl." Patty smiled faintly. "What do you know, I am a teacher, and I love my students."

She sat back down, and Jessie said, "That's nice, Patty."

Jessie then turned to Jeremiah. "I know you have stories to share."

Jeremiah stood, his voice steady but filled with emotion. He cleared his throat. "The letter and gift Mom sent me were just as amazing as everyone's. She had a gift of love and a gift to see a little of the future. She told me to trust my heart and go where I was led."

He paused for a moment, and the room fell silent. "I think all of you know that I am blessed to preach, and I know it is a gift as well as a calling. Mom sent me a red Bible with a note that said, 'This Bible is red, and it is unique, but what will be special for you is when you read it, it will be a "READ" Bible. R_E_A_D.'"

Jeremiah smiled at the murmurs of awe from the group. "Yep, it was amazing to me too. Mom said in the letter that I was always on my knees when I played on the floor, and she said she witnessed me with my hands together on my knees beside my bed on numerous occasions. She said it might have been for play, or it might have been real feelings in me, but..."

Jeremiah's voice faltered, and he paused. "She said she could feel the Lord's presence when she held me in her arms."

Christy, her hand over her heart, whispered, "Oh, that sends chills up my arm."

Jessie wiped away a tear, looking at her brother. "That's beautiful, Jeremiah!"

Dusty, wiping his eyes, asked, "What did Mom leave in that chest for you, Jessie?"

Jessie chuckled, the tears still glistening in her eyes. "She left me a toy stethoscope and a real pin to put on my shirt. It says 'CAREGIVER.' I still have those items."

Jessie's voice grew soft, her heart full. "This has been a special time for me. I really appreciate the sacrifice you all made to be here on this special day. I hope you can stay and spend the night if you don't have to hurry home. I hope everyone had a good time. I feel like we have a lot to be thankful for."

As they were going inside, Eric suddenly heard a scream. He turned to Jessie. "Jessie, did you hear that?"

Jessie paused, trying to listen. Another scream echoed through the air. "HELP!" The faint sound of a woman screaming from down the road reached them.

Eric grabbed Jessie's hand. "Come on!"

They ran down the road, breathless by the time they reached the neighbor's driveway. The woman stood there, frantic. "Something's wrong with my husband!"

Eric knelt beside the man, who was lying unconscious in the driveway. He turned to the woman. "Call 911 now!"

Eric climbed onto the man's chest and started CPR. Jessie kneeled beside him, ready to blow a breath into his mouth. The woman had already called 911. "The ambulance is on its way!" she cried.

Eric continued with chest compressions, Jessie giving the man another breath. Suddenly, the man started to cough. Eric quickly turned him onto his side, making sure he wouldn't aspirate. The woman gasped, covering her mouth with her hands. "Thank God!"

Eric instructed her, "Stay back and make sure the ambulance sees you."

About three minutes later, the ambulance arrived. The lady, still crying, thanked them. "Thank you!" she called as the paramedics lifted her husband onto a stretcher.

As the ambulance drove away, Jessie turned to Eric. "That was amazing! Eric, you did a great job!"

Eric smiled. "We did a great job. We make a great team."

Eric stopped suddenly, then turned and faced Jessie. Jessie asked, "Is something wrong?" Eric responded," Nothing is wrong, everything is right. I know I've talked to you about joining the military earlier, but I have been praying and asking for guidance." He was quiet for a few seconds, but excitement was in his voice as he continued , "I know now what I am supposed to do." Eric could feel Jessie tense up. He looked into Jessie's eyes and said, "I'm feel a calling to serve God by helping people, just like we did today. This is where I am suppose to be." Jessie's smile was warm as she hugged him tight.

Eric stopped suddenly, then turned and faced Jessie.

Jessie asked, "Is something wrong?"

Eric responded, "Nothing is wrong, everything is right. I know I've talked to you about joining the military earlier, but I have been praying and asking for guidance."

He was quiet for a few seconds, but excitement was in his voice as he continued, "I know now what I am supposed to do."

Eric could feel Jessie tense up. He looked into Jessie's eyes and said, "I feel a calling to serve God by helping people, just like we did today. This is where I am supposed to be."

Jessie's smile was warm as she hugged him tight.

When they walked back home, everyone was waiting in the house. Jeremiah had seen them running down the road and witnessed the rescue. As Jessie and Eric walked in, Jeremiah greeted them with a smile. "We have some heroes in the house!"

Everyone clapped, and Eric shrugged. "We're in the medical field; we're not heroes."

Jeremiah smiled. "You gotta watch out for those quiet people like Eric. They may surprise you."

Jeremiah saw Jessie standing alone for a moment and walked over to her. "Jessie, that was amazing. I'm so proud of you and Eric."

Jessie smiled softly. "Thanks, but you know we couldn't save that man unless God was there. He is the only one who can save, but I'm glad He uses us. It feels good."

Becky approached Jessie. "This has been a good day. I wanted to thank you for letting me crash your party."

Jessie smiled. "You are always welcome. I hope you come back. By the way, forgive me for being nosy, but are you Jeremiah's girlfriend?"

Becky laughed. "Not really. We're real close friends, but who knows what the future holds?"

Jessie winked. "You two are very suspicious to me, but I can live with that for now."

Becky laughed, her eyes sparkling.

Jeremiah, who had been watching from a distance, spoke up. "I need to take Becky home, and we have some miles to cover, so we'll say goodbye. It's been a blessed day."

The next day, Jeremiah saw George at the store and walked over to him. "How have you been doing, George?"

George looked up from his work and smiled. "I'm doing good. My daughter, her husband, and the grandkids visit me often, and my daughter calls me almost every weekend. My son has recently gone through a divorce, and he's considering moving in with me for a while." He paused before asking, "How's your family?"

Jeremiah smiled. "George, my family is terrific! Thanks for asking."

George nodded thoughtfully. "You know, I think we are all searching for answers in the world. We want to know who we are, why we're here, and if we're worth anything."

Jeremiah raised an eyebrow. "Did you get your answers, George?"

George thought for a moment, then answered, "I did get some answers, but more questions keep coming up. So, I just keep living and learning."

Jeremiah smiled, impressed. "You're exactly right. You have a great understanding, George. Maybe you'll have the opportunity to teach others."

George gave a nod. "Maybe so." He waved as he went back to work.

That night, when Jessie and Eric lay in bed, Jessie had a peaceful look on her face. She picked up the folded letter from her bedside table. Eric, noticing her calmness, asked, "What do you have, honey?"

Jessie held the letter to her chest for a few moments, as if it were something sacred to her. She let out a soft breath and said, "Eric, I want to share something with you." Her voice was soft and serious, catching Eric's full attention as he maneuvered to sit up in bed.

She continued, "I was only nine when my mom passed, but she must have felt some great trust in me to leave me three letters."

Eric, surprised, said, "Oh, I thought you had two letters."

Jessie nodded, her expression thoughtful. "I haven't shared this letter with anyone, but I will share it with you now. She told me that I would understand when the time comes, because she couldn't talk about it out loud. I didn't know exactly what that meant, but when I found this letter at the bottom of the chest, I understood."

Eric asked gently, "Why didn't you read it when you were younger?"

Jessie took a deep breath. "Mom wrote on the envelope that she trusted me not to open it until I was much older. I guess, over the years, I forgot about it. But hearing everyone's stories today made me think about it." She paused, then began to read the letter aloud to Eric:

"Jessie,

I trust that you are much older now and will understand this letter. I want you to know that I did not spend a lot of time with you or the other children in the last month of my life because I didn't want any of you to see me when the pain was so bad that I couldn't even cry. I gritted my teeth a lot and prayed to die quickly. Some cancers can be fixed with surgery or medication, but some are inoperable. I missed spending time with you and the other children, but I thought of you all every minute. I also want you to know that your dad and I are still young, and I didn't want him to be lonely. I told him I wanted him to remarry. My only request is that he marry someone who will love our children, and that was one of my final prayers.

The last thing to tell you is that you can trust the Lord with everything. He will answer you in His time, so that's why patience is a virtue. And always give thanks and praise to God for all He does. Sometimes things won't make sense in your life. You may wonder why things happen or wonder what to do, but it will come in time. Don't ever give up on your goals and dreams, and help other people as you can along the way. I can't imagine anyone loving my children as much as I do, but Jesus did. He gave His life freely for God's children. I love you so very much!

Mom"

Eric wiped away a tear and asked softly, "Does that make you sad?"

Jessie, her voice quiet, answered, "I miss my mom, but she gave me such a beautiful gift of peace in my heart." She stared at the letter for a moment, holding it close. Eric, ever supportive, put his arm around her. "You had a special mother."

Jessie smiled faintly, tears in her eyes. "Oh, Eric, thank you for saying that. She was certainly special to me."

The next morning, Becky came to the store to look for Jeremiah. When she saw him near the western belts, she walked over and said, "Hi, Jeremiah."

He greeted her with a smile. "Hi, Becky. Are you looking for something western today?"

She hesitated. "No, not really. I wanted to ask you something."

Jeremiah, sensing something was off, said, "Oh, okay. Let's go over to my office." He offered her a seat, his voice soft and inviting. "What's on your mind?"

She stood up, then quickly shook her head. "It wasn't important, and I shouldn't have come by. I need to go."

Jeremiah, concerned, stepped toward her. "Wait! Whatever it is, it can't be that bad."

Becky sighed, clearly distressed. "Yeah, it's embarrassing. I just need to go." As she walked out of the office door, she added, "Hope you have a good day." She hurried out the door, leaving Jeremiah standing there, confused.

He placed his hand on his cheek and whispered, "I wonder what that was all about."

George, who had been nearby, asked, "Is everything okay, boss?"

Jeremiah, still puzzled, answered, "Stop calling me that." He explained what had happened. "Becky came by and said she needed to ask me something, but then she just got up and said she couldn't and walked out. It doesn't make sense."

George chuckled. "Well, as smart as you are about the Bible and life in general, I think you missed the boat when it comes to women. She probably wanted to ask you out."

Jeremiah raised an eyebrow. "Oh yeah, why would she want to do that?"

George grinned. "Because she likes you. Maybe you should call her, ask her out, and see how she responds."

Jeremiah, still unsure, said, "We're just friends. We've been friends a long time."

George winked. "She might feel something more than friendship now." He walked away with a smile, leaving Jeremiah deep in thought.

That evening, Jeremiah sat in his chair at home, pondering George's advice. He picked up the phone to call Becky but laid it back down, unsure of what to do. Looking out the window, he saw the sun setting. He spoke to himself, "Why would she want to go out with me? What if it hurts our friendship because I'm not sure I feel the same way?"

The next morning, Jeremiah almost called Jessie for advice, but thought she might make a bigger deal out of it. He walked into the store in a daze, unable to shake the thoughts of Becky. George walked up and greeted him. "Good morning."

Jeremiah replied, "Good morning." After a beat, he added, "George, I almost called Becky last night, but there were so many questions in my head. I wasn't sure what to do."

George, ever straightforward, said, "You won't know until you try."

Jeremiah, deciding to take the plunge, went to his office and dialed Becky's number. When she answered, he said, "Hello."

Becky's voice was warm, but there was a hint of nervousness. "Jeremiah, I'm sorry I came to your store and acted crazy, but I'm fine now."

Jeremiah paused, gathering his thoughts. "Becky, would you like to go out to eat tonight?"

There was a brief silence on the other end, and Jeremiah's heart raced. "Hello, Becky? Are you still there?"

Becky's voice came through softly. "Yes, I'm here. I'd be happy to go out with you."

Jeremiah let out a quiet sigh of relief. "I'll pick you up at 6."

As they sat down to eat, Becky smiled at him. "This is nice."

Jeremiah smiled back. "Yeah, it is nice."

When he drove her home, he walked her to the door. She turned to him, her smile warm and genuine. "I enjoyed the evening, Jeremiah."

He smiled, his voice soft. "Me too. Would you like to do this again sometime soon?"

Becky smiled, her eyes twinkling. "I think I would enjoy that."

Jeremiah leaned in and kissed her on the cheek, his heart fluttering as she walked inside. He turned to walk back to his car, a smile on his face.

The next day, Jeremiah called Dusty to share the news. Dusty, ever teasing, said, "Aren't you about thirty? Is this your first date?"

Jeremiah laughed. "First of all, I'm not about thirty. And second, I've talked to girls before, but they're too forward. Becky is different. I know her. We've been friends a long time, but she doesn't come on strong, and I'm thankful for that. I always thought of her as my best friend, but now...I'm feeling a little different."

Dusty's voice softened. "It's a good thing to be married to your best friend."

Jeremiah hesitated. "I didn't say anything about marriage."

Dusty laughed. "Just enjoy her company and see where it goes. Take your time."

Jeremiah, still unsure, asked, "What if it doesn't work out, and I lose my friend?"

Dusty's tone grew serious. "What if it does work out? Sometimes, you just gotta take that chance, or you'll always wonder why you didn't. I think you said Mom told you to trust your heart. That applies to life and love."

Jeremiah smiled. "Thanks, Dusty. For a young brother, you're pretty smart."

Dusty laughed. "Yeah, I know."

Jeremiah chuckled. "And humble."

Two years passed, and Jeremiah continued to work at Dusty's western store and serve his church. He'd even added two more rooms to his house. One September evening, he invited his dad and siblings over for a get-together. He told everyone to bring dress clothes because he had something special planned, but wouldn't elaborate.

That night, when his family arrived, Jessie was buzzing with excitement. "What's the fancy place we're going to while we're here?"

Jeremiah grinned. "I think we should all sit down for dinner, and I'll tell you everything."

The long dining table was set, and Jessie remarked, "This is like royalty dining."

Jeremiah laughed. "Not hardly. I can't imagine the king eating meatloaf, green beans, corn, tomatoes, cream potatoes, biscuits, and pecan pie."

Everyone laughed and filled their plates. Jeremiah said the blessing, and just as everyone started eating, Joe asked, "What's the big news, son?"

Suddenly, there was a knock at the door. Jeremiah excused himself and answered. When he returned, he walked in with Becky, his arm around her.

Everyone gasped when they saw the shiny ring on Becky's finger. Jessie's noticed. "Oh my gosh!"

Eric asked, "What is it?"

Jeremiah grinned, his voice calm. "Before Jessie spoils my surprise, I'll just say that Becky and I are getting married the day after tomorrow, and we hope you all will attend."

For a moment, the room was dead silent. Then, Jessie jumped up, hugging Jeremiah and jumping up and down in excitement as she hugged Becky. "I knew it!"

Becky laughed. "Well, you kind of started it when you asked me if I was his girlfriend. I thought I should be. We've been friends a long time."

Eric laughed. "Well, Jessie, you did it again!" The room was filled with laughter.

Jeremiah stood, raising his glass. "I have to say something, if I can get through it without crying."

Dusty teased, "Not many men would say that."

Jeremiah smiled, looking at his family. "This family, my family, is amazing. We've been through an amazing journey. At one time, we were all searching for answers. As my friend George said to me once, he found some of the answers, but more questions came up, so he just kept learning and living. Patty has found her answers about the Lord, but she'll still have questions and will keep learning. She and Mark have two precious ones to fill their life and answer their questions. Jessie and Eric had a loss with their second child, but then they were blessed with a little girl, Mary, as well as their sweet little Joseph, who is growing like a weed. Dad has a wonderful mate, who has helped him through some tough times. Even though she inherited this big family, she is still married to him." The room burst into laughter.

"Dusty and Christy found each other through a little horse statue. I'm still not sure why she took the time to bring it to him, but I'm thankful. I found this beautiful woman when she came to the store and tried to ask me out, but she was too scared. I was too ignorant to figure it out, but we've gone through some adventures, some mysteries, and I believe we've been blessed."

Everyone raised their glass in unison as Jeremiah added, "Thank you, Jesus, and thank you for our Mary."

www.ingramcontent.com/pod-product-compliance
Lightning Source LLC
Chambersburg PA
CBHW050342030726
47503CB00008B/2575